Blue Angel

by

Nadine Monaco

This is a work of fiction. Names, characters, places, and incidents are either the product of the author's imagination or are used fictitiously, and any resemblance to actual persons living or dead, business establishments, events, or locales, is entirely coincidental.

Blue Angel

Cover Art by *Debbie Taylor*

The Wild Rose Press, Inc.
PO Box 708
Adams Basin, NY 14410-0708
Visit us at www.thewildrosepress.com

Publishing History
First Champagne Rose Edition, 2016
Print ISBN 978-1-5092-0491-5
Digital ISBN 978-1-5092-0492-2

Published in the United States of America

Jennifer laughed as she reached the tree, spun around its trunk, and plopped to the ground out of breath. Paul followed her lead, but then leaned over and playfully wrestled her until his body covered hers and her arms were pinned above her head. She was still laughing, until she looked up and they locked eyes.

The moment was fiery, intense, combustible. Her throat tightened as she held her breath. He's going to kiss me again, and I want him to, she thought quickly, her heart pounding more rapidly than it had from the race. His eyes roamed over her face, going from her eyes to her lips to her hair. When his gaze fixed on hers again, she saw the incredible desire there.

Then, to her surprise, Paul rolled off her and stood up. He brushed the dirt from his knees and offered her a hand. Jennifer sat up suddenly, perplexed then embarrassed. She took his hand and let him hoist her up from the ground.

Paul leaned forward as he plucked a piece of stray grass from her hair. "See what happens when you try to race someone who's athletically your superior," he said, his face now relaxed and composed. She would have paid a million dollars to know what he was thinking at that moment. His opaque eyes held no clue.

"Yes, but who taught you everything you know?" she said lightly, trying to figure him out. The *New York Times* crossword puzzle would have been less challenging and complicated.

"Good point. I think I'm in your debt." He moved a slow arm across his damp forehead and wiped away the sweat. "Let me pay up."

Dedication

To Navy wives everywhere

Prologue

He stood at attention, spine straight, chin up, eyes forward. Even though his future depended on the events of the next few minutes, Lieutenant Paul Davis faced the Naval Board of Inquiry with traditional military stoicism. He didn't care what the group of senior officers decided. It didn't matter to him. He already knew the truth. He'd killed his best friend. The hearing today was just a formality.

Paul gritted his teeth as he worked to keep his shoulders back and maintain the needle-straight position. Heavy beads of sweat trailed down his back, further dampening his formal dress white uniform. Even though his mind was moving a mile a minute, he revealed no emotion. That wasn't his way. He kept all his feelings inside.

Paul blinked hard through the brightness of the hot June sun that spilled through high dust-covered windows. His leg ached and his knee throbbed under the pressure of standing still, waiting for the verdict. It had been this way since the accident. He pushed the pain to the back of his mind. Jeff was dead, for God's sake. He could stand a little pain.

The inquiry to determine the cause of the accident had taken several weeks to complete. The investigative team had taken apart every inch of the plane—or what was left of the special two-man fighter jet Paul and Jeff had flown that day.

As the military justices concluded deliberations, Paul could feel angry eyes upon him from the back of the crowded room. Carol Lyons, Jeff's mother, blamed him for the accident and the death of her eldest son.

Like Paul, she wasn't interested in what the court had to say. She already knew what she needed to know. Her son was dead, and Paul was alive. That was enough.

Papers rattled in the still room as the court came to attention. Paul drew a deep, sharp breath and waited for their words.

The senior officer on the military bench beckoned Paul to step closer and he complied.

"After reviewing the evidence, we find Lieutenant Paul Davis innocent of any wrongdoing in the death of Lieutenant Jeffrey Lyons on May 15." He looked directly at Paul as he spoke. His voice was clear and without sentiment. Too many accidents happened to young flyers like Jeff Lyons for him to become emotional. "Lieutenant Davis may report back to active duty as soon as he is fit."

"No, no…" The horrid, blood-curdling screech of a wounded animal filled the stuffy courtroom. "My boy is dead. It's his fault. He has to pay for what he did to my son."

"Carol. Stop. It's done," the young woman beside her said soothingly, wrapping her arms around the distraught older woman. She glanced up at Paul, her tired blue eyes full of pain and sadness. She cursed his soul, too. He couldn't expect any better.

As the slender blonde guided the grieving woman from the court, his stomach clenched, and burning liquid rose in his throat. Jennifer would have been Mrs. Jeff Lyons by now if there was any justice in the world. She would have made a beautiful bride.

He tried to swallow again to get rid of the bile-like taste in his mouth, but the knot in his throat forbid it. It choked him, but he refused to react to it. He would have been the best man at Jeff and Jennifer's wedding. They should have been on their Caribbean honeymoon right now, right this damned moment. He closed his eyes for a fraction of an instant to pull back the control. Later, when he was alone, he could let it all out.

His heart continued to race like a revved engine as he cleared his mind. But he couldn't push out the image of a small velvet-covered box at the back of his nightstand. He still had the matching rings Jeff had entrusted to him. He didn't know what to do with them now.

At that instant, if he could have changed places with Jeff, he would have. He would have done anything to remove the despair from Jennifer's eyes.

Chapter One

Twenty months later

Vacations were for relaxing, but Jennifer Wade didn't feel like relaxing. Tomorrow would be her last day on the island, and she was anxious to return home. Her physical therapy practice was finally taking off, and she needed to get back to her patients. Her hard work was paying off, and she couldn't let up now. There was too much at stake, too many responsibilities that couldn't be ignored.

It was almost noon, and after relaxing on the beach at Waikiki for more than an hour, she was restless again. The warm waves rolled lightly onto the shore, and the white foam of the surf retreated back to the ocean. It was a calming, relaxing sight, and she closed her eyes to enjoy the sound and feel of it. She smiled happily as the sun beat down on her back, making her feel toasty, warm, and relaxed. While she'd tried to fight it, told herself again and again that vacations were a terrible waste of time, she had to admit she'd had a good time on the island. Somehow the tropical magic had taken over, and she'd grudgingly enjoyed herself.

She would have laughed if someone had told her when she'd arrived that she would miss Hawaii. She would. The morning had been like every morning on the beach—absolutely beautiful. She moved from her prone position and swirled around, digging her big toe into the powdery sand as she scanned the shore. She removed large black sunglasses from her face and lifted a palm to shield her eyes from the high sun. Each day the sky had been the bluest blue she had ever seen. Turquoise water merged into cloudless heaven.

She tightened narrow bright pink bikini straps behind her neck and reached for a plastic cup filled with iced tea. She sipped the cool liquid and followed the sound of deep laughter. A hundred feet away, bronze-skinned volleyball players tossed a hard white ball over a net. With eyes fixed on the players, she put the drink down and grabbed for the small bottle of sun lotion beside her. They were in excellent shape, she mused, looking from one player to the next. She liked and respected good bodies. It was her business.

She could hear the smack of the ball as it was slammed and punched over the delicate net. It was good aerobic exercise, exercise she encouraged her patients to participate in. As a physical therapist, she worked to heal sore and injured bodies, to make them better, stronger. She wished all the people she treated at work were as enthusiastically athletic as this bunch.

She and Jeff had played volleyball together. It was he who had patiently worked with her when it seemed abundantly clear she'd never learn to serve the ball correctly. When she'd succeeded, he hadn't been the least surprised. Her throat tightened at the memory. Before she could stop herself, her eyes began to well. *No—stop that.* She dragged the back of her warm palm against her damp lids. There had been too many tears already—and crying wouldn't change a thing.

An ocean breeze caught her attention, and she

turned to the water and closed her eyes, allowing the warm air to wash over her face. Okay, the vacation hadn't been a bad idea. It had given her time to think and clear her mind, to work through the sadness that hadn't subsided. It had helped a little. She needed to heal herself, and pretending she felt no pain hadn't done the trick.

****

Paul took a long breath and exhaled deeply.

He'd been watching her for more than an hour, sitting high on the beach where he could see her, but she couldn't see him. It had been months and months, a lifetime ago, since he'd seen her at the military inquiry. She looked good—beautiful like always. The way she had been before the accident. The way he liked to think of her. Her hair, shoulder-length and loose, fell in waves of glinting silver. Her eyes, he knew, were a deep mesmerizing blue. She had the best smile, the best laugh. At the moment, she looked relaxed and rested and that made him happy. She deserved a little peace.

He wanted to talk to her, to tell her again how sorry he was. He swallowed and closed his eyes. What could he say to her that she'd want to hear? Not the truth, never the truth. He'd die before he'd let Jeff fall off that pedestal in Jennifer's mind and heart. Even though she looked content, there was a restlessness about her. All he could do was cause her more pain—and that was something he refused to do.

He'd always had feelings for Jennifer, feelings that weren't right for his best friend's girl, feelings he'd worked hard to cover up and ignore. Now, the best thing he could do—for the both of them—was walk away and forget he'd ever seen her.

****

It was almost time for lunch, but she wasn't quite ready to give up the morning. Jennifer toyed with the fringe on the side of her beach towel and reached for another sip of tea. From the corner of her eye, she watched the activities on the beach and the gentle beckoning water. She crossed her bare legs and uncrossed them. She was anxious again and irritated by the emotion. She owed it to Lori, her business partner, to come back ready and able to give one hundred percent to their growing physical therapy practice. Lori had been doing her part and more to build their patient base. Certainly, Jennifer had carried a heavy patient load, but building a business meant getting out there, talking to people, promoting their services. Now it was her turn to do her fair share.

Unable to stay put, Jennifer kicked up some sand with the tips of her toes as she moved to stand in the grainy powder. She bent down and picked up her shades and a short white cover-up. Slipping the light cotton fabric over her tanned arms, she stretched and tucked polished toenails into casual open-toed sandals.

With light steps she strode to the shoreline, kicking off her sandals to wade ankle-deep in the foamy surf. The cool white curls tickled her toes and she kneeled to examine a pastel-colored seashell. When the next wave rolled in, she stood and dropped the shell into the surf and ventured further into the clear turquoise water. The horizon seemed to go on for an eternity. Early in her stay, she'd taken a morning tour to the other side of the island where surfers came from around the globe to catch an endless curl. This water was different, at peace with the world and as still as glass.

If it hadn't been so calm, Jennifer never would have seen her. At first she thought it was a dolphin frolicking in the easy water, perhaps a little too close to shore. She lifted her shades to the top of her head to get a better look at the friendly fish. Then she saw her, long dark hair on a small thin body and a single arm flailing high in the air, crying out for help.

It took less than an instant for Jennifer to react. The glasses fell from the top of her head as she dove furiously into the brisk Pacific water. The cold water shocked her system, but she ignored the biting chill. She moved her arms purposefully, stroke after stroke, each taking lifesaving seconds. The white cover-up was holding her up and was discarded mid-stroke. She breathed when she could, but spent her energy gliding through the salty ocean. She gasped when she reached the right spot in the water. The little girl was gone. Where was she? Precious seconds were wasting as Jennifer plunged deep into the water below. Her eyes burned from the salt as she searched under the calm surface. Was it too late? She pushed the pain away and kept going.

Finally she saw a cloud of black hair and grasped at the tiny body below. As she grabbed the soft flesh, her stomach cramped, like a knife slicing into her side, and the water became an enemy to them both.

*I've got to get her, I've got to save her…*The words screamed in her head, but the muscles cramping in her lower abdomen fought against her. The little girl escaped from her hold as Jennifer hunched over and tried to push the pain away. Only sheer willpower and determination allowed her to ignore the gut-wrenching agony and pull the small child back into her arms.

Gritting her teeth and quelling the cry that wanted to explode from her lungs, she forced her feet to propel the two of them back to the surface. As she sucked in sweet air, she hoisted the little girl to the surface. With one arm laced around the child's neck and shoulders, she attempted to backstroke with the other. After several feeble tries, she realized she was doing nothing better than a poor excuse for a doggie paddle. The thought of giving up, of letting the vast ocean win, was unfathomable. She tried to paddle again but only began to sink. Before her head crept beneath the surface, strong and steady arms grabbed her shoulders and hoisted her back up to the surface.

"Get her! Please, God, get her," Jennifer pleaded, while the little girl's head bobbed lifeless in the water. Their rescuer was way ahead of her pleas as she felt one arm go around her shoulder and under her arm, and capture the chest of the unconscious young swimmer in the process.

Jennifer breathed in mouthfuls of welcoming air as her body moved raggedly to the waiting shore. The moment her feet dragged against the grainy wet sand beneath the shallow water, she pulled from her rescuer's grasp and struggled to shore. The water felt thick as she moved aching, exhausted legs to the dry sand.

When she lifted her drooping head, she saw him. She blinked in utter surprise and dropped to her knees. Maybe her eyes were playing tricks on her. Paul Davis.

Like an expert paramedic, he laid the little girl on her back and tilted her head into the sand to open the air canal. He closed his mouth on the small child's to breathe life back into her lungs. Her eyes remained closed. He ignored the gathering crowd. Chest compressions came next, palms pushing rhythmically on the flesh below her delicate rib cage. Miraculously, water sprayed from the tunnel beneath her throat. She gagged and choked as life poured back into her body. Seconds later, she was sobbing.

Jennifer cupped her face in her hands, too stunned to think, to feel anything but relief. Her lashes closed tight for a moment. When she opened them again, she faced concerned dark green eyes.

Crouching beside her, Paul clutched her shoulders and held them tight. "She's going to be all right. We got to her just in time." His gaze narrowed as his eyes swept over her face. Then, his brows furrowed with worry. "Your eyes look glazed. Did you take in too much water? Are you okay? Jennifer?"

Jennifer nodded slowly as a frantic raven-haired woman in her early thirties rushed to the scene and dropped to the ground, spraying sand everywhere her feet landed. The little girl opened her eyes wide and burst into fresh tears. "Baby, oh baby. Mommy was so scared." She turned to her daughter's rescuers. "Thank you so much. I...I don't know what I would have done if you hadn't saved Melissa's life."

The woman's eyes filled with gratitude before she bent over the little girl, softly caressed her knotted dark hair, and embraced her in her arms.

All of a sudden, Jennifer felt her knees turn to mush, and she collapsed on her bottom. The cramp in her stomach intensified, and she gripped her abdomen, trying to stand and fight off the offending pain.

"Sit down. Rest." Paul held her shoulders and coaxed her back down.

"No, it's better if I walk," she replied under her breath, always the physical therapist, and allowed him to hoist her to her feet. Still dazed, Jennifer tried to stand tall and erect.

Slowly, she breathed air into her lungs and worked to relax the angry muscles in her stomach. Her feet felt slightly disconnected from the rest of her body, but she followed the lead of the man directing her.

After making light footprints in the dry sand, the pain dissipated, and she tried to walk on her own. Paul wouldn't release his hold. "Take it easy. This isn't a road race." Despite the growing anxiety that had spread throughout her body, his voice was calming and reassuring.

She raised her head and couldn't see through the curtain of blonde hair falling over her face. Her chest ached and she feared she was going to get sick right then and there. "I'm all right." Dropping her head again, she took in heavy breaths. She'd swallowed a good deal of water. It left a retching feeling in the pit of her stomach.

Paul stopped instantly when her head fell again. "Are you going to be sick? Do you feel faint?" He brushed the tangled mat of hair from her face and checked to see if she'd gone into shock.

Jennifer closed her eyes to his scrutiny, and shook her head from side to side. "No, no. I'm just a bit nauseous now, really, and a little shaky." She faced him again, her mind spinning with a thousand thoughts. She paused and focused on his concerned eyes. "Thank you for helping out there. I got that lousy cramp, and if you hadn't been there…" Her voice stopped and faltered. The alternative was too terrible to consider.

He wiped a band of wetness from his forehead and smiled nervously. "I spent summers during high school as a lifeguard and never had to rescue anyone, not even a toddler in the kiddy pool. I knew that swimming and CPR training would come in handy one day, though."

Jennifer glanced down at Melissa, sitting with her mother, wrapped in a thick bright beach towel. She nodded her head. "Well, I think we're all fine now."

"Thank you, thank you both." Melissa's mother interrupted the twosome. Her face was still white and her eyes filled with the agony of what might have been. "Melissa is all I have. I just went to get her a drink on the boardwalk, and she was eating a sandwich. I told her to stay put. She's usually so good. It was dumb of me, but I wasn't gone more than four minutes." She spoke like a speeding train, wringing her hands as she went on. "I'll never do that again. I'll never let her out of my sight."

"It's all right now." Paul reached out to the woman, touching her fingers, trying to calm her. "It might have been a two-person effort," he said, grinning hesitantly at Jennifer, "but everything turned out just fine."

"Thank you," she said again, before returning to the little girl who was already wiggling her way out of the blanket to play on the beach.

Finally, they were alone.

It had been easy to talk minutes ago, but now it was just the two of them and the awkwardness settled in.

"It's good to see you," Paul said after a long, drawn-out moment. She could hear the tension in his voice, even though he'd spoken just a few words.

"It's good to see you, too, Paul." It was so odd to

stand here like this. Once they'd been the best of friends, and now it was like talking to a stranger.

"So, you're okay?" he asked again, his voice still tight and controlled.

His nerves were catching. "I'm fine," she said a little quickly. "I don't think I really swallowed too much water." She shifted a few paces from him. Her toes curled, then clenched under her feet.

He took a deep breath. "I meant in general."

"Oh." She tilted her head, combing damp hair with her fingers. Momentarily, she was at a loss for words. What could she say to him? There was so much history, so much sadness. Her pale brows knit together as a thousand thoughts and sensations rocked her. "Fine. I'm fine, Paul."

"On vacation?" he asked.

"Yes." She nodded. The tense conversation was quickly beginning to unnerve her. "You?"

He paused before he spoke. "Not exactly. I've been stationed at Pearl for the last few months."

During flight school he and Jeff had talked about getting stationed in Hawaii together, at Barber's Field. They'd planned to fly, learn to surf, and hang out at the beach. It had all sounded so wonderful.

Had it really been only two years ago that the three of them had sat laughing and joking in O'Brien's Pub, discussing final details for the wedding? Both she and Jeff had warned Paul about decorating their car after the ceremony, and Paul had only grinned. Memory after memory came flooding back with full force and her head began to pound.

"It was good to see you, Paul." She turned away. Even though she had so many things to say, it was easier to close her eyes to the past.

"Don't go. Not yet." He reached for her arm and held it.

She lifted her head to meet his anxious gaze. "Yes?"

"Jen." His voice cracked and he took a deep breath. "I need to talk to you, about Jeff, about that day."

She wanted to move on, to move past the sadness. Talking would help, but she wasn't ready, not nearly ready. She swallowed hard as she shook her head. "No, I can't."

"Jennifer, I did what I could," he said in a rush.

She paused and stared at him. "What?"

"I promise you, I did everything I could." There was so much pain in his eyes. "It wasn't my fault."

For a moment she was speechless. *What was he talking about*? "Jeff, I…"

He looked sad and hurt at the same time. "I know you hate me."

Her throat constricted, but she shook her head slowly from side to side. "No, Paul, I don't hate you, I never hated you." She paused again and sighed. That day, that awful day, hadn't been just about her. "I never blamed you for what happened."

"You didn't?" His mouth gaped open. "But I thought you…"

"No, well, maybe for a moment, I wondered," she admitted. "But I never really thought it was your fault." She'd read the preliminary investigative report; she'd pored over it line by line. Even then she hadn't been looking to cast blame. She'd only wanted answers.

"But…Carol. The day of the inquiry…"

She shivered from the memory. Never had she

experienced a worse time in her life. The realization that the man she loved—the man she was going to spend her life with—was dead, made her mindless with grief. "It was an awful time for all of us. She was so upset and wasn't thinking clearly."

"You wouldn't talk to me. You could barely look at me."

"I couldn't talk to anyone. I fell apart. Even today, I find it too hard to talk about."

She knew the military report had shown Paul had done everything possible to save Jeff, his RIO—radar intercept officer—even risking his own life in the process. But she'd wanted to find something, anything, that would explain why the man she'd loved was dead. The sensible, logical part of her had understood the facts. Her heart still couldn't fathom the fact that sometimes terrible things happened to the people you love.

She'd been to a counselor. He'd only told her what she'd already known. It was time, time to get on with the rest of her life. The answer was simple, and just as impossible. How could she ever pick up the pieces again and go on?

"I know we should have been there for each other." She shook her head slowly as he started to pace. She remembered he did that when his nerves were on edge. "I owe you a long overdue apology. I'm sorry for how I treated you, Paul. I wasn't handling anything very well at the time. I couldn't focus on anything else but my own grief."

"Jen…" He started to protest, but she raised her hand to still him.

"No, you didn't deserve it. But please know I

wasn't just shutting you out, I was shutting out the whole world." She paused for a second to catch her breath. Her shaking fingers pressed against her racing heart. "I have to admit that, in an odd way, I did want to blame you for the accident. I mean, I knew if it weren't for you Jeff never would have been in that plane." She watched his face fall, then reached for his hand and clutched it. "But I was wrong. For just a moment, I was grasping at straws. You didn't twist his arm to fly with you, and neither one of you could have known what was going to happen. He was thrilled to get the chance to fly that demo two-man F-18—and I was thrilled for him. As a RIO, he would normally never get that opportunity. He took care of radar and weather equipment, and while he loved doing that, it wasn't piloting a jet. He'd never been able to go solo in a regular F-18 like you. This was his chance." She swallowed again and caught her breath. "I know my silence made you feel guilty. That wasn't fair to you at all."

"It's okay," he said softly.

"No, it's not," she protested. "It wasn't right. Months later, I wanted to contact you, but I just…it's been a tough time."

"I know."

Her gaze followed his pacing. "Your walk is still a little off." She remembered from the inquiry. Most people wouldn't have noticed, but to her, his injury was difficult to miss.

"It's not bad."

"Does it hurt much?"

"No, not much." He shrugged his shoulders as he shook his head, and Jennifer knew he was lying.

"I can recommend some exercises," she offered.

"Nah," he continued, shaking his head. "I've had enough doctors and PTs poking and prodding me to last a lifetime. I'm afraid I haven't much faith anymore."

"A good attitude's important."

He swallowed. "Yeah, I know."

"Have you flown since?"

"Yeah, but it's kind of a long story. I'm grounded again."

"Oh?"

"During maneuvers, I had a real bumpy landing. It stiffened up again."

"I'm sure your height didn't help any. A six foot two man doesn't belong in the cramped cockpit of an F-18."

"Yeah, well."

"How long has it been now?"

"Four months."

"Wow, that's a long time." They both knew what time away from the cockpit meant to a pilot.

"Tell me about it." He sighed again. "It's been really weird, Jen."

She saw the flicker of hot emotion in his eyes. The accident had left a permanent scar—and he'd been alone to deal with it. "You miss him still, don't you?"

"All the time," he said with complete honesty, a touch of hoarseness in his voice.

"Me, too," she whispered, and then choked.

"He was my best friend, Jennifer." His throat clogged on words that were obviously difficult to say. "When I think of all the years we planned and dreamed, I thought we'd be flying forever."

Her eyes moistened as she reached for her mouth

and covered it with her hand. It was strange how overwhelming grief could be. She paused to catch a breath that lodged deep in her throat. It was important to clear the air, to put the unhappy events of that late spring day behind them and go on. "I know how much you cared about each other. He said you were the best pilot he knew. You made a good team. I know you did everything you could that day. Maybe we can sit and talk, catch up, over lunch? I'm staying at the Hilton Hawaiian Village. It's right behind us."

He lifted his arm and swiped away the tears gathering at the corner of her eye. She could see a lump lodge in his throat. "I'd love to. In fact, all this water rescue business has suddenly made me very hungry." They laughed at that, and the tension broke between them.

"I'm not exactly dressed for lunch, though." For the first time since she'd dragged herself back onto the beach she realized that all that stood between her and her birthday suit were three tiny triangles. She self-consciously wrapped her hands around her chest. "And what about your jeans? They're still sopping wet."

The faded, form-fitting jeans clung to him like a second skin.

He shrugged his shoulders. "They'll dry," he responded, not taking his eyes off of her. "Hold on a second." He jogged a few yards up the beach and retrieved a navy blue cloth gym bag off the sand. He unzipped the bag and sifted through its contents as he made his way back to Jennifer. He pulled out a large gray cotton T-shirt with the word "Navy" embossed on the front and handed it to her.

"I'm sure this will more than cover you up."

Jennifer held up the shirt that brought back so many memories. Jeff and Paul had been best friends since as far back as either of them could remember—little boys in grade school. Together, they'd decided to attend the Navy's OCS—Officer Candidate School—and when Paul said he wanted to go jets, Jeff decided to reach for the clouds, too. They'd graduated top of their class at flight school in Pensacola, and then they'd landed in the same training squadron in Beeville, Texas, just as they'd planned. They'd had the world by the tail.

It was during a family holiday on South Padre Island, several hours from Beeville, that her father, an aerodynamics instructor at OCS, had run into Jeff and Paul on the beach. Jeff had been one of her father's best students, and he'd introduced his star pupil to his eldest daughter. Growing up in a military family, Jennifer had sworn up and down she'd never fall in love with an officer, but that first night they met she did just that—hook, line, and sinker.

Brushing the memory aside, she slipped the shirt on quickly. "Thanks."

"You're welcome, Jennifer."

As he spoke, he took her hand and together they traipsed through the sand, toes hot and squishing on the island powder, heading toward the hotel behind them.

An hour later they were sipping mai tais around the hotel pool and carrying on like old friends.

"So what happened to Mary Beth? I thought she had you lassoed and hog-tied for good." Jennifer laughed as she thought about the pretty redhead Paul had been dating before the accident. Of course, she'd been the last of many, many woman Paul had been involved with over the years. So unlike Jeff, who had looked forward to marriage, a home, commitment, Paul was the free and easy bachelor. She and Jeff used to kid him that the woman who would one day win his heart would certainly have her hands full. "That lady had marriage written all over her face. She wanted you bad."

Paul raised and lowered his shoulders. "Maybe that's why it didn't work out." His mouth formed a grin. "Maybe I like to do the chasing."

"You always were a chauvinist, weren't you?" she said, giving his forearm a little shove. "I remember that first week we all met at the beach. All those girls, Paul. Honestly, I swear we could never keep track of all your romances. Jeff used to say he'd never seen a slicker guy with the ladies."

"I'm not, really. I've just never met anyone who I wanted to settle down with. Anyway, you know I always said that Jeff was the luckiest guy in the world." He hesitated for an instant, and his eyes softened a bit. "Since the accident, I guess I just haven't felt very…social."

"I know." She propped her elbows on the table and placed her chin in her open palms. "Course, I don't know if you guys should get involved with women. I remember how my mom was while Dad was flying during the first Gulf War. She couldn't sleep, and she hung on every tiny tidbit of information she could get her hands on. She was a nervous wreck. It was a hard time for all of us." She shrugged her shoulders.

"Yet you got involved with Jeff."

She nodded. "But you remember how I fought it. Tooth and nail. No dashing young officers for me." Her lips tightened into a thin smile. "I guess you can't help

20

who you fall in love with."

"And we're a persistent breed of animal," he said softly.

Her eyes met his solidly, and then she couldn't help but grin. "Yes, you are." She paused for an instant. "Of course, we'd planned on leaving the glitz, glamour, and utter craziness behind and have a regular sort of life. After Jeff's commitment was up, he'd settle down with a nice normal flying job with one of the big commercial airlines."

"Yeah," he said after a long pause. Paul swallowed hard as he glanced toward the surf before facing her again. "It really is great to see you." He cleared his throat as he changed the subject. "When are you heading home?"

"Tomorrow."

"Any plans for your last night in town?"

She shook her head. "None to speak of. Not really."

He smiled from ear to ear. "Well, you do now. Tonight I'm taking you to the best luau in Hawaii."

It sounded like fun. Before she could agree, she heard a voice in the distance calling out her name.

"Jen, Jen, someone's anxious to see you." Jennifer and Paul turned in unison to watch a young dark-haired women traipse down the steps from the hotel lobby with an infant and a toddler in tow. As they approached, the infant smiled broadly when it spied Jennifer, stretching pudgy arms in her direction.

****

Paul froze for an instant and blinked hard. The sun was partially in his eyes, so he shielded his brows as his stunned gaze fixed on the baby. Jeff's baby, it had to be. Even with fat rosy cheeks and wispy fine blond hair, the baby had to be his best friend's child. Its eyes, nose, mouth…he'd know Jeff's baby anywhere.

Jennifer had had Jeff's child. It couldn't be, but the truth was staring him straight in the eyes and gurgling for attention.

The dark-haired woman gently placed the tot in Jennifer's open arms and lightly tousled its fair curls. "Hello," she said as she looked up at Paul.

Then she quickly turned her attention to Jennifer. "I was going to take the kids for a walk, and then we saw you sitting out here." She lowered her shoulders in an exaggerated manner, and exhaled loudly. "I don't know how you've done it all week. I swear you've taken both the kids eighty percent of the time, so I could gallivant around the island. I've done so little compared to you, and I'm exhausted."

Jennifer smiled patiently at her friend. "I lived in Hawaii when my Dad was active duty, remember? I've already seen all the sights you visited. I didn't mind taking care of our little hooligans."

Paul's eyes shifted from the baby to Jennifer, then back to the baby again. "Jen…" He choked as his voice disappeared.

She kept her eyes from Paul, obviously wanting to put off what she knew she couldn't avoid for more than a few more seconds. She took a deep breath. "Paul, this is my friend and roommate, Becki, and her little guy, Tyler. This," she added, planting a kiss on the baby's cheek, "is Jake, my son."

"I…I didn't know," he said, stumbling over his words, stating the obvious.

Jennifer turned to her friend. "Becki, Jake and I are

going to go down to the baby pool with Paul." She ignored the quizzical expression on her friend's face. "We'll catch up with you later." Her eyes shifted back to Paul. "Want to walk?"

After Paul nodded his assent, she rose from her chair, snuggling the baby in her arms as she moved from the small café table. "Hi, Buster Brown. Did you have fun with Becki and Tyler this morning?" Not expecting a response, she brushed her lips against his soft forehead. "Oh, I bet you did."

"He didn't know, did he?" Paul asked, finally finding his voice again. It cracked under the strain of the moment. Jeff had been his best friend. Even if the pregnancy was supposed to be a secret until after the wedding, he wouldn't have kept the news from him. They'd shared secrets most of their lives.

"No, he didn't. I didn't…until after the accident." She spied an open table right next to the baby pool. "Over there, okay?"

Paul felt as if his soul had shrunk into oblivion. Jeff would never know the joy and wonder of the perfect bundle Jennifer now carried so lovingly in her arms. There would be no playing catch in the backyard, no days at a ballpark together, no heart-to-heart father-son talks. And Jeff would have been thrilled by the news. He'd wanted a large family with Jennifer. "Why didn't you say something earlier?"

"I knew you'd be upset…like you are right now." She snuggled the baby closer. "I love how he feels. His hair is so soft and warm, and he smells like fresh sunshine." Her smile took over her face. "Jake is amazing. Not that it hasn't been hard being a single mom. It's really tough, but I love him. It's such a cliché to say this, but he is my life. He helped fill that big empty void." She plopped down by the side of the baby pool, and then eased Jake into the water in front of her.

The child squealed with glee as his legs were submerged into the water. He immediately slapped his chubby palms flat down in the still pool, obviously enjoying the cool water as it splashed and rippled all around him. "He absolutely loves this little pool. Every day we sit here, and he has a ball."

"I can see he's a wonderful baby," Paul said with a nod, working to quell the mix of emotions that fought within him. He swallowed hard as he tried to catch his breath. "It's just not fair. Jeff should be here with you, with Jake. The boy deserves a father."

"Well…we're doing okay, Paul," she said as she stroked Jake's wispy cap of blond curls, now soaked from constant splashing. "I wouldn't have chosen life as a single mom, but I don't know what I would have done without my little boy. I have a few friends close by and my favorite aunt is less than an hour away." Her smile shined bright as she met his eyes. "With Jake and my work, I stay pretty busy. There's not much time for anything else. I don't want you to worry about us, Paul. Life isn't always easy, but we're doing just fine." Her smile grew wide and welcoming.

"There's hours until the luau," she continued with a grin. "There's this little cove I used to go to as a kid. Why don't the three of us go there? If you're willing, we can take turns snorkeling and watching Jake. I want you to get to know the best baby in the world."

Chapter Two

The sun set slowly over the vast Pacific coastline. Tall, graceful palm trees stretched the length of the shoreline and swayed in the warm breeze. Clear blue water lapped up on the shore and kissed the soft white sand, as pale pink and blue pools formed lakes of color in the twilight heaven. It was impossible to tell where sky and sea separated into two elements. The large orange sphere that looked close enough to touch melted easily into the deep blue ocean.

Relaxing tropical music played in the distance and Jennifer twisted her head to find Paul standing at the outdoor bar, waiting to get drinks to start their evening. Jake was spending his evening with Becki and Tyler. It was the first night during her vacation that she'd left the baby with her best friend. Back home, she and Becki often shared babysitting duties. It made life easier for the both of them.

During the afternoon, Jennifer, Paul, and Jake had visited some of the little hidden coves and bays on the island to do some snorkeling. She was amazed how easily Paul had hoisted Jake onto his hip and carried the happy child to the various locations they'd explored during their action-packed afternoon. He was a natural with kids and Jake took to him immediately. Later, they'd trailed through the surf, stopping to admire the hibiscus in bloom and the forests filled with lush ferns, philodendron, eucalyptus, and bamboo. Lingering in one of the island's hundred rain forests, she'd marveled at the carpet of scarlet anthuriums that spotted the ground. They'd found secluded areas of beach and walked where it seemed civilization was a million miles away.

She felt alive again, more alive than she had in a long, long time. She had a right to feel good, and she tried to push aside the guilt that wouldn't let go. *How could she enjoy herself when Jeff was dead*? He wouldn't want her to go on mourning him forever. He would have wanted her to pick up and get on with her life.

But what would he think about her afternoon with Paul and the son he would never know? She liked that she and Paul were friends again. It was the way things should be. She swallowed hard and wished she could ignore the strong feeling of attraction she felt for him. But there were moments during the day when her thoughts had been anything but platonic and fraternal. She'd always found him attractive—even sexy—but that was it. They were friends, buddies, and she'd been in love with Jeff.

It was normal and natural for her to feel close to Paul. After all, because of Jeff, they'd been through so much together. She tossed a handful of windblown hair over her shoulder and scolded herself. She was being silly, that was all. It was simply the excitement and surprise of seeing an old friend. There could never be anything but friendship between her and Jeff's best friend.

****

From the tropical bar, Paul stood and watched

Jennifer relax on the soft grass beside the beach and cast her eyes to the setting sun. She looked content, and he was pleased. Life couldn't be easy for her. Throughout the afternoon, he'd picked up bits and pieces and had put them all together. Since Jeff's death, she'd buried herself in her work and her son and didn't leave much room for a social life of any kind.

While it was obvious she loved her little boy, it was also obvious Jeff's absence had left a deep hole in her life. He prayed she'd never learn about the foolish choice Jeff had made that had changed all their lives.

The early evening breeze tousled her shoulder-length blonde hair and teasingly wrapped it around her face. He loved her carefree expression. Her lightly tanned skin looked golden against a thin white cotton blouse. A short denim skirt revealed long shapely legs that somehow looked even sexier than they had in the bikini she'd worn earlier in the day. Just a few hours ago, he'd promised himself not to dwell on old emotions. It was crazy to want someone who'd never want him back. And what kind of guy would go after his dead buddy's girl—especially when there was a kid involved, a kid as great as Jake?

Accepting tall, elegant-looking glasses from the bartender, Paul meandered back through the small crowd gathered on the sand waiting to enjoy the luau.

"Hi." He bent down to present her with an exotic pink drink complete with a wedge of pineapple and a red and green umbrella. "For you."

She smiled and stole a quick sip. "Potent stuff. What is this?"

He sat down next to her and sampled his drink. His eyebrows rose. "Bartender's special. He calls it Passion

Delight."

"Do we dare?"

"Absolutely," he responded with a friendly wink.

"I don't mean to press—but I'm a little worried about that walk of yours." She tasted her drink again and waited for him to respond.

When he didn't, she went on. "It's not as if it's really obvious, but it's important to let injured limbs mend completely. I'd hate to think you hurt yourself again rescuing me and that little girl today."

As she spoke, he memorized the shape of her eyes, the slant of her jaw, the pout of her lips. God, she was gorgeous. Gently, he brushed a disobedient piece of blonde hair from her cheek, and warnings went off in his head. *She was Jeff's girl, Jake's mom.* If any woman was off-limits, it was Jennifer Wade. "I'm fine, really. Let me tell you what we're in for tonight."

He wanted to change the topic. He didn't want to dwell on unhappy remnants of the past. He'd spent too much time doing that on his own. "First we have drinks." He held up his hourglass-shaped glass and clinked it to hers. "Then there's a traditional island dinner complete with poi." He watched her nose wrinkle. "What's wrong with poi?"

"Have you ever had it?" she asked, still making a face.

His eyes flashed with amusement. Her face was so expressive—and so cute. "No."

"Don't ask, then."

"All right, I won't," he said, as he stretched out his legs and smiled. "I'm really having fun tonight, Jen." He turned to her and gently squeezed her hand. She nodded, and her smile made him uncomfortable again.

Why did he keep having those thoughts about her? They were all so incredibly vivid. He felt like a traitor. Lord, he'd been there the night Jeff and Jennifer met and had watched their romance bloom into the kind of love most people only dreamed about—and he couldn't help but be a little jealous. He remembered how she'd hated falling in love with an officer, especially a flyboy. But Jeff had won her heart before she'd had the chance to realize what was happening.

"After a sumptuous dinner, there's a great show and dancing." Paul clenched his jaw and tried to think of something else, anything else. *Get a grip, Davis.* It can never be. He owed that much to a dead man's memory.

****

"I must confess, I can't remember the last time I had such a good time." Jennifer smiled into his eyes and looked around at the group of people gathering for the luau. The tantalizing smell of grilled chicken and island fish drifted through the air, mixing with the romantic scents of ginger and jasmine. The purring sound of the ocean made her sleepy and relaxed. How long had it been since she'd felt so rested and peaceful?

"It's been much too long," she added with a sigh. She kicked off her sandals and stretched out her tanned legs. She kneaded her toes into the powdery white sand. "Of course, tomorrow it's back to work and the real world." She smiled again, banishing from her thoughts the long list of work-related activities that awaited her when she got home. "But at this moment, I'm just going to think about now and today."

"Would you like a lei for the lady?" An elderly tawny-skinned woman with straight black hair and warm, wise eyes held an armful of beautiful floral necklaces in front of Paul. He surveyed the colorful strands and chose one made with soft pink cattleya orchid blossoms. "I think that one will look especially lovely."

The older woman revealed missing teeth that didn't hamper a genuine smile. With a careful hand, she removed the lei from her arm and handed it to Paul. "The perfect gift for your wife. Enjoy the luau. Aloha."

As the older woman strolled away, Jennifer raised her drink to her lips to hide flushed cheeks. The woman had thought them husband and wife.

In a white polo shirt and snug beige khaki slacks, he certainly fit the bill for good-looking husband material. If she were a different kind of person, had a different kind of life, who knew? He was undeniably sexy: dark green eyes, strong masculine jaw, chiseled chin. She rolled her eyes at the absurd thoughts running through her head. As if she had time for any of that. Paul was certainly not husband material for her. But today he'd made her happy and content. He was a good person, and she was glad they could become friends again.

They were soon summoned to a large buffet spread with colorful and tasty island delights. Beautiful young men and women in festive native costumes introduced her to sweet and sour chicken, savory barbecued pork, and a collection of luscious fruit such as papayas, passion fruit, and guavas. When they reached the poi, Jennifer grimaced, but took a small taste of the goo that looked like gluey paste and tasted about the same.

"Yummy?" Paul laughed as she pursed her lips, and scooped up a fresh piece of pineapple to rid her mouth of the aftertaste.

When they returned to their blanket and started to sample the unusual foods, Jennifer was delighted by all the tasty items on her plate. She was the first to admit to being a finicky eater, but everything there tasted delicious. She bit into a guava and searched frantically for a napkin as the juice squirted and drizzled down her chin.

"Here. Let me help." With the aid of a nearby cloth napkin, Paul blotted the syrupy juice as she laughed.

"Oh, no, what a mess." She grimaced slightly and lifted her hand to help him.

"No, not a mess at all," he murmured.

His eyes roamed her face and she could see desire there. It was more than a flicker of emotion; there was something hot, intense, surprising between them.

Her pulse quickened, and the air became thick. The napkin fell from his hands, and he caressed her cheek with callused fingers. Gently, his mouth lowered onto hers. A thread of excitement raced through her from the top of her head to the tips of her toes.

It was a short, sweet kiss, over in a moment, but she would remember his lips, his mouth touching hers. His warm raspy breath on her cheek broke the connection.

He bit back a curse. "Oh, God. I'm sorry. I shouldn't have done that."

She was more than a little startled, too. But at that moment when his lips touched hers, she'd wanted it to happen. To pretend annoyance would be a lie, and she wasn't a liar. "It's all right. Really," Jennifer whispered back, her pulse beating rapidly.

"No, it's not all right. Jeff was my best friend. I

don't know what I was thinking. I had no right."

"Paul, I…"

"While I thought of Jeff as my brother, I never thought of you like a sister," he admitted. "I know there's a line. Even though I've always been attracted to you, I understood the line."

"It's all right," she repeated.

He ran his fingers through her windblown blonde curls. "Jeff was one hell of a lucky guy."

****

The next few hours passed in a hurried blur. As the sky became a soft midnight blue, lit by a full moon and a blanket of bright, twinkling stars, the nightly celebration of life ended with a flourish.

The crowd slowly started to dissipate, still worked up from the night's energetic performances. Jennifer was reluctant to move, and groaned as she stretched in place. The evening was over, and while she was tired, she didn't want the night to end. "That was a wonderful show." Her eyes met his and held. "I've had a great time today."

"Too tired for a short walk on the beach?"

"No, that sounds great."

When his hand moved to guide her, she shivered slightly from the contact. Sparks, red hot and electric, flickered between them.

While she'd always known Paul was attracted to her—his admission that he'd never had sisterly thoughts about her wasn't a surprise—she was startled by the fierce attraction they now shared. It was thrilling and terrifying, all at the same time. It would have been smarter to end the evening now, but she didn't want that to happen. She wanted to spend her last few hours in paradise with Paul, strolling from the luau to the light surf on the shoreline.

The sand was as fine as powdered sugar as her toes dug into the tender talc. They easily walked five hundred yards down a strip of white foam. The romantic scent of jasmine and roses filled the warm evening air, as did the sweet hum of island birds nestled in for the night. They came to a cove secluded from the rest of the beach and detoured from their path. Palms, shrubs, and ferns in the deepest, darkest green set off a backdrop for vibrant pink and yellow blossoms. Moonlight dripped through outstretched leaves and cast haphazard streaks of light in the small isolated pool they'd discovered.

She kicked off her light leather sandals onto the grass and strode into the crystal water up to her knees. "Oh, Paul, this is so beautiful."

"Like it?" She was pleasantly startled by the light footsteps behind her.

"Love it," she murmured back.

"Come on." He lightly pulled at her arm, urging her out of the water, and she was surprised to find his touch once again sent her heart pumping.

She'd thought there wasn't a romantic bone left in her body. The love of her life was gone, and she buried herself in her son and her work. At the moment, work seemed light years away.

They journeyed through the dark, verdant foliage. Suddenly, her head tilted, and her eyes narrowed with concentration. "Do you hear that?" She grabbed his arm and held him still.

"What?" He turned and watched the excitement in her eyes.

"Listen." The faint sound of falling water brought a broad smile to her lips. "A waterfall. I hear it, I just know it."

"Let's go," Paul said with a quick wink.

Jennifer ignored the beautiful clusters of flowers at her feet as she and Paul strode through the lush island flora. She was glad he was game for this adventure. But then, she remembered he was a man game for just about anything, as they pushed aside growing palms and stepped lightly onto virgin grass.

She liked him. Very much. Too much. The thought spread through her veins and landed in her stomach with a nervous thump. She came to Hawaii to take it easy. With the way she was feeling about Paul, nothing would be easy.

She tore a leaf from foliage in her path, and shredded it in her fingers. She was being foolish, of course, getting ahead of herself. She would leave the island tomorrow, and this time with Paul would be just a memory. She'd face the real world tomorrow.

The sound of pounding water got closer and closer, louder and louder. At the same moment, she and Paul stepped feet-first in the lagoon surrounding the waterfall. The water was above their ankles and Jennifer ventured in a little farther. "It's not very deep," she shouted above the roar of the falling water. "I think we can get pretty close."

"I think we can get even closer than that." His eyes flashed with mischief as he scooped her up and carried her toward the waterfall. She thought to struggle for a moment, to insist on being put down, but she liked his well-built arms around her as they lifted her in the air and held her close to his hard, warm body.

34

"How close are we going to go?" she yelled, as they were feet away from the glistening sheet of clear water. She knew the answer before it was spoken, and braced herself for a brisk, unexpected evening shower. Her arms tightened around his neck, and she hastily shut her eyes. The water sprayed like light rainfall at first. Then, he pulled them under the curtain of continuous water, and they were engulfed in a sea of liquid moonlight.

"You must be crazy!" she hollered, but the words were lost in the watery thunder. The water was cool and revitalizing, and Jennifer's heart fluttered as the endless downpour drenched every part of her. She sputtered as he moved them to the other side of the fall, where they were bound between the curtain of water and the smooth high cliffs from which it fell.

"If I'm crazy, it's all because of you." His eyes were intense with yearning. And it was contagious. *What was he doing to her?* It was crazy. But at the moment, she *felt* crazy.

As if he had no control over his actions, his mouth lowered onto hers. Automatically, her lips opened and she enjoyed the delicious feel of his touch. Her hands and fingers tightened around his firm neck. He was gentler than she'd imagined he could be, as she allowed him to hold her tightly. There was no doubt, only desire, as he kissed her.

As if she were a treasured diamond, he placed her gently on her feet. The chilled water felt delicious around her legs and sent shivers down her spine. The kiss continued as his fingers trailed across the nape of her neck, and caressed the skin above her collarbone. They were alone, but they could have been anywhere—

home plate at Yankee Stadium—and she wouldn't have noticed.

She relished the sensitive touch of his mouth on hers. As if it were the most natural thing in the world, she linked her arms around his waist, imploring him to hold her closer. His hands slid down her back, molding and caressing her curves. His kiss became more powerful. It would be impossible to turn back even if she'd wanted to.

Every nerve was raw, exposed, on fire. Her body shuddered with passion.

It had been so long since she'd felt desire; the sensation was almost foreign to her. But the embers were starting to blaze higher and hotter than ever before. And he felt it too; the hardness of his body giving away his mounting passion.

When his mouth left hers in search of tender skin on her throat and neck, Jennifer twisted to give him the access he wanted.

Her mind filled with thoughts of ecstasy, and she willed him to possess her body. His palms felt coarse as they stroked her face, her arms, her hands. Her eyes closed as his mouth sought hers again, seduced and intoxicated by the pleasure he was giving her.

Slowly, the buttons at the front of her blouse gave way to the pressure of his fingers. As the material separated, the brisk wet air on her bare skin was stirringly seductive. His hands slipped behind the garment and explored the wet skin on her back as he expertly unhooked her bra. Even over the thunder of the falls, she could hear and feel his uneven breathing on her cheek while he held her closer, meshing their clinging bodies together through the damp mist.

He tossed her now-transparent shirt and bra on the ragged edge of a jutting stone. Jennifer gasped as he caressed her breasts with his clever hands, and then with his equally clever mouth. With an even building rhythm, he massaged her swelling nipples with his tongue.

Caught up in the desperate passion that consumed them both, Jennifer longed to feel his warm, wet body against her own slippery flesh. In seconds, she unbuttoned his shirt, molded to his well-muscled form, and touched the soft matted hair on his chest with her fingers.

As she yanked to unbuckle his narrow leather belt, he lowered his hands to unzip her snug skirt. The material loosened; suddenly her hips were free of the clingy denim fabric. For a brief moment, she felt vulnerable, almost afraid. This was so unlike her. She had spent so much time being angry at the world—angry at Jeff, at Paul, at the Navy. Now, in this instant, she couldn't get enough of him. Everything else was a dreamy haze.

When she tried to speak, to say his name, she only managed a groan. Her heart pounded as he captured the tender skin at the side of her neck. Paul tenderly lifted her again and carried her through the streaming falls. She hung on tight and kissed him as he placed her onto the grassy area protecting the grotto.

His hands slowly, seductively stroked her legs, moving higher and higher up her thighs. Like a master violinist, he played her beautifully, knowing which chords to play hard and which to play soft.

While his hands outlined and caressed her slender hips and buttocks, a dull ache began to grow inside her body. To quicken his pace, Jennifer unzipped his slacks and tore the dripping pants away from his body.

As he leaned hard against her, Jennifer knew his desire equaled hers.

"Oh, Jen, you feel so good." Paul groaned into her neck, continuing to seduce her with his magic fingers.

Jennifer grasped Paul tightly, her fingers digging into his shoulder, as his fingers slowly caressed her belly and drifted lower, onto the soft down between her legs. Her silk panties were tossed onto his crumpled sodden khakis. She reveled in the exquisite pleasure as he massaged and stroked the intimate parts of her body. The moment was an eternity, as they kissed and caressed each other. She wanted to know every part of him, to know what made him paralyzed with pleasure and want.

The grass beneath them smelled fresh and sweet as they moved about in the damp mist. She wanted him, oh God, she wanted him. Jennifer gasped as they rolled from one position to another, finding new, undiscovered flesh.

Finally, she closed her eyes and waited. She needed him inside her body, desperate for them to finish what they'd started with blind madness and hot desire. Then crash, they rolled right into the cool grotto water.

Sputtering and choking, they coughed as they pulled themselves from the water. The heat had cooled, and the madness had passed.

"Jen, are you okay?" Paul took her fingers and helped her to dry land.

"Yes." She wiped water out of her eyes and took a step back. She desperately needed some distance.

"I guess we got a little carried away." He took a deep breath and narrowed the gap between them. "Look, I'm sorry…"

"No, you don't have to say that." It wasn't his fault. They'd both strayed and gotten caught up. "It was a moment. We're friends. Let's just…" Her lips bent slightly as she searched for the right words. "Blame it on the water gods."

"Ok, the water gods," he agreed as he grabbed for their clothes. "They can be tricky little suckers."

Chapter Three

Paul slammed down the health report on the old doctor's metal desk. He was fit for duty, damn it. He'd spent three months of temporary duty taking it easy in Hawaii. That was plenty of R&R. What more did they want from him? Now he was at his next duty station at Miramar, the large Naval Air Station north of San Diego, and ready for action. He didn't need any more therapy, particularly from some old coot at San Diego's mammoth Navy medical complex.

The gray-haired doctor sitting across the desk just shook his head and smiled sternly as Paul continued ranting and raving. To be told he'd be grounded for at least another six weeks was a bitter pill. It wouldn't change the diagnosis and treatment, though.

"It won't do any good, Lieutenant," the doctor said firmly. He'd clearly dealt with more than a couple frustrated flyboys in his career. "You don't step one foot inside an F-18 until your leg is deemed one hundred percent healthy by your new physical therapist."

Paul argued for a few more moments, more to make himself feel better than anything else, then stormed out of the examination room. Once inside the changing room, he grabbed his starched white uniform slacks and yanked it on. *You're losing it, buddy. Calm down.* He took a deep breath as he slowly zipped up his regulation pants.

Uneasily, he sat down on the long oak bench and picked up the spit-polished white shoes that lay beneath the sturdy clothes rack. Still sitting down, he pulled his short-sleeved white cotton shirt off a nearby hanger and adjusted the epaulets, the black bars at his shoulders. It had felt good to be back in his dress uniform this morning. His tirade had been more disappointment than anger. Okay, his knee wasn't in perfect shape, but his limp was hardly noticeable. Even Jennifer—and she was a physical therapist—said it was barely apparent. His mood shifted from agitation to guilt as she took over his thoughts. Jennifer, Jeff's fiancée, Jake's mom…the woman he had no right to care for, but did.

His head was a jumble of raw feelings and hot emotions as he thought about the night they'd almost made love. He was still a little stunned by the events of that fantasy-filled evening. Their sanity had returned the moment the water had cooled them off. They'd gone too far too fast.

Later on, when Jennifer was safely back in her hotel room, Paul had played the evening back in his head again and again. How could he be so damned disloyal to Jeff? How could he have acted on those feelings for Jennifer? God help him, but he'd wanted her more than he'd ever wanted anyone or anything in his life.

He'd been stunned by his utter lack of control, but even more shaken by feelings of confusion and loss; he couldn't get her out of his mind. Her skin was so soft, like a dewy rosebud. And that hair, he loved the way it felt as it had glided up and down his chest and stomach. It was a miraculous satiny combination of silver and wheat and as shiny and lustrous as a blanket of stars. She'd hated the spray of freckles that dusted across her nose. He'd found them—and her—downright alluring.

The image of her that day was still crystal clear in his mind. The plain white blouse that hung loose around curves that were anything but plain. A mid-thigh denim skirt that emphasized slender, fit legs that went on forever.

His fingers trembled as he struggled to hook the top of his collar. He'd had great pleasure, too much pleasure, discovering what was underneath those clothes. Their frenzied passion at the falls had made his head swim.

He tried to shrug it all away. A crazy moment in time. Just those damned water gods at play. But it was impossible to pretend making love to Jennifer wouldn't have changed his life. She'd made him feel alive and whole, helping him fill an emptiness that had been missing in his life for a long time. She'd been occupying his mind ever since.

He ruffled his freshly cut hair with an agitated hand. It was a damned shame. For a little less than twenty-four hours, he'd been on top of the world with her.

Although it had felt so right—*they* had felt so right—he knew it was wrong. She'd loved Jeff, and Jeff had loved her. He'd had no business doing what he'd done that incredible night.

Paul clenched his jaw and kept rationalizing the situation in his mind. With his career in such a jumble, it wouldn't be fair to bring somebody else into his complicated mess—especially somebody he cared about so much. Besides, he needed to concentrate on getting his leg to that one hundred percent mark the doctor was talking about, didn't he? Time was running out; if his leg wasn't shipshape soon, he'd lose his right to fly and would spend the rest of his Navy career as a flight deck officer. God, how could be spend the rest of his life grounded?

He wiped damp palms down the length of his pants. He wasn't the right type of guy for her anyway. His track record with women was certainly proof of that.

Jennifer knew all the gory details. She didn't need or want a man like him—especially when she had a baby to consider. He smiled as he thought of the happy little baby with Jeff's eyes and lopsided smile. An odd tug at his heart gave his emotions an unfamiliar jolt. He wasn't much of a kid person, but Jake made everything seem a little bit fuzzy. He'd love to be a part of that little boy's life—for Jeff's sake as well as his own. His mouth became cotton-dry. That sweet little boy deserved better than he could ever give.

Jake needed a man in his life who'd give him the moon, and Paul wasn't in any position to make promises. He knew himself too damn well.

A lump caught in his throat, and he closed his eyes. He had to face the truth without her—without anybody else. He'd almost opened up to her, but it wouldn't have been fair to burden Jennifer with his problems. While he'd been furious at the doctor, he'd been even more furious at himself. He needed to get back in the cockpit again and soon. If he didn't, he'd lose his nerve for good this time.

Every muscle in his body tightened. God, just the idea of flying again caused his palms to drip and his stomach to turn to mush. *You've lost the edge. You're a coward.* The words shouted in his brain. It had been his life, his dream, and he wasn't going to let it go. He couldn't.

****

"Lori, I'll do the veteran group and you do the pilots." Jennifer paced as she spoke into the phone. As she listened to her partner's explanation, she toyed irritably at a wisp of blonde hair that had escaped the barrette that held back a wave of curls. "I thought it was all arranged."

"I'm sorry, Jennifer, but you impressed Commander Taylor so much during your presentation that he specifically wants you to work with his guys," the soft voice on the other end of the phone disclosed. "Come on. It's only for six weeks. And if they're happy with us, it could lead to larger contracts. Isn't that the reason we pitched to the Navy hospital?"

Of course it was, she agreed. When she and Lori started their private physical therapy practice two years ago, they'd decided to play like the big boys. Not only did they see patients at their office, they marketed themselves as freelancers to hospitals, nursing homes, and other large organizations.

Six months ago, Jennifer had treated the son of an admiral. The senior officer had been so impressed by her care that he'd recommended Jennifer and Lori to the physical medicine staff at the largest military medical complex in the city. They'd handled some of the overload at the hospital, and now they were getting patients of their own. Commander Taylor had been one of their overload patients. He'd like the results so well—the healing of torn ligaments in his left leg—that he'd decided to send some of the men in his command to Jennifer and Lori. Now for the next six weeks, she would be catering to a bunch of flyboys.

She moved the receiver to her other ear and grumbled back her acceptance of the situation. The next six weeks could be a turning point in their practice if they were successful. She needed this to work—for herself, for Lori, and most importantly, for Jake. If everything went well, they'd be able to hire additional therapists soon. Then she could enjoy the financial aspects of her hard work and spend the time she needed to with Jake. It was difficult to keep up with all the bills, and being a single mom was trickier than she'd ever imagined. The foundation she was laying now would set the course for the rest of their lives.

After she hung up the phone, Jennifer drifted toward the bay window in her living room. She nibbled on a polished nail as she squinted at the deep pink sky, a backdrop to the dark rocky mountains in the distance. Pilots—the word sounded so lonely in her mind. Jeff. Her throat grew taut as she thought of her dead fiancé. It had been more than a year and a half since the accident, and there were still times she couldn't make the hurt go away. She brushed a stray tear from the corner of her eye and was irritated by the emotion welling up in her.

No, not again. She was stronger than that now. She wanted to live in the present, not dwell in the past. She'd been stunned how the pain had softened for an instant when she'd been with Paul Davis.

Hawaii. She'd been home only two weeks, but it seemed like a lifetime ago. His spark of excitement, of hot smoky passion, had made her forget for a day. The following morning had brought back the reality and the pain. She'd been unfaithful to Jeff, and with his best friend. God, how could she have let it happen?

It had happened because there'd always been that flicker of attraction between the two of them. They'd both felt it, both ignored it. There'd never been any doubt she'd adored Jeff, so she'd brushed aside the touch of chemistry she'd felt for his devil-may-care best friend.

She crossed to the kitchen and grabbed a diet soda from the refrigerator.

Thank goodness he was thousands of miles away. A man like Paul Davis could turn her life upside down, just when she was finally getting it right side up. As she took a gulp of the cold cola, she plodded over to the couch and plopped down on her new chintz sofa. It had been a catharsis—a release from the past for them both. It didn't mean she loved Jeff any less. Still, it was good Paul was far, far away. She didn't need a complication like him in her life.

The next six weeks would go by quickly. She smoothed back her silvery hair and considered the situation. Very quickly.

****

The late April breeze was crisp as Jennifer maneuvered her light gray sedan down the curvy lanes of Highway 5. She kept the car windows down as she sped up the highway, allowing the early morning wind to whip her fair hair around her face. At a stoplight, she pulled a large barrette from the glove compartment, and secured her now-tangled shoulder-length mane. She laughed as she peered into the rearview mirror, and unruffled the short wisps of her bangs. It seemed she spent half her life keeping her hair out of her way.

Her gaze caught the now-empty car seat in the back. She missed Jake, but he would be full of giggles and laughter when she picked him up from the sitter later in the day.

Since the light was still red, she flipped open the notebook of charts and records Lori had left for her. She'd meant to read up on her new patients last night, but she'd drifted into an early slumber in front of the television.

She closed the book as the light changed. There would be six weeks to get to know her patients. She grimaced at the thought of twelve egotistical Navy pilots, and then grinned wryly at her biased categorization of what her father called the Navy's finest, her future patients.

As a Navy brat, Jennifer had learned at an early age to keep her distance from the overly flirty flyers. It took a certain kind of craziness to do what they did. Barely sixteen, she remembered a tall, dark, and handsome aviator trying to coax her into bed with some sorry line about the risks he took in the air every day and that each flight might be his last. She'd laughed at that first of a hundred come-ons from men just like him.

Like her father, Jeff had been an exception, a wonderful exception to the rule. Over the years she'd discovered she'd been right ninety-nine percent of the time about the rest of them.

There was no reason to doubt her current crop of patients would be any different. Some had injured limbs in accidents, and others just needed to strengthen and firm stretched and tired muscles. She grumbled. Well, she wasn't about to hand-hold and coddle a bunch of flying jocks. That type always expected lots of nursemaiding. Not from her, she thought determinedly as she swung her compact car into the hospital parking lot. Even if she did have that very contrary soft spot for them—because of her dad and Jeff. That was all behind her now. They only brought loneliness and heartache.

Jennifer zipped around to the staff parking lot and gave her name to the attending marine at the front entrance. Before stepping out of the car, she adjusted the large tortoiseshell barrette at the nape of her neck and reapplied fresh lipstick. Under a light dusting of face powder and blush, her cheeks glowed from the cool wind from the drive. Hurriedly, she tidied her light gray wool blazer and cornflower-blue blouse. Just after swinging open the car door, she smoothed faint wrinkles from her matching straight skirt, and picked up the mandatory white lab coat she would wear during work, as well as a bulky tote bag that contained the rest of her life.

After today, she'd be wearing jeans and sneakers with her white coat, but on a first day she liked to dress up and make a good impression.

She walked steadily toward the main entrance in medium-heeled shoes. Only for the briefest instant did she wish for her Reeboks. To Jennifer, looking professional was important—particularly on her first day. At a diminutive five foot three with a child's blonde hair and an irritating sprinkle of freckles across her nose, she could easily be mistaken as a teenage hospital volunteer in casual clothes.

As Jennifer glanced around the enormous medical complex, she squinted while surveying the pretty pink buildings that belonged in the nearby park instead of a place for sick people. In the early morning, the sky was stunningly bright. The welcoming sun poured through tall oak and poplar trees, throwing stray patches of light on the dirt path and surrounding turf.

She strode onto a walking promenade that led to a staff entrance and dug a pair of sunglasses from her pocketbook. The partially shaded walkway was edged with a carpet of brightly colored impatiens. A small patch of lavender forget-me-nots huddled under a stately red maple. The grass had been freshly mowed and smelled spring-like. The early dew hadn't completely vanished, or perhaps an early morning gardener had already begun work for the day. The green lushness reminded her of Hawaii—and a night, sweet and desperate, filled with romance and longing.

In the last two weeks, she'd done her best to forget what had happened with Paul Davis. Unfortunately, as she took in the fresh smell of nearby wild jasmine and carefully tended gardenias, his name made her shudder with memories. For a crazy moonlit moment, she'd thought him the furnace to reheat a heart that had cooled. He was the kind of man to make a woman almost forget other men. Almost. But that was the illusion of a beach and midnight dip in a tropical paradise thousands of miles away.

If they hadn't been so enthusiastic, it could have been a disaster. Making love to Paul was about the last thing she needed—but oh, she had wanted him. In the daylight, she could see more clearly. She wasn't ready for another relationship, especially one with a pilot. Especially one with a pilot named Paul Davis. She glanced heavenward. She wasn't ready for the risks and the pain. Or the guilt. And for Jake, she needed somebody with staying power. A child needed security, stability. If she were to get involved in a relationship again, it would have to be with a man she could count on. But she was getting ahead of herself; it would be years before she could even consider allowing another man in her life.

"Jennifer, over here." A familiar voice called from behind her, and she pivoted on her heels to greet her physical therapy partner.

Lori Hampton raced up the dirt lane carrying an armload of papers. With bright red glasses, dark unruly hair, and a purple and orange jumpsuit, she looked like a psychedelic punk rocker. When it came to physical medicine, though, Jennifer couldn't have a better partner and her patients couldn't have a better therapist. Lori was an expert in the field, succeeding in treating the untreatable. The football player with the shattered knee could attest to that, as well as the young ski champion who'd been wheeled into the hospital with multiple leg fractures and walked out several months later under his own steam. Lori didn't believe in the impossible—that was her number-one secret to success. Jennifer learned more from her in a week than she had in three years of practice.

When Lori reached her, she wrapped her arms around Jennifer's shoulders in a warm hug. "I missed you, Jen. First you go away, then I go away. Visiting the in-laws was a terrible bore, but they sure fussed over their granddaughters. It will take me weeks...no, months...to undo the damage. I hope Hawaii was wonderful. You should get out in the sun more often. You look wonderfully radiant. Meet anybody interesting, or is that just a great tan?"

They strolled up the walkway arm in arm. "Interesting?" Her face flushed. Normally she was comfortable talking to Lori about anything. Just five years her senior, Lori was as much a trusted big sister as she was a business partner. Lori knew all about Jeff, and had cried with her about his death.

Lori stopped dead in her tracks and grabbed Jennifer's arm to prevent her from striding ahead. "What happened? Who is he? God, it's been so long."

Jennifer exhaled a long, hot breath and then nibbled on her upper lip. Lori watched her response and lifted her eyebrows in retaliation. "Stalling will do you no good."

"Okay, okay." She glanced down at her feet before spilling her news. "I ran into one of Jeff's friends in Hawaii."

"Good friend?"

"His best friend," Jennifer replied with a weary chagrin.

"And?"

"And…" She sighed again. Now wasn't the time for this. Maybe never was the time for this. "Things got a little hot and heavy." With the declaration, Jennifer started back up the path to the hospital. Lori was by her side in an instant.

"Wait a second," she said, halting her again. "You can't say something like that and just walk away."

"We'll talk later." Jennifer flashed her an awkward half smile.

"But I want to hear all about the steamy part." She groaned as her eyes widened with curiosity.

Jennifer sighed uneasily. "Later, I've got too much on my mind this morning to dwell on an event that I'd rather forget."

"All right, all right. But I want to hear everything later." She hesitated a moment as if to shift gears. "Have you had a chance to go over the files I dropped by your apartment?" She continued talking when Jennifer shook her head. "Well, you've got a real mixed bunch. But from what I can tell, there's no one hopeless in the group."

"I've been trying to prepare myself for their stories about being at 30,000 feet." She shook her head, feeling her pony tail swish across the back of her neck. "It's funny, but as a kid I used to love Dad's tales." Of course, that had been years before Jeff and the accident.

Her father had been a fighter pilot twenty years ago. As a little girl watching her dad perform barrel rolls in the sky with his squadron, she'd been fascinated by flying. She'd considered learning to fly herself, but weekends volunteering at the local hospital and then four years of college to become a physical therapist didn't leave much time. Still, it didn't surprise anyone—except herself—when she'd fallen in love with Jeff Lyons. And now he was dead. A stupid accident that wasn't anybody's fault. It was that simple. It happened to a lot of good pilots. She'd hated flying from that moment on. She rubbed her eye, preventing a single tear from welling up. "But there are only so many flying ace stories a girl can hear in one lifetime."

"And I'm sure you'll be hearing a few more than that." Lori opened the staff lobby door and walked in front of her fair-haired partner. "You know this place pretty well by now, don't you?"

"Um, yes." She was momentarily distracted by the fast pace of the hospital. At times, doctors and nurses were mere blurs of white. The medicinal, antiseptic smell that dwelled in the corners of every hospital was in full strength here. She realized quickly they were near the emergency room. "I've seen a few patients here. Right now, I'm working with a little boy, Billy Wilder. You know, the thirteen-year-old. He was an overload patient, but he's been doing such a good job with me, they wanted me to stay on his case."

During the next few minutes, they reached the physical medicine department and inspected the facilities and equipment. Then Lori went one way and Jennifer went another. Everything seemed to be in order. She'd borrowed a classroom for the first part of the morning's activities. In the future, she would see the pilots individually for therapy. Today she was going to present a rundown of the program and give them the opportunity to ask questions. From experience, she knew there were always questions, the same questions. She would also fill in blanks left on the charts. The charts. She glanced down at her gold wristwatch, then at the loose pile of papers and files scattered on the desk. She shook her head, irritated at herself. There was no time now; they'd be here in a minute.

In the midst of straightening her files into a neat pile, she was distracted by heavy footsteps and a deep booming voice. Before looking up, she recognized the tenor. "I just wanted to make sure you had everything you needed, Miss Wade." The warm voice of Commander Taylor was accompanied by a smile just as welcoming. "You know how things can be. I'd hate to provide you a room and find that it had no tables and chairs."

She crossed in front of the desk and extended her

hand, which he accepted with a sound handshake. "Everything seems to be in order, sir. Thank you."

In their first meeting, he had impressed her as a man who easily took charge. She wasn't surprised to see him checking out the facilities personally.

"I also wanted to warn you that some of my squadron would rather have duty at the North Pole than be in your therapy program. I don't believe we have any volunteers. The next six weeks is an experiment for all of us, and they don't want to be here."

She nodded her head in agreement. "I understand. No one wants to feel like a guinea pig." This was a new kind of program. The Navy normally didn't have the funding to keep their men in therapy programs unless they were practically crippled. This program was as much preventive maintenance as physical therapy. To Commander Taylor's dismay, many of his officers routinely functioned at eighty or ninety percent. He'd decided that wasn't good enough anymore.

"If it's all right with you, I'd like to say a few words to my officers this morning before you get started." He glanced up toward the door as the group of twelve disgruntled men entered the classroom.

Jennifer smiled in agreement and watched as the men filed through the door. She watched for limps, shuffling, something not quite right in their gait. She looked at their faces, and tried to forget they were pilots.

The automatic smile plastered to her mouth melted the moment she saw him. Color drained completely from her face. The excitement from the first day on a job, which normally sent her blood pounding, settled at the bottom of her feet. His name lingered in her throat, but for the moment, she was speechless.

Then his gaze shot to the front of the room and their eyes locked. Paul Davis. *Oh my God, Paul Davis.*

It was the booming voice of Commander Taylor that reminded her she was not in Hawaii and they were far from alone. Paul's eyes were on her as his commanding officer again explained to the group why they had been selected for the program. She heard the words strengthen, improve, be the best, but she was not listening.

He was here….in San Diego? Nothing would have happened if she'd known he was to be one of her patients. My God, he'd come so close to being her lover. The fact that he hadn't been was barely a technicality.

She toyed impatiently with a button on her crisp white lab coat. She'd expected him to still be soaking up the rays in Hawaii. Behind the plain metal desk, heat rose in her body, and she forced a smile back on her face. The work, she needed to focus on the work.

****

He read the hot emotion in her eyes. With his heart pounding, he'd seen the shock and anger in her gaze. She didn't want to see him again. She was upset they'd happened and wanted to forget what they'd started. He knew just how she felt.

At the same time, he didn't know if he could put Hawaii behind him, behind them. He closed his eyes and breathed deeply. He was torn, torn between loyalty and friendship, and memories of a passion that just wouldn't fade.

When it was Jennifer's turn to speak, Commander Taylor took a seat in the back of the room and gave her the floor. She swallowed hard, then strode to the front of the desk and leaned against it.

"Gentlemen, it's a pleasure to be here today." Her tone was crisp and professional, and she made every effort not to meet *his* gaze. "During the next six weeks, I'll be working with each of you in daily individual therapy sessions. I've spoken to your doctor, and I've read some of your charts. Our job is to make you as fit as possible. Most of the program consists of exercises and equipment you're probably already familiar with. My job is to teach you how to exercise properly, to work on the muscles and problem areas that need help. I'll be meeting with each of you individually this morning for some preliminary fitness tests."

She picked up a copy of the morning schedule and displayed it to the group. "Please find your name on the schedule and meet me in the gym in your sweat clothes at your designated appointment time."

****

"Okay, stretch and flex your leg until I tell you to stop."

Jennifer felt strong thigh and calf muscles under loose Navy blue sweat pants. They belonged to a man of average height, but built like a Sherman tank, he appeared taller. His thighs were as strong and wide as telephone poles, and his arms and barrel chest were the result of dedicated weight lifting. If it weren't for curly strawberry blond hair and a small boyish nose, Lieutenant Scott Montcliff would have looked overpowering. As it was, he seemed more like a teddy bear. "Let me know when your leg feels tired, or if it starts to hurt."

He nodded at Jennifer and continued. He'd gotten a

nasty sprain a few months ago. The leg still bothered him at times—he wasn't the type to complain, but instead to grin and bear it. When his jaw tighten in a grimace, she grabbed his leg in mid-lift. "Okay. Enough already. This is only a prelim." He relaxed on the exercise bench beneath him, breathing deeply. "So are you a draftee into this program?"

He smiled broadly. "Is it that easy to tell?"

She nodded. "Lift your arm to your chest and start flexing." His arms were even stronger than she'd originally determined. "Good."

"Do I have any volunteers, or was everyone ordered here?" She already knew the answer, but wanted his take on the situation.

The glimmer in his hazel eyes told her she'd have her hands full. "Most of us were dragged here kicking and screaming. Wait until you start with the next guy."

She glanced down at her schedule and bit her lower lip. Scott was her second-to-last patient of the morning. "What can you tell me about Paul Davis? Stop now and let's go for a short walk." She led him to the treadmill and set the timer and speed before he began.

"Want to know all about the troublemakers?"

"Something like that." She plugged the rate into the running machine.

"I've known him off and on for a couple of years. He was in a bad accident a while ago flying this hot demo two-man F-18. Boy, that baby could really fly— so much sexier than an F-14. Unfortunately, even though it had passed all tests, it still had bugs. His RIO died. He was in Hawaii recently, on temporary duty. I understand he's mad as a hornet to be grounded."

Her mouth went dry. "Is that so?"

"You know the kind. Always flies by the seat of his pants. The first to volunteer for any job with an element of risk. Works hard, plays harder. Likes fast planes, faster women. You know the type. Nice guy, though," Scott added, comfortably keeping up with the machine. "He'd give you the shirt off his back."

Color vanished from her cheeks for the second time that morning. She could feel it. But she kept her gaze glued to the electronic recorder, afraid of what her eyes might reveal if she looked at her patient. The shirt off his back, that's what Paul had given her. And what had she given him? Her stomach rumbled from the memory.

"Course, he hasn't been the same since his accident," Scott went on, occupied by his thoughts. "That happens, they say. But you know those wild guys. They don't stay down for the count for very long."

The timer started buzzing and the automatic track stopped. Jennifer jotted down the results, keeping the pen tight in her fingers. "Thanks. That will be all for now, Lieutenant."

He bent down to stretch his legs. "Scott, please. If you're going to whip my butt into shape, I'd like us to be on a first-name basis."

His grin was infectious and she returned it. "Scott. You can make it Jennifer, then."

"Hey, Monty, you're eating into my time." The voice sent shivers through every inch of her body. Without turning to the door, she knew whom it belonged to.

"Speaking of the devil."

Paul traipsed forward and shook the other man's

hand.

Jennifer stood back, bracing herself against the running machine. At that very second, she was certain her heart was beating faster than any patient who had used the stationary track.

His eyebrows raised into two perfect arches. "Oh, really?"

"Yeah. I was warning her."

"I don't need any warning, Scott. I'll see you tomorrow at nine. Bye." Her voice and her brain disconnected as a flurry of emotions raced through her soul. Paul didn't move until he heard the swinging door stop after Scott's departure. He shifted toward her slowly. "I didn't think I'd be seeing you again so soon, Jennifer."

"I didn't either."

"I guess this is a surprise for both of us." He closed the distance between them to mere feet.

"It was for me." She cast her head down, but was unable to prevent herself from looking back up at him.

"You didn't seem too happy to see me in there." He tilted his head toward the makeshift classroom.

She tried to back away, but it was as if her feet were glued to the floor. She turned again to meet his eyes. "I wasn't," she murmured.

He reached to grip her forearm with a gentle but firm hold. "I don't want you to feel bad about what happened between us."

"Why didn't you tell me you were coming here from Hawaii?" The angry words spilled from her mouth, and he released her. "If I'd known...nothing, Hawaii wouldn't have happened." She spoke quietly, shaking her head. "It shouldn't have happened anyway."

"I didn't know I was going to be transferred here then. I never wanted to hurt you, Jen. I'm sorry."

"I've never felt so awful about anything in my entire life," she cried in a burst of emotion. Her hope to stay cool, calm, and collected shot out the door. "It was a rotten thing to do to Jeff's memory."

"Jen, I'm sorry," he repeated again, because it was obvious she hadn't heard him. "I'm really sorry."

"I have felt so guilty…" She sighed, exhaling in one big gust.

"Don't, please," he said, moving to comfort her. "You have nothing to feel guilty about."

Her eyes flew open as she backed away. "How can you say that, after we…"

"Jennifer, it just happened. If there's any blame to be had, it goes to me. I should have stopped; I shouldn't have started in the first place." He put his arms around her, and she didn't shift away this time.

"I feel like I've betrayed him." She choked and her eyes welled up. "I loved him so much, Paul. How could I let that happen?"

"Because you're human," he answered simply, gently stroking her hair.

"No, that's not good enough." She pulled away and shook her head resolutely from side to side.

"Then how about because I'm utterly charming and irresistible?"

"What?" Her eyes shot up to his.

"Jen. I'm kidding," he said gently, as he reached over and cradled her tense shoulders in his hands. "I won't let you beat yourself up over this."

"I wish it was that easy."

"It can be." He smoothed his fingers over her cheek. "We both cared so much about Jeff. We were probably the two most important people in his life. I don't know if this makes any sense, but I think sometimes strong emotions can develop from a shared pain. It doesn't mean we didn't love Jeff; it just means there was a moment when we…"

"I know what we did," she interrupted.

"I can't pretend I haven't been attracted to you, because it wouldn't be true. I always thought you were special and that Jeff was a hell of a lucky guy. But, I never intended to cross over the line; our friendship, the past we share, means a lot to me. I'd hate for that to change."

"I don't know what to say, Paul."

He captured and held her fingers. "Say you'll let bygones be bygones," he implored. "I don't expect to be in town for more than three or four months. My stay largely depends on how successful your therapy program is for me. But I'd really like to spend some time with you and Jake while I'm here."

"You don't need to do that. I know hanging out with an eleven-month-old isn't your style. Jeff wouldn't expect that."

"I want to do it because I want to do it, not because of any obligation." His lips turned upward. "I mean, I can teach him all kinds of good stuff."

She laughed at the notion. "Like what? How to wolf whistle and pick up women with sorry come-on lines?"

"For starters." His eyes gleamed with mischief, then he pointed to the universal. "Is this where the torture begins?"

Chapter Four

She walked over to the fitness equipment, and nudged him over and onto the massage table adjacent to the universal. "Please raise your left pant leg and pull it over your knee. I'm going to help you loosen up for the tests."

"This is better than I expected." He strained his neck to watch her massage the muscles of his calf. "What are you doing down there?"

She pulled at a tightened muscle, and he rested his head back on the table. "Please stop talking. I need you to relax your lungs during therapy," she commanded with a voice she hoped was full of authority. "You want to get better, don't you?"

"I didn't know the leg and the lungs were connected."

"Well, actually, it's the vocal cords, yours in particular."

As Paul relaxed, Jennifer went to work. She began to massage the lower part of his calf, going up his leg slowly and methodically. The muscles beneath her grasp tensed and pulsed with each stroke of her hand.

She wanted to make their therapy relationship work. She couldn't risk the success of this critical project on hormones and infatuation. She owed it to Lori and to Jake. Securing a long-term commitment with the Navy hospital would do tremendous things for their business and their future. She had to make it work—and putting aside her unwanted feelings of attraction for Paul had to be a top priority.

She prodded his sturdy upper thigh. "Hey, Lieutenant, this is serious business. No sleeping on the job," she said playfully, her voice a bit strained as she continued to rub his tight muscle.

"Sorry." He blinked, lifting his head to meet her gaze. "I didn't know therapy could be this much fun. It hasn't been in the past."

She pulled his legs around so he was forced to sit up, his feet dangling to the ground. "I doubt you'll be saying that for long. That was the only fun part, I'm afraid. The rest is work," she announced as she headed to the universal.

With ease, Paul hopped off the massage table and followed her to the large piece of exercise equipment. "Now you're going to work that leg like never before. Sit here." She gestured toward the leg curl bench. "And start lifting the bar with your legs until I stay stop."

Paul swung his leg over the bench while eyeing her suspiciously.

Her lips curled in an easy smile. "Don't worry. I've never lost a patient." She moved from the machine and watched as he began lifting the weighted equipment with his legs. "Let me know if it hurts."

Paul nodded and started lifting the weights at a steady even pace. After fifty lifts, his face began to flush, and Jennifer knew it was time for him to quit.

"Okay, okay, don't be a show-off," she said, holding the bar so he couldn't lift it again. "It would be terribly embarrassing if you pulled a muscle in my care."

"So what else do you want me to do?" He wiped his forehead with the hem of his T-shirt. "Do you have some miracle exercises and workouts that are going to make my leg perfect again? You know I'm not so keen on this physical therapy business. I've been through it about a million times in the last year, and so far, not so good."

She cocked her head and tried to stifle a smile. "Oh, we've got some special techniques up our sleeves. Maybe I can change your mind."

He shrugged his shoulders as the mahogany color in his hair intensified under the high ceiling lights.

"The doc says avulsion fractures can be mighty nasty—not to mention all the muscles, tissues, and ligaments that were a mess." He stuck his leg in front of him and briefly examined the skin around his knee and ankle. "It was black and blue for weeks. Doesn't look too bad now. If it weren't for the tightness…"

Her brows knit together, and she twisted her head to get a second look at the offending joints. "As I told you before, the stiffness is a symptom." The muscles in his body tensed under her scrutiny. She realized the pressure and stress to be fit was immense. If his leg wasn't one hundred percent perfect, he wouldn't be flying again. And there were a hundred pilots who'd be glad to take his place in the cockpit.

"We can fix it, Paul," she added, trying to reassure him.

"I hope you're right. You're not the first PT to tell me that."

Her eyes met his and her heart melted—again. "But I trust you, Jen."

"Yes, well. It seemed to heal very well, no

problems with the fracture." She stepped back several paces, digging her hands deep into wide lab coat pockets. "I noticed from your file you've started and stopped therapy with a half dozen therapists."

"Yeah, it was all a big waste of time."

She pursed her lips together. "No miracle cures are being handed out here. It's going to take some time, but if you stick with me, you'll see results."

He smiled lazily. "Not that I have much choice in the matter, but okay, I'm yours."

She tried to keep her expression serious and business-like, but he made it exceedingly difficult. "If we work hard, we can do it."

The blonde hair knotted at the back of her head began to come free, and she poked it back into place with a bobby pin. He made her stomach flip-flop and her head completely jumbled. She wished he'd stop smiling at her that way—even if he only meant it in friendship. She had to concentrate on her business. And that was that.

She glanced down at her note pad at the few scribbles she'd made during the last half hour. "Let's get to work then." She inhaled deeply, trying to sort out the thoughts tumbling in her brain. "I...I'd like to see you do some racewalking."

"Racewalking is for sissies, not he-men." His grin was followed by a wink.

God, she loved—and hated—that wink. "Your commanding officer and staff doctor don't agree with your diagnosis, Dr. Davis."

"Hey, I'm almost as good as new."

"I'm sure you're right, but in the meantime, I prescribe the therapy, not you. You fly planes. I provide physical therapy." She scanned her notes again. "Start with one mile and work up."

"Starting when?"

"Starting today, Lieutenant." She smiled as she ruffled through some files, then handed him a sheet of paper. "I also want you to try this diet."

"Diet?"

She grinned, liking the fact that he was taken aback. "It has nothing to do with weight, Paul." That was an understatement. He had an incredible body. "It's a holistic approach to care."

"Holistic? You've got to be kidding."

Her brows raised, and she eyed him with seriousness. "Don't knock it until you've tried it. It's low in fat, and semi-vegetarian."

"But I like meat."

"I know, but you can cut back on it for a while." She stifled a grin that tugged at the corners of her mouth. "Also, no alcohol."

"No beer?" he asked with mock distress. They both knew he'd never been a big drinker.

"Paul, you and I both know you're just being argumentative now."

His grin widened. "You love it, and we both know it." He then quickly lifted her chin and touched his lips to her cheek. "Bye, Jen."

Jennifer watched as Paul strode from the room, and only then did she focus on the slight limp in his walk to the men's dressing room. Her mouth was dry as she followed his leisurely jaunt. She would do everything in her power to make Paul's leg well again.

When he started flying again, she'd be a distant memory. Even though she knew it would be for the best, she couldn't help feeling more than a little disappointed by the thought.

****

"Yuck, Jake, macaroni and cheese belongs in your mouth, not on your head," Jennifer said with a grimace, as Jake continued to practice the fine art of eating with utensils. She quickly grabbed the sticky spoon from his chubby fingers and decided to demonstrate the process one more time. "You go like this." She smiled widely as she scooped up a spoonful of the cheesy mixture and pretended to place it in her mouth.

"Yum, yum. Now you try it," she said optimistically, handing him back the spoon.

Jake looked entirely too pleased to have control of his silverware again, and Jennifer eyed him wearily. Table teaching was a lot tougher and messier than she'd expected. She felt like putting on a smock every time they sat down for a meal.

"Maybe Mommy should show you one more time," she said, reaching for tiny hands that tightly gripped the spoon. Before she could pry the spoon free, the doorbell rang. "Talk about being saved by the bell. You really lucked out there, buddy boy. It's probably Mrs. Martin; I owe her money for watching you the other day," she said, rising from her seat in front of him. "Now, remember the spoon goes in your mouth, and please don't throw any more macaroni on the floor," she added, knowing the words would be lost on him. "Mommy will be right back."

Jennifer gave him a warning look that made him giggle.

Unfortunately, she was a pushover, and the kid already knew it. Jennifer sighed as she grabbed her purse and headed to the front door.

"Mrs. Martin, thanks for being so patient with me," she said as she opened the door. But, instead of greeting gray hair and kind brown eyes, she was face to face with killer green eyes and a smile that would make any sane woman's heart do a flip-flop.

"Paul…hi."

His smile widened and turned into a charmingly sheepish grin. "I know I should have called first. I mean, you've probably seen enough of me for one day."

"No, no, that's all right," she replied, finding a voice that had dropped to the pit in her stomach. "Won't you come in?"

He nodded and entered her home. "I looked you up," he said, as he shifted out of a light khaki jacket. "I realize it's rude to just stop by like this, but…" He stopped mid-sentence and his brows furrowed as he studied her face.

The intensity of his stare unnerved her. "Is there something wrong, Paul?"

He reached over and pulled a thick blob of orangey cheese from her hair. "I always thought you had lovely hair. New beauty treatment?"

"No, just dinner," she said, with a shake of her head. She knew she must look like a complete mess.

"Gee, and I thought you had such nice table manners," he answered with his infectious grin.

"I've been trying to teach Jake the fine art of using a spoon and fork. It's been a battle and I'm losing horribly, I'm afraid." She took his jacket and led him into the main part of the apartment. "The lesson was nearly over when you rang the doorbell, so just take a seat while I finish him up." She moved toward the kitchen and gasped when her eyes fell on the baby. "Jake, what did you do?" she cried aloud, and Paul dashed into the room as he heard her moan of distress.

Every inch of Jake's beautiful curly blond hair was covered in gloppy macaroni and cheese. The offending bowl was still perched on the top of his head like a jester's play crown. "I don't believe it." She rushed over to retrieve the bowl, then surveyed the damage. It was like a gooey cheese bomb had gone off on top of his head.

"Maybe this will help, but I'm not so sure," Paul said as he grabbed a paper towel roll and handed it to Jennifer. He stood back a good distance from the scene of the crime. "I think you've lost more than the battle here, Jennifer."

"Paul, I know you came over for a nice visit, but maybe some other time would be better." Paul had no experience with children and would probably be thrilled to escape this disaster. Besides he was used to women with shiny tresses, not hair dotted with cheddar. "If you'd like to make a hasty getaway, nobody's feelings would be hurt, I assure you."

"No way," he said, edging slowly into the demolition area. "Tell me what to do. My godson needs me now."

Her lips turned up in a smile. It was sweet that he was trying. "He's not your godson."

"Yeah, but I kind of think of him that way. I hope that's okay."

"Sure," she said, with a self-conscious shrug. "But I don't think it would be fair to subject even an honorary godfather to Jake the cheese monster at the moment."

She moved to unhook Jake's tray from his high chair. She assessed her son's condition a final time before lifting him from his seat. "He's such a mess, I'm going to clean him off in the sink."

While she tried to hold him away from her body as she transferred him to the kitchen basin, he reached for her and ran gooey fingers through her hair. From the corner of her eye, she could see the blonde strands cling together in a greasy mess.

"Thanks, sweetie," she said with a laugh, knowing annoyance or irritation would be futile. Babies would be babies. "That's just what mommy needed."

"I'll take him, Jen." Paul grabbed a large kitchen towel and wrapped it around Jake as he took the baby from Jennifer's arms. Before she could protest, Paul had him safely encased in the towel, gently capturing his hands so he could do no further damage.

"Hey, that's pretty good." Jennifer said, as she dashed over to the sink and quickly filled it with warm water. Together they slipped the towel off Jake as they eased him into the makeshift tub.

"Could you hold onto him for a second?" When Paul nodded, she ran to the bathroom and emerged an instant later with baby soap and shampoo in colorful Winnie-the-Pooh containers.

As Jake playfully splashed the water surrounding him, Paul smiled with a look of accomplishment. "Hey, with a little teamwork, it's not so bad."

She pretended to grimace. "Easy for you to say when you haven't been christened with the sly fingers of an almost one-year-old." She squeezed some soap onto a washcloth and began attacking the project at hand—little hands and toes.

"Nah, it's those lightning-quick fighter pilot reflexes of mine," he retorted easily, reaching out to help her balance her young son in the slippery sink. "No match for even the most sly infant."

"Naturally." She poured a little shampoo into her palm and began the first of what would be many applications.

Macaroni and cheese was a tough opponent.

"Speaking of developing fast reflexes, I thought I might give Jake a head start." He released Jake's arm after verifying that Jennifer had him securely in her grasp. He jogged back to the entryway of her apartment and picked up a large crumpled paper bag from ToysRUs.

"What's that?" With all the macaroni and cheese commotion, she never even noticed he'd come to her door with his hands full.

"A little something for my favorite baby." He pulled a large dark box out of the shopping bag. "I haven't been in a kid store in ages. There's so much stuff, it's kind of overwhelming."

"Yes, toy stores can be mighty scary places nowadays. The manufacturers make sure of that." She tried not to smile as she imagined Paul the fighter-pilot bachelor making his way through the mile-long aisles of the toy superstore.

"I know you probably have a bunch of these already, but I figured one more wouldn't hurt." He pulled a large gray plastic plane from the bag and showed it to the baby. Paul smiled widely as Jake's soapy fingers eagerly reached for the gift.

"It must be in his blood already. Fighter pilots are

born, not bred—right, kiddo?"

Jennifer's heart clutched and her mouth went bone-dry. While she couldn't escape her past, she had no intention of flaunting the daredevil excitement and adventure of flying in front of her son. All flying had brought her was pain and loss. It would play no role in her life or the life of her little boy. She didn't want to make a big deal about it, but her position was clear in her mind.

"I know you mean well," she said, trying to keep her tone casual, "but I'm trying to keep Jake's exposure to flying and planes to a minimum." She worked to take the toy jet from Jake's hands, but he determinedly held on tight.

Paul chuckled as he watched Jennifer try to wrestle his gift from Jake's insistent grip. "I think this is another battle you're going to lose, Mom. He loves it."

"That may be so, but I don't," she muttered through gritted teeth. A moment later, she gave up the fight, knowing the longer she scuffled with him the more he'd want it and remember it. She faced Paul's grinning face. While she didn't want to seem ungrateful, she couldn't relent on this point. "We don't have any planes or Navy memorabilia at home. I don't like Jake exposed to it."

"What?" His grin dropped into a quizzical frown. "You make it sound like a virus or something."

"You think I should celebrate flying in my life?" she asked matter-of-factly.

"No, but are you going to pretend it's not a part of his life?" He ran a finger over Jake's soapy head.

She shook her head. "It isn't a part of his life."

The sparkle in his eyes was gone. "If you say so,

Jen. But his dad was a pilot. It's going to be hard to escape and hide from it."

"I'm not trying to run away from anything." She looked away from Paul and focused on Jake's snow white cap. "I just don't want to flaunt it, that's all."

"I'm not talking about flaunting anything. I'm just asking if you're planning on hiding from this, because it's going to be a hard thing to do. One day, Jake's going to want to know who his father was."

She couldn't prevent a look of annoyance and exasperation from crossing her face as she met his eyes again. "Jeff was not just a pilot. It doesn't begin to define who he was. He was smart, he was funny, he was kind. He would have been a terrific dad."

"I know, Jen, I know," Paul replied softly. "It's just hard to see you avoiding the thing that made Jeff so happy—that really is a part of Jake's legacy."

"Well, it's harder for me to be constantly reminded that if it weren't for flying, my son would have a father," she snapped before she could catch herself. Taking a breath, she tried to get control of her emotions. "I'm sorry. You didn't deserve that."

"That's okay," he said without further argument. "I know I don't have any right to march in here after all this time and push you when you don't want to be pushed. But I cared about Jeff, and I care about you and Jake. I want you to be happy…"

She could read the sincerity and sympathy in his tone. He was trying to understand, even if they didn't need any help. "I appreciate that, Paul, I really do, but Jake and I are fine." She worked to relax the muscles that had tightened throughout her body. "So, let's finish getting the cheese monster all cleaned up. I think another two suds-ups will do."

Paul yanked up his shirt sleeves to dig into the lather again.

"If you both behave, I'll pull out a quart of vanilla ice cream in the freezer," she promised.

****

She needed him; there was no doubt about it. After leaving Jennifer's apartment, Paul played back their conversation in his head.

Of course, he didn't blame her for mourning Jeff's death. When his best friend died, Jennifer had lost the father of her son and the man who would have been her husband. She deserved the right to grieve as long as she needed to—and if she needed to keep jets out of Jake's life, he had to respect that.

His own place seemed especially quiet after leaving Jake Central. Paul smiled as he tossed off his clothes and rubbed his sore knee as he headed for bed. At the end of each day, his leg always felt like hell. Still, he couldn't help grin when he thought of young Jake happily covered in gooey cheese. While he wasn't used to such frantic antics, he enjoyed the lively activity of Jennifer's home. Being a single mom had to be difficult, but Jennifer was doing a terrific job with Jake. She couldn't mask the sadness in her eyes when she talked about Jeff.

The emotional wall had come up a dozen times in the hour and a half he spent with her and Jake. In Hawaii, there'd been a comment here and there about the busy nature of her life. Her hectic schedule left her pretty much isolated and alone. While he didn't blame her for wanting to spend all her free time with her son, she needed more than to be with Jake exclusively. He chuckled to himself. Not that he was an expert on parenting and relationships, but it just made sense, even to his bachelor mind. He grinned again as he thought of Jake, Jake who looked so much like Jeff. God, genetics was an amazing thing.

Paul felt his throat tighten as he closed his eyes and pictured Jeff and Jake together, the way it was all supposed to be. He owed it to his best friend to spend time with Jake, to help provide the male companionship that every little boy needed. In his gut he knew Jake needed him in his life and Jennifer did, too.

Of course, his feelings for Jennifer didn't make the situation any easier. He was crazy about her, and she was only looking for friendship—or so she said. While he didn't want to cause her any more pain, he knew she was only fooling herself. Hawaii had meant something to both of them. They'd made each other feel alive and whole. It would be impossible to wipe away all those incredible feelings, even if he wanted to, and he didn't want to. But for Jake, he would do it. For Jake, he would do anything.

Chapter Five

She liked the sound of children's laughter. In a hospital, it was a mighty rare thing, and Jennifer reveled in the glee. It made her feel good. Patients like Billy Wilder made her feel good.

Billy had stood with leg braces last week. For a kid who shouldn't have been able to even move his legs again, he was performing a miracle.

As Jennifer slid into the children's orthopedic wing the following day, Billy was reading a paperback sci-fi novel in the corner. It would be more difficult than she'd initially thought to get him out of his slump. Four days ago, he'd learned his father's sea tour was to be extended an additional fourteen weeks. To the thirteen-year-old, fourteen weeks might as well have been fourteen years. When he'd found out the news, his progress had come to a dead halt.

"How's my favorite patient today?" Jennifer asked as she approached the boy sitting by himself.

"Hey, Miss Wade." He sighed heavily, putting down the book and looking up to face her.

Jennifer sat at a table next to the boy, still unsure how she was going to deliver her pep talk. Like several of the children with serious injuries, Billy spent his days at the hospital, only going home at night. He attended classes in a large room provided by the hospital for study, and was popular with the other teenagers in his group. During the past few days, Jennifer had heard bits and pieces about Billy's depression from his teacher, as well as other student patients. He was now at an important point in his therapy, and she was afraid he'd start to lose ground if he didn't get back in the swing of things soon. Earlier in his program, she'd spent much of her time cautioning him from trying too hard, working himself to exhaustion. She wished a little bit of that Billy sat in front of her right now. "It's important you don't skip too many therapy sessions. We don't want those bones and muscles to forget what we've been re-teaching them all these months."

"I know," he responded with a deep sigh, closing soft blue eyes for an instant as he relaxed. "But I can't seem to get motivated anymore."

"I realize it may not seem like it now, but your dad's going to be home before you know it." She tousled his wavy brown hair and ignored the gruff look on his face.

"You're right, it doesn't seem like it," he tossed back.

Jennifer stared back at the boy who had been filled with drive and determination. He'd said a million times he wasn't going to have one bad day ruin his whole life. He had set a goal to walk again, and up until a few days ago he'd been doing everything in his power to succeed. She knew he wasn't afraid to face a challenge head-on. If she could only lift him out of this awful blue funk, they'd be on track again. "Hey, I know what it's like having a father gone for months and months at a time. Sometimes it seems they don't even exist."

"He couldn't come home after the accident. The

captain said they needed him too much," Billy replied with a shrug, but his feelings on the matter were far from cavalier. "He was supposed to be home next month, and I'd planned to be standing on my own by then."

"So what's stopping you?" Jennifer moved forward and took his hands in her own.

"I had a goal. I even circled it on my calendar. I was going to meet Dad at the carrier, and I was going to stand and greet him." He sighed again. "Now there's no rush."

Jennifer wanted to rid his mind of that crazy logic he was spouting. "Maybe you could be running by the time his ship docks."

"Yeah, right," he answered, his expression as glum and dejected as ever.

A change of tactics was what she needed now, and she smiled as she came up with the perfect solution. "I don't think I mentioned it to you earlier, but I'm working with a group of pilots off the *USS Valiant*. Mostly, they fly F-14s and F-18s. I think one guy flies an S-3."

Immediately Billy perked up. "Wow, Tomahawks and Hornets," he exclaimed, referring to the fighter aircraft, and the men who flew them. He leaned back in his chair, and for a moment seemed to forget his problems. "Someday I'm going to fly an F-18," he said with a resurgence of energy and confidence.

"Really?" Mission accomplished. The boy pepped up right before her eyes. "You have to be in great shape to fly one of those jets."

"Yeah, I know," he declared a little defensively. "But I can do it."

"I'm sure you can. I know you can," she replied, rising from her seat to the nearby soda machine. "Want one?"

"Okay," he said as she fed quarters into the machine. "My Dad was going to be a pilot, but his eyes weren't good enough. He likes being a flight deck officer, though." He paused for an instant as he accepted the cola can from Jennifer. "I still want to fly. I have pilot-perfect vision."

"One of the fellows in my group is an old family friend." Jennifer found it difficult to keep a straight face with that description of Paul. "He's busy working at Miramar and then coming over here for therapy, but maybe I can have him stop by and visit with you. I mean, he knows just about everything there is to know about piloting the plane you want to fly one day."

"That'd be great." His voice rose again with excitement. She was happy to see the old Billy was back.

"Of course, you realize there is a catch." She raised her brows and grinned.

"There's always a catch," he answered with a good-natured smirk and she was glad to see his spirits continue to improve.

"I expect you to get back with the program in earnest tomorrow. No more pouting at me, your teacher, or the other kids." She playfully punched his arm. "We all miss the Billy we've grown to know and love."

"In the meantime, how about you play me a fast game of hearts," he said slyly, pulling a deck of cards from the backpack behind his wheelchair. This was the Billy she knew and adored.

"Always prepared I see. All right. One very fast game." As he started dealing the cards, Jennifer leaned back in her seat and tried to relax. While she didn't relish the idea of asking Paul for a favor, if it got Billy back on track again it would be worth it.

It had nothing to do with wanting to spend more time with Paul, nothing at all.

****

The card game with Billy turned out to be one of the week's highlights.

Commander Taylor's pilots were one frustration after another. Scott Montcliff, always complaining, turned out to be far from the sweet teddy bear she'd first pegged him to be. A grizzly bear was more like it. If one more aviator tried to sweet-talk her into giving him a clean bill of health, she vowed she'd scream.

While she could deal with all the difficult and cajoling patients, she didn't know what do about Paul. Early in the week, he'd casually stopped by her home and rescued her from a Jake food disaster. Now, every day since then, he'd dropped by with some silly excuse for his visit—he had a craving for a malted and couldn't bear to eat alone; he'd read this terrific book and wanted to share it with her right away; he saw this cool sippy cup with Jake's name already on it and knew it was meant for her kid.

It was obvious Jake adored him already, and in just five days, she'd come to look forward to his little impromptu visits more than she'd imagined was possible. While she'd reminded herself a hundred times in the past few days that all she felt for him was friendship, she couldn't completely convince herself of that fact.

Hawaii kept creeping into her mind; the way his lips had felt on hers, the way his fingers had caressed every inch of her skin and set her on fire, the way he'd made her feel alive again. Then, to make matters worse, he'd mixed in a dose of genuine affection for her son and good old-fashioned fun. Yesterday, he'd dragged her to a local playground and had placed Jake in the middle of a sandbox full of babies. Her son had had a terrific time throwing sand all about with the other little ones, and she was embarrassed she'd never exposed him to such an apparent treat. She was forced to admit Paul was good for them. If she could only keep it all light and friendly, she'd be all right.

By four o'clock Friday afternoon, she was ready to call it a week. Every one of her new patients had received a therapy plan and had started his workout schedule. She knew that 99.9 percent of them thought a therapy program was a waste of time and she was being optimistic at that. She pushed open the exit door with a determined nudge and was flooded by bright afternoon sunlight. She reached deep into her purse for black sunglasses and put them on.

She toyed irritably with a knot of hair around her cheek and walked with determined resolve. She was going to show them—particularly Paul. He went along good-naturedly with her program, but he thought it was a lot of mumbo jumbo. She'd make his darned leg stronger than Superman's when she was through with him.

What made her most agitated of all was that no matter how she tried, she couldn't even begin to look at him with the objectivity she wanted. In therapy, she worked closely with her patients—too closely when it came to him. While he was giving her the space she needed—he hadn't mentioned Hawaii, the waterfall, a night filled with passion and desire—he was too friendly, too likable and, darn it, made her laugh too much. He took the chill out of her veins and replaced it with hot pulsing blood. At the moment, she wished for a job that would put her at one end of the planet and him at the other.

The sun was slowly beginning to drop in the marine-blue sky as Jennifer stepped along the hospital path she'd journeyed up early that morning. Her gait was leisurely, and her spirits lifted as she unhooked the black barrette at the back of her head and let her silver hair fall carelessly around her shoulders. She clutched the oversized white lab coat in one hand and carried a large canvas bag in the other. The faraway spread of mountains on the horizon sat lazy and regal in the distance. A skyline of red-tiled roofs sat quiet and unobtrusive, nestled comfortably around the sparkling harbor. There wasn't a cloud in the sky, and sailboats, white and welcoming, breezed through the restful water.

She waved at a group of young children playing catch in the wide open field facing the front of the medical complex. Further down the path, she spotted some joggers. The fitness course was used by hospital staff and patients alike. It was a pretty, scenic, peaceful run, offering a great way to clear the head and see the city at the same time. For a moment, she considered changing into running clothes, but reminded of the bag full of charts, she knew she'd better head home and start poring over the pounds of paper she was carrying after a week of note-taking and observation.

Then, she saw him—a tall, dark-haired man race-walking on the dirt course—and her resolve melted. Paul had changed into white running shorts and a faded Navy T-shirt. He was limping slightly and moving incorrectly. He was going to hurt his leg. She raised her sunglasses above her forehead to get a better look.

He stopped in mid-step when he saw her approach.

"Hi." His smile was easy and absolutely beguiling. "I like your hair like this." He reached to touch a tip of the silver gilt. "Come out here to twist my leg some more?"

His hair was ruffled by the wind, and short locks waved across his forehead. His face was moist with perspiration. He breathed heavily and moved a rough hand through damp hair. Disheveled and sweaty, he never looked sexier. She ignored the tease and tried to force herself to concentrate. Pretending he had horns, fangs, and a long furry tail would have been a simpler task.

"That's right. You didn't know this, but I keep a voodoo doll of all my patients, and when they get difficult, I just pull out my handy witch's needle. It's not a pretty sight, I assure you." She couldn't help smile. "Actually," she said, trying to remember he was a patient, "I've come to give you some more grief."

Jennifer pointed accusingly at the offending limb. "That leg. You aren't doing it one bit of good by working on it that way."

"What do you mean? You said to racewalk. I'm racewalking."

"Sure. But I want you to exercise your leg the right way, the way I showed you, not your way." Her hair cascaded downward as she leaned over to touch his stiff and swollen ankle.

She shook her head. People rarely listened to their bodies. The way Paul had been exercising and his puffy ankle were certain indications that his leg was hurting. "Your body tells you when to stop. Spread the pressure out more when you move. Don't force the ankle to work overtime right away. It won't like you, and it will fight back. Use your arms and the rest of your body. The ankle will come along in time. Don't be so impatient."

A small family of sparrows scurried by, looking for crumbs. They chirped at the twosome as if asking for leftovers. Jennifer chuckled, having nothing to offer and watched curiously as Paul strolled a few paces to rest on the trunk of a gnarled oak.

"Why don't you show me again?" His voice held a challenge, his eyes an invitation. "That really is the best way for me to learn your way of racewalking."

She lifted her foot in low pumps. "Not today, I'm afraid. I met with Commander Taylor a little while ago so I already changed out of my casual stuff."

She stood straight again and faced him, trying to avoid distraction from the glimmer in his eyes and the tempting curl of his lips. "Anyway, it's not my way, it's the right way," she replied firmly.

"So you said." He nodded his head toward her carryall. "Don't you have anything appropriate to wear in there?"

She considered his question for a moment. "Actually, I do." She always kept a spare set of workout clothes with her.

He crossed his arms across his chest. "I don't mind waiting." He watched her face and spoke again before she could beg off again. "That is, of course, if you want to prove that there really is something to your little therapy program." His eyes held a challenge.

He baited her and she snapped at it. "Okay. Fine, I'll be back in a few minutes." With a sound between a huff and a haughty moan, Jennifer flounced away with her carryall and lab coat in tow.

****

Paul admired what moved under Jennifer's businesslike gray suit. He leaned solidly against the tree again and smiled wider than a Cheshire cat. He'd expected a stodgy old male therapist five days ago. The rotten person who would keep him on the ground. His anger had faded when she'd entered the conference room that morning.

He was trying to keep his distance in a not-keeping-his-distance sort of way. Something wonderful had happened to the two of them in Hawaii. He'd tried, but he just couldn't let it drop. The spark refused to go out—even though they were both trying to put it on hold. All right, he'd work to maintain the status quo for a while.

She needed the time and distance. Of course, she had every right to be wary and apprehensive. If he could have stayed away, he would have. But there was that fire and magic that wasn't going to go away. He saw it in her eyes and felt it in his soul. It wasn't going to be simple at all.

Paul's eyes widened with pleasure and appreciation a few minutes later as the slender blonde skipped out the door and jogged down the walking path to meet him. Pale cotton shorts replaced the plain straight skirt. A matching T-shirt demurely flattered the curves he found so intriguing and appealing. And her bouncy pony tail was back.

"All set?" Jennifer asked as they started out, explaining the proper way to racewalk, addressing him like a patient in therapy.

"Sure." He started at a slow pace next to her, watching her movement closely.

****

Jennifer was pleased as his legs lifted off the ground. The muscles weren't fighting anymore, and his leg was responding positively to the proper movement. After they had gone once around the one-mile trail, they stopped on a bench near the emergency room, and took a breather.

"Hey, take it easy," Jennifer warned, smiling, her defenses down. Exercising always made her relax. There was something about those endorphins. She liked the way her muscles pushed and strained. Her breathing was deep, but regular. Her disheveled hair whipped around her forehead as she pushed herself to the limit. She glanced at her patient. Where he was concerned, she didn't know what the limits were, and she was afraid to find out. "You don't have to win a marathon today, you know."

"Right," he said agreeably, his head down, while resting on elbows balanced on his thighs. He reached down and plucked a black-eyed Susan from its hiding place under the bench. He placed the stem behind Jennifer's ear and rolled her curls through his fingers. "But I bet I can still beat you."

Jennifer turned her head and looked Paul straight in the eye, a mischievous gleam in her baby blues. She couldn't resist a challenge. "Oh, really?" she replied smoothly and then bounded from her seat. "To the water fountain at the edge of the park," she screamed, pointing down the hill through a bench-studded grassy area. "And you better racewalk."

Jennifer laughed as her fit legs carried her down the path, and he was trailing far behind her. But before she was even halfway to the target, she heard heavy steps and deep breathing. Paul easily passed her, and made it to the fountain yards before Jennifer.

Jennifer laughed as she reached the tree, spun around its trunk, and plopped to the ground out of breath. Paul followed her lead, but then leaned over, and playfully wrestled her until his body covered hers and her arms were pinned above her head. She was still laughing, until she looked up and they locked eyes.

The moment was fiery, intense, combustible. Her throat tightened as she held her breath. He's going to kiss me again, and I want him to, she thought quickly, her heart pounding more rapidly than it had from the race. His eyes roamed over her face, going from her eyes to her lips to her hair. When his gaze fixed on hers again, she saw the incredible desire there.

Then, to her surprise, Paul rolled off her, and stood up. He brushed the dirt from his knees and offered her a hand. Jennifer sat up suddenly, perplexed then embarrassed. She took his hand and let him hoist her up from the ground.

Paul leaned forward as he plucked a piece of stray grass from her hair. "See what happens when you try to race someone who's athletically your superior," he said, his face now relaxed and composed. She would have paid a million dollars to know what he was thinking at that moment. His opaque eyes held no clue.

"Yes, but who taught you everything you know?" she said lightly, trying to figure him out. The *New York Times* crossword puzzle would have been less challenging and complicated.

"Good point. I think I'm in your debt." He moved a slow arm across his damp forehead and wiped away the sweat. "Let me pay up."

"Huh?" Her hands nervously hung into the thin pockets of her pale pink shorts. "I don't think…"

He smiled as he leaned over to stretch the muscles in his thighs. "My intentions are honorable, I assure you. The canteen doesn't close for another forty-five minutes. How about I treat you to a snack?"

Her stomach growled at the mention of food. It was strange that some days she couldn't wait until lunch, and other times she missed the noon meal entirely. Today was one of those days. "Fine, but no more racing. Let's take it slow this time."

"Can't take any more, huh?"

Her reply to the challenge in his sharp eyes was a quick dash up the hill and a sprint through the hospital building to the canteen at the back of the reception and records building.

Jennifer stopped when she landed on an empty redwood picnic bench and quickly sat down on the seat. "What took you so long?" She breathed deeply when he arrived moments behind her. "You sure you're only twenty-eight? You were going so slow I would have thought you were twenty or thirty years older." She laughed as he teasingly grabbed her shoulder.

He put a leg up on the bench next to her. "You cheat. What ever happened to one, two, three, go and the requisite racewalking?" He lowered his foot and plopped down beside her. "I'm not even sure you deserve a treat now." He laughed as he reached beneath her hair and lightly squeezed the nape of her neck.

Sparks again. She eased out of his grasp and tried to ignore the way the lightest touch, the slightest movement, caused ripples to move through her body. She masked the emotion with a giggle.

"Okay, Okay. I promise I'll give you fair warning next time. Actually, I only did it out of medical necessity." She added with a smirk, "I needed to see your response time."

"Right." His voice was as smooth and rich as aged bourbon, but with a lot more bite. "If it's a response you're looking for…" His words trailed, and he released the lazy blonde curl he'd taken possession of moments ago. He ran restless fingers over his bare thighs and turned to look at the chalkboard menu. His foot impatiently kicked at the pebbly gravel on the ground. "Recommend anything?"

Her eyes scanned the chart, but she was anxious to know what he was thinking. He wanted her so much; she knew it, she felt it. "The churros and pretzels are good. The chili is too hot. But, of course, you're getting the garden salad."

His posture relaxed, and his eyes took on a playful glimmer. "I want the chili, though."

"Well, I don't think…"

"Ease up a little. I promise I'll be completely holistic all weekend long, but right now I'm craving chili."

"All right." She gave in easily. "But you better get a pitcher—a big pitcher—of water to go with it."

Jennifer watched as Paul disappeared into the

canteen. Damn, why was he such good company? She was fooling herself if she thought exercising with Paul was just in the name of good medical care. She cared for him. She wanted to get to know him better and better. And she couldn't shrug off the guilt that accompanied that knowledge.

Across from her, a young man with a cane dressed in hospital clothes was being fretted over by a pretty dark-haired woman.

"I wasn't sure what to get, so I got a little bit of everything," Paul said as he approached the table. He placed three containers full of food on top of their picnic bench.

Her mouth opened wide. "I hope you left something for the other people." She shifted through the boxes. "My gosh, you have four churros, three pretzels, two bags of popcorn and two chili dogs."

"I figured the chili with the hot dogs would be all right."

She lifted two enormous cups of cola from the bottom of a carton. "I'm sure with this much soda to help it down." She watched as he bit into the smothered frankfurter. "Don't tell me you eat like this all the time?"

"I don't, but I didn't know what you wanted."

"I thought this was supposed to be a snack?"

"It is, so dig in."

Jennifer obliged by eating a chili dog, a churro, and half a pretzel. "I'm stuffed," she said, after eating a knot in the pretzel.

"Guess I ruined your dinner?"

She wiped her mouth with a paper napkin. "That's okay. I hate to admit it, but I love junk food."

"You?" His gaze ran admiringly over her from head to toe. "It doesn't show. You always look great."

She tried to ignore the look, but it moved her like a touch or caress.

"Thanks. But if I ate 'snacks' like this every day, I'd look more like a whale. I try to keep stocked up with healthy stuff in the apartment. I want Jake to have good eating habits."

A cafeteria worker pulled the menu off the wall, closing up shop. Night was just around the corner. "It's getting late..." Paul said hesitantly, glancing up at the hazy dusk sky.

"Yes, it is." She nodded her head a little.

"Thanks for the workout. I think it really helped."

"I'm glad," she answered with a grin. Before long he'd see the results of their joint effort, and the thought pleased her. "Thanks for the food. While my stomach probably won't appreciate it, I did."

"I'll walk you back." Paul picked up the cardboard containers and tossed them in the large metal trash receptacle.

"I have a favor," Jennifer spoke hesitantly as they reached the front of the main hospital building. "I need to pick Jake up from the sitter, so it will only take a few minutes of your time. There's a boy I'm working with in the children's ward. He's just wild about flying and pilots."

"An interest you don't share," he murmured.

"To each his own," she returned easily. "He's been down a bit lately. His dad's deployed, and he's feeling out of sorts. I think he could benefit from a man's attention. If you have a few minutes, would you mind saying hello? I know it would really pep up his spirits."

His magnetic grin made her weak-kneed for an instant. "Sure."

It took a split second for her to gather her possessions and adjust the items in her oversized tote. As they walked through the hospital to the orthopedic ward, Jennifer ignored the heavy antiseptic and medicinal smells that wafted through the corridors. Hospitals were hospitals, after all.

"Billy is a really nifty kid. You'll like him." She spoke evenly as they ambled down the straight narrow halls. She smiled at a young man hobbling down the corridor with a walker. "About six months ago, he was hit by a drunk driver while riding his bicycle. The prognosis wasn't good. In fact, it was horrible. But Billy didn't believe anyone." She smiled warmly at the memory. "He's a tough kid who decided he wasn't going to spend the rest of his life in a wheelchair. He stood for the first time a few weeks ago."

Paul nodded with respect. "And the kid's feeling down? He should be elated."

"He was until he found out his dad's cruise has been extended for another fourteen weeks. He got word the other day. He thinks it's an eternity."

They found the thirteen-year-old in the crowded dayroom playing a game of solitaire before dinner. His mother would be picking him up after work. In jeans and a polo shirt, he looked like any ordinary boy, until you saw that the chair he was seated in had wheels.

"Hi, Miss Wade. What are you doing here at this hour?" The little boy with light brown hair looked curiously from the blonde woman to the tall man beside her.

"This is my friend, Lieutenant Paul Davis. He's the

F-18 pilot I told you about earlier. I mentioned you were interested in flying, and he said he'd be glad to talk to you about everything and anything you want to know about his work."

Paul pulled out a small metal chair next to the boy and sat down beside him.

"It's nice to meet you, Billy." Paul extended his hand to shake man to man.

"You, too," Billy replied, his face brightening. "I really want to fly an F-18 like you someday."

"It's a fast little plane." Paul clearly enjoyed the excitement in the boy's expression. "I'm happy to talk to another flying enthusiast."

Jennifer put her hands behind Billy's chair. They didn't need her to spur on conversation. Their immediate rapport was very apparent.

The dayroom was packed full of people as Jennifer admired the big open space. The hospital did a nice job of making communal spaces like this comfortable and appealing. There were a number of teenagers as well as some elderly veterans enjoying the room. Sitting in a far corner were two elderly patients playing cards and grumbling about each other and the world at large. She smiled as she watched them poke back and forth at each other. She imagined they'd been friends for most of their lives.

Jennifer spoke up. "I have some progress reports to review. I'll just be over at the other table. If you'll excuse me?"

Paul gave her a quick wink over Billy's shoulder and the boy seemed to barely acknowledge her departure. A moment later, she plopped down a stack of manila folders at a small empty table a few feet away.

****

"You fly today?" Billy asked, maneuvering his chair to face the man beside him.

"No, not today," Paul answered, a knot lodged in the middle of his throat. He swallowed hard, trying to mask his discomfort. Finally, he shrugged. "To tell you the truth, Billy, I've been grounded for a while."

"How come?" Questions etched across the boy's thin face.

"I had an accident," he said flatly, trying hard not to avert his eyes from Billy's curious gaze.

Billy leaned forward a little in his chair and the wheels below him shifted slightly. "A bad one?" he asked.

"Yeah, a real bad one." His sigh was heavy and from the heart. "My RIO died."

Billy paled for an instant. "Oh, my God, that's horrible. You must have felt terrible."

Paul's brows rose as he nodded his chin. "It's hard to describe."

Billy hesitated before he spoke again. "Lieutenant Davis, it wasn't your fault, was it?" The question stumbled out a little awkwardly.

"No, Billy, it wasn't. Just a dumb mechanical error. Nobody's fault, really." His throat burned for an instant, and then the pain began to pass.

"Well, then how come you aren't flying right now?"

His palm rubbed on his problem limb. "I hurt my knee and ankle in the accident. Then I reinjured my knee a few months ago in a tricky landing. I still have a little stiffness. That's why I'm seeing Miss Wade. I'm hoping she can help me get my leg back in working order again."

"I can tell you she's a great therapist," Billy said with confidence, glancing over at the next table to the pretty blonde who was intently poring over papers.

"I don't know, Billy," Paul answered with mock seriousness. "She says you were going like gangbusters on your program and then came to a dead halt."

"That's not her fault," he protested quickly, shooting forward.

"Yeah?"

"Yeah, it's my fault." He shoved his back hard in the wheelchair and ran a nervous hand through his short hair. His eyes shot up to Paul. "Did she tell you about my dad?" Paul nodded and watched as Billy's lips tightened in a scowl. "I hate the Navy sometimes."

"Join the club," Paul said jovially, giving Billy's arm a playful shove. "But that's still no reason to put a halt to your therapy. The Navy's your dad's career, whether you're walking or not."

"I know." His jaw tightened. "It still makes me mad."

"Of course, you could turn his delayed return into a positive." Billy scowled before Paul could finish offering his suggestion. "Just hear me out. If your dad was going to be back in port on time, you couldn't possibly be walking, could you?"

He shook his head. "No, he was supposed to be back in a few weeks. I wouldn't have been able to do too much walking by then. It would have been too soon."

Paul lifted his index finger as if a light bulb had gone off in his head. "But you could be walking in fourteen weeks, I'll bet. Just imagine his pride if you met his ship walking—I mean, really walking." Paul hesitated for a second. "Particularly if you make it a surprise for him."

"You think?" Billy asked, his mind obviously spinning, liking Paul's idea.

"Hey, if you work hard you can do just about anything."

"Okay, I will," Billy replied, a new fire in his eyes. "You'll see."

"I haven't any doubt," Paul answered back, reaching over and grasping Billy's shoulder with a friendly tug.

"So when do you think you'll be flying again? Maybe you'll take me up sometime—after I'm walking, that is."

Paul paused, and then hedged. "I'm not really sure, Billy."

The boy offered a lopsided grin. "I bet you're really anxious to get back. I know I would be."

It would be so easy to lie and just nod his head and smile. He just couldn't do it, though. The kid trusted him. "Most of the time," he confessed, rubbing his eyes as he was suddenly tired.

Billy's face screwed up with puzzlement. "Just most of the time? I thought you'd be aching to get back."

Paul released a weary breath, then met the boy's unwavering gaze. "To be honest, Billy, the accident really threw me. Like I said, my buddy died. I'm a little nervous to get back in the cockpit."

"No way," Billy tossed back, not believing what he was hearing. "You are gonna fly again, aren't ya?"

"You better believe it." Paul perked up, refusing to

let his fear creep in. "Sometimes in life you really have to push yourself—even if you don't want to, even if it hurts."

"Okay then, I have a deal for you," Billy interrupted, looking a little too pleased with himself for Paul's comfort.

"What's that?" Paul asked with a small smile, wondering if he'd just created a monster.

"When I walk, you take me flying," he announced with a very self-satisfied grin.

"I don't know, Billy," Paul countered, wondering what he'd started today. He felt cornered by a teenager. What was the world coming to? "It's been quite a while since I've been in the cockpit. Your mom might not like the idea too much."

"Oh, she won't care," he said blithely, then hesitated as if thinking it through a bit more. "But just in case, how about you start flying the day I start walking? Then we'll be able go up together soon after that."

"Well, I do have a friend who has a plane at Montgomery Field." Paul mentioned the small airfield frequently used by San Diego's private pilots.

Billy clasped his hands together and looked terribly pleased with himself. "I guess that's settled, then."

"We'll talk about it. No promises yet." Paul caught the satisfied look on Billy's face and scratched his temple. "I don't know what just happened here. I thought I was the one giving the pep talk."

"You did," he replied, continuing to look pumped up, "and now we both owe each other one." Billy proceeded to resituate himself in his chair. "Would you tell me about your most daring mission?"

****

Jennifer glanced over to the other table, trying not to stare at her two male patients. It looked like her plan had worked, and Billy would be ready to start again with his therapy plan with renewed gusto. He was talking a mile a minute now, barely waiting for Paul to respond to his questions before he asked another one.

A breath caught in her throat as she considered the conversation she'd overheard. She hadn't meant to eavesdrop—well, maybe a little—but she hadn't expected to discover what she'd learned. Paul was afraid to fly.

The information startled her, but she was almost relieved by the news. Maybe he would quit flying and become a flight deck officer. Considering the crash, nobody would blame him. But Paul would blame himself, and anger and self-doubt would eat him up. Even though it meant he wouldn't die like Jeff, she couldn't feel good about the situation.

A moment later, Jennifer was distracted by a strong acrid, smoky odor. Her eyes blinked as they watered, and she touched her fingers to her scrunched nose. She'd always been sensitive to smells, loving a garden, hating cutting onions.

Her eyes flew open and her mouth dropped when she took in the sight before her. To her astonishment, there was smoke coming from an electrical outlet near the two elderly card players. Amazingly they hadn't seemed to notice the smell, or the crackling electrical noise, but she did.

All of a sudden, the curtain framing the nearby window started to smoke. It all happened so fast. The old men finally took notice. One was trying to snuff out the fire with a magazine, but if anything, he seemed to fan the flames.

"Oh, my God, Paul," she screamed, fighting the choking feeling in her throat. She didn't know precisely where he was, only that he was near and she needed his help. Jennifer spun around, fighting hair that flew around her face. She scanned the room. An extinguisher? Where the hell was an extinguisher?

Before she could blink, the curtains framing the picture window was on fire. In seconds, the room was a smoky blur. Almost immediately, the ceiling sprinklers started squirting water, but the light spray was not enough to calm the blaze that was climbing up the far wall of the dayroom. As if operating on auto-pilot, Jennifer ran to the door and pushed the emergency buzzer. A deafening alarm pierced through the halls of the ward.

Unable to wait for help to arrive, Jennifer began to assist patients out of the room. She started with the wheelchairs, moving the non-ambulatory individuals out of the stifling air. Then, she began grabbing arms, pulling those too confused or too frightened out of their chairs and into the adjoining hall. There were so many people; it was hard not to panic. She prayed she'd be able to get everyone out of the room in time.

Chapter Six

"Stay calm. Help will be here in a moment. Everything's going to be fine," Jennifer yelled over the rising hysteria, ignoring the perspiration gathering at her forehead and neck. "If you can walk, please leave through the exit immediately. If you can't, we'll get to you right away."

Jennifer moved quickly, maneuvering patients out of the room as fast as they could go. There were no wasted steps, every motion was done for a reason. *Where were they?* It had been a full thirty seconds since she'd sounded the alarm and no help had arrived yet. She was a trained physical therapist, not a firefighter.

The room was starting to get murky, and her eyes were tearing and itching. She ignored the hot, burning sensation, and scanned the room. Except for the two elderly card players, everyone had been evacuated. They weren't ambulatory, so she scoured the room for wheelchairs. Not one was left in the room, and each man weighed at least one hundred and fifty pounds. She wished she were stronger. There was no way she was going to be able to lift and carry them out of the room, and time was getting short. It didn't take much smoke to cause serious respiratory damage in men their age.

When the alarm sounded, Paul had picked up Billy Wilder and carried him out of the room. He'd followed suit with some of the other patients. Thank God, they were safe. Jennifer took a deep breath and choked as her eyes fell on the two needy patients. She blinked back hot, burning tears and wiped her face with the sleeve of her once-bright pink top. There was only one thing left to do.

Through a growing curtain of smoke, Jennifer made her way to one of the elderly men, who was coughing and sputtering, and attempted to lift him out of his seat. She couldn't make him budge. Damn, Jennifer hissed through clenched teeth, taking a deep breath and gasping through the smoke. What was she going to do now?

Like a commando coming in for a surprise attack, Paul dashed from behind her and almost effortlessly scooped up one man and then the other, holding them on his shoulders. A moment later, they were in the corridor and Paul was gently lowering the men to vacant seats in the hallway. At that same instant, staff members came barreling through the door with fire extinguishers and hoses. Right behind them, nurses and orderlies wheeling gurneys zoomed to the scene.

Patients being attended to, Jennifer breathed a welcomed sigh of relief. It was over. The fire was out, thank heaven. She closed her eyes and welcomed the arrival of clean fresh air to her lungs.

She inhaled and exhaled deeply several times, breathing through both her nose and mouth. Quickly, her eyes opened and automatically scanned the hallway for Paul. With all the doctors, nurses and orderlies, she couldn't see him through the crowd. *Had he gone back in?* Panic rose in her chest and her heart started to sprint.

She clutched the collar of her shirt and dread

seeped into her body. Were there others in there she hadn't seen? What if he'd gotten stuck in there somehow while trying to help? She looked frantically from side to side. *Where was he?* She was about to go for assistance when she spied his dusty Navy shirt across from an open window down the corridor. With his head cocked back and eyes closed, Paul was visibly shaken, his breathing heavy and sporadic.

A rush of relief washed over her. He was all right. Jennifer darted down the corridor and grabbed his arm. For an instant, she clung to him like a lifeline and swallowed fear that had threatened to strangle her. If anything had happened to him, she didn't know what she would have done. The thought was too horrible to consider.

"Paul." She stammered his name and tried to lead him over to a nearby chair. He wouldn't budge. Slowly, he turned his head and looked at her with red and watery eyes. When their eyes met, something between them ignited. The emotion sent shivers—terrifying and exciting—through her body.

"Jen." His voice was hoarse and raspy as his fingers moved to brush a tangled wave from her cheek. "Thank God you're okay." His touch was petal-soft and as light as a delicate caress. "I hate when you're being a hero."

She coughed into her sleeve as the tips of Paul's lips turned upward. The muscles in her body that were finally beginning to calm tightened again. "Tell me about it, Mr. Swoop Down and Save the Day. Just because you think your leg is in perfect shape, doesn't make it true. Being a hero is not part of your therapy program, Lieutenant."

"They're going to be all right, aren't they? All of them?" Paul asked, through a husky cough. Like hers, his clothes were damp and sticky and reeked of smoke. His legs, finally accepting the stress, eased out from under him until he rested on the cool tile floor.

"Yes, I'm sure." She grabbed a blanket from a nearby gurney and draped it around his shoulders. She kneeled across from him, and again forgot her promise to be professional and distant. "You were amazing. You saved their lives." She shook her head from side to side and swallowed hard. If Paul hadn't been there to help, there was no telling what could have happened to the others. "They were too heavy; I didn't know what to do. They would have had some kind of terrible respiratory damage if you hadn't gotten to them when you did. They might have died, Paul." She pushed back curls that skimmed across her cheeks. "I was so worried when I didn't see you right away."

"I knew you cared, Jennifer."

"Of course I do."

"I guess that emergency rescue class came in handy again. It's good to know it wasn't a waste of time." His voice grew huskier as he talked. "What is it about the two of us, Jennifer Wade? Remember that little girl on the beach? Are we jinxed? Do catastrophes follow us around?"

His eyes were smiling, and almost simultaneously their lips turned upward. Moments later, they were laughing.

As their laughter died down, Jennifer began to feel anxious again. The thought that she could have lost him moments ago was so raw, so real. The concerned, caring look in his eyes said he felt the same way about her. She was in real trouble.

Awkwardly, she stood up and noticed he was rubbing his knee. The weight of two adult men wasn't going to make it feel better.

"Do you need a wheelchair?"

He looked down as he massaged his leg. "Nah. It's just a little tired, that's all. I'll just rest here a minute."

"We don't take chances around here, Lieutenant." She turned to one of the orderlies and requested a wheelchair and a room for Paul. The group of patients was fine; she could tell from a quick scan of the corridor. Everyone had been attended to. Even the elderly men Paul had rescued were breathing hard, but normally.

Jennifer stood up and straightened her back. Her heart was beating like a tom-tom.

When the wheelchair arrived, Jennifer and the young orderly helped Paul up and into the chair. He sighed comfortably as they made more of a fuss than was truly necessary. He relaxed and enjoyed the short ride to an empty room with Jennifer and the young orderly at the helm.

The room was bright, airy and smoke-free. An open window allowed a fresh breeze to flow, and the late-afternoon sunlight warmed and embraced them. The orderly situated the wheelchair near the bed, and Jennifer asked that a doctor be sent for immediately.

"I want a doctor to check you out for smoke inhalation." Too anxious and high-strung to sit, Jennifer paced down the short space from the door to the bathroom. A moment later, her anxiety was replaced with anger. A fire; damn, a fire. Those curtains had gone up like kindling. She breathed deeply, holding her chest as she coughed, wondering whatever happened to flame-retardant fabrics. "The weight of those men must have been terrible for you." She glanced up into watery eyes as she attempted to dust the smudges from her cotton top.

It seemed as futile as cleaning the soot from the inside of a chimney.

Paul started to lift himself from his chair, but her harsh look kept him in his place. "Okay, I'll stay where I am. But I don't know about you."

Jennifer stopped pacing back and forth. "What do you mean?" She coughed again, refusing to consider that Paul was not the only person in the room suffering from the smoke and fire.

"Listen to yourself, and your eyes are blood-red."

Her eyes stung, but she'd ignored the urge to rub them. She slid into the bathroom and flipped on the light switch. Her eyes, red and teary, grew wide as she discovered the condition of her face and hair as well as her clothes.

She was a dark and sooty mess. Her neat and prim ponytail was no more. Loose strands danced frantically around her face. She wiped at the gray residue across her nose and found it a pointless exercise. "Oh my gosh, you didn't tell me how appalling I look." She twisted her head and gave him a menacing frown before turning on the warm water faucet and grabbing for the container of liquid soap that hung above the basin. She scrubbed her face until the slick dirty feeling disappeared.

Drying her face, she looked at her reflection again and decided her hair was a lost cause.

"How's the cough?" he asked as she reemerged

from the bathroom, her face shiny clean, tendrils around her face damp from the thorough scrubbing.

"What cough?" she demanded through a gritty, raspy voice.

"I think you need a doctor more than I do." He crossed his legs and smiled. "This is a dangerous place. I think I'd be a lot healthier jumping out of a plane."

"Just stay put." She gave him a sideways glance. "We'll let a doctor decide."

Five minutes later, the hospital administrator, a smallish man with thick wire-framed glasses, a sharp nose, and a pointed chin ran into the room, wringing his hands in a very agitated manner. He pulled a handkerchief from his back pocket and mopped a perspiring brow. "This has never happened before. A fire in our hospital. Who ever heard of such a thing?" His brows knit together, and he moved his hankie to attend to the wetness above his upper lip. "Our insurance company is furious. We should have had our annual electrical inspection months ago. They insist you both spend the night for observation."

Jennifer faced the man and met him eye to eye. There was no way she was going to waste a night in the hospital. While she knew Becki could watch Jake, she had no intention of spending the night away from her son. "That's ridiculous. The lieutenant, maybe, because he has a bad leg, but I'm perfectly fine."

Paul's lips turned in an amused grin. "My leg was good enough to beat you in a race an hour ago. I'll pass, too."

"You don't understand." The small man's mouth twitched. "The insurance company insists. I implore you to comply, Miss Wade. And Lieutenant Davis, if need be, I'll have to get your commanding officer to issue you an order. As soon as you get situated in your rooms, I'll send a doctor to look in on you."

The next five minutes of arguing were a waste of time and energy. With an irritated shrug, Jennifer finally relented.

****

Hours later, Jennifer grabbed a tissue from her nightstand and dabbed her nose; her eyes filled with warm, wet tears. It was one of the saddest things she had ever seen.

"Tell him you're his mother," she pleaded aloud with the character on the television screen. *Madame X* was her all-time favorite movie. When she started flipping the dial more than an hour ago, she felt duly compensated when she found the tear-jerker from the nineteen-forties. Every time she saw the movie—which was at least a dozen times now—she wanted the ending to change. She was always a bit disappointed when it didn't.

Jennifer sat cross-legged on top of the starched white hospital sheets. She still couldn't believe they'd insisted she spend the night.

She was perfectly fine, for heaven's sake. But at least she was being entertained. Jennifer dabbed her nose and wiped her eyes as she grabbed the back of her awful hospital gown. The ridiculous construction invited an irritating breeze from behind every time she shifted.

The quiet steps of doctors and nurses and the mild hum of stretchers down the long empty corridors were the only sounds in the large sleeping wing. Only the faint sound of singing crickets could be heard through a crack in the window. She reached for the glass of apple juice a nurse had brought twenty minutes before for an evening snack.

She took small sips of the juice as she continued to focus her eyes on the black and white screen. When she returned the empty glass to her nightstand, she reached again for a tissue and blew her nose. She discarded the crumpled tissue a moment later and fingered distractedly for a fresh one, eyes still fixed to the older woman and younger man on the screen.

"How about a dry sleeve and some wine?"

Jennifer jerked her head toward the voice surprising her in the night. *Paul.* "You scared me. Don't do that," she scolded with a sniffle.

He continued from the entrance and walked into the room a few paces. "Sorry about that. The nurse said you were up watching a tearfully sad movie, so I thought I'd come and see what a tearfully sad movie was. Like the outfit?"

He lifted his arms to display his bedtime apparel.

Jennifer giggled as she scanned the blue and white striped pajamas that needed to have the sleeves rolled up and the pants hemmed. A gray mismatched terrycloth robe completed the outfit.

"At least it covers you." She made a feeble attempt to close her impossible gown from the back.

She heard a sob from the screen and the television once again captured her attention. "This is the best movie," she murmured.

"Look what it does to you, though." He leaned across the bars surrounding the bed to dab her eyes with the sleeve of his terry robe. "You're a mess."

"I wouldn't talk if I were you," she muttered,

casting her eyes over his bedclothes. "Anyway, it's a wonderful movie."

"What a softy."

"I'm not," she said with a snort and grabbed his arm to use again as a towel. Releasing him, she asked, "Didn't you say something about some wine?"

He stepped into her bathroom and returned with plastic cups filled with Chablis. "Here."

"Thanks, but you shouldn't be having that."

"We're both off-duty right now and this is a special occasion."

"Right," she said with a laugh.

"How's Jake?"

"Fine," she responded a little wistfully. She'd called Becki ten times for updates and he was doing just fine without her. "I miss him. We've never spent the whole night apart before."

He warmly rubbed her shoulders. "Afraid he's having a wild party with his pals?"

The thought made her laugh out loud. "Yeah, something like that."

Dialogue on the TV caught her attention, and she focused again on the screen. "This is the saddest part of all. She's going to die before she tells him the truth."

"How do you know? Have you seen this before?" He lifted his cup for a sip of the inexpensive dry wine.

"Of course. It's much more fun that way."

"You're crazy." He rumpled her hair with his hand.

"Shhh." She sniffed loudly as the story ended—the way it always did. As the final credits were shown, she leaned back and stretched her legs out in front of her. She wiped her eyes for the final time. "Now wasn't that great? They don't make movies like that anymore."

"Thank goodness. You'd be walking around red-eyed all the time." He picked up the remote control and started to flip through the radio channels. He stopped when he found a station playing jazz music from the big band era. "This I like."

Sitting in the chair beside her bed, Paul picked up her hand and held it as the band played "As Time Goes By."

"I love this song." Jennifer sat back, her hair floating around her face as she relaxed to enjoy the music.

"Yeah, a softy would," he teased lightly, brushing his fingers on the tender skin of her hand.

When the band started to play "Moonlight Serenade," Paul undid the bars around her bed. He took her hand and urged her off the starched white sheets. "Dance with me." It was more command than invitation, but Jennifer still found the request hard to resist.

Before she could protest, she was standing on the cool linoleum of the hospital floor swaying to the sound of the romantic ballad.

With lulling music in the background, she could hear the steady pumping of his heart. He was warm and smelled freshly of soap. She buried her head in his chest and tried to ignore the sensations that were enveloping her. Her body was responding, but so was her heart. That was the part that scared her the most. If it were just the sex, the physical attraction, she wouldn't have been so terrified. But she was starting to feel with her heart and her head—and the risks were just so great.

Today, she'd been absolutely horrified that Paul

might have been injured in the fire. She'd never felt a panic quite that intense before. At the time, she'd been too stunned to think much about the emotions he was stirring in her. During the last few hours, though, she'd given it more thought than she'd ever confess, and she didn't particularly like the answers that kept cropping up in her mind.

In the cocoon of his arms, she felt so safe and protected. She forced her eyes shut; God, was she falling in love with him? The thought sounded ridiculous as it played in her head. He wasn't the kind of man she wanted. He wasn't the kind of man to love only one woman. He was the type to take risks, break hearts, and never make promises. He lived one day, one moment at a time. That wasn't for her, especially not when she had responsibilities, a son she owed stability and permanence. No, it was impossible. It would be years before she'd be ready to open her heart again.

If the situation had been different, she would have wanted to close her eyes and just drift away in his arms. Instead, she was aware of every sensation and motion. Paul's solid chest, equally masculine arms, and strong lean legs swaying with her to a romantic beat were hard to ignore.

She'd noticed the five o'clock shadow that had formed on the lower half of his face. It lent him a rugged, dangerous quality that made her knees suddenly weak. God, she wanted him to make love to her. And, as his hard body moved against hers, she could tell the feeling was mutual.

"What did the doctor say?" Jennifer asked in a voice slightly above a murmur. She kept her head where it was, resting lightly on his chest, letting him lead her on the floor to the music. She wanted to think of anything except the sexy thoughts that just ran through her brain.

"I'm as right as rain," he said, with a smile in his voice. "He also couldn't believe that I was in a therapy group, a strong, incredibly healthy he-man like me." His voice was soft and melodic as his fingers stroked through her hair.

"Is that what he said?" she murmured. Her eyes fell on the open window that framed a bright crescent moon before moving to his gaze. What she saw there made her shiver with need.

"Something like that." His hands slipped inside the back of the gown, and started to skim the delicate skin across her shoulders.

His mouth brushed across her halo of hair. A tingle of excitement started at the tip of her toes and rose until the fire was everywhere. His fingers stroked the baby-fine hairs at the nape of her neck. They were no longer dancing, just standing, holding, waiting.

Gently, he lifted his free hand to hold her chin and her breath caught in her chest.

"Tell me to stop…if you want me to stop," he whispered, just before their lips met. She didn't argue, she didn't protest, she didn't want to. Her lips opened to welcome his tongue, as he delved into her mouth.

Emotions burned bright as he moved from her lips and journeyed to her neck with hot, quick kisses. She sighed as he fingered the back ties of the hospital gown. With the slightest pull, it would open.

"Jen?" He breathed into her ear, the need in his voice so urgent.

She looked deep into his eyes, eyes full of passion

and wanting. "I don't know," she gasped, so aware his desire mirrored her own.

"Jennifer…"

She closed her eyes and her jaw tightened. Why couldn't it all be simple? "I'm sorry."

"You don't need to say…"

"I do, Paul. I'm attracted to you, and I don't want to be," she admitted with painful honesty. Pretending otherwise would be futile. "I like the rules we've established; I feel comfortable with you as my friend and as Jake's godfather. It feels right. You and I together like this doesn't."

His eyes penetrated hers. "I know that I shouldn't have the feelings I do. Jeff was my best friend. I'm only going to be in San Diego for a few months—and I don't know where I'll be stationed next. But I have to be honest. My feelings for you aren't platonic. I don't know if I have the right to want more, but I do."

Her heart pounded frantically in her chest. Why did he have to be so darned honest? "Paul, I know how much you cared about Jeff and how awful you feel about the accident. But you don't have to feel responsible for Jake and me."

"That's not what this is about, Jen. I mean, I think Jake needs a man in his life, but if this was just about an obligation to Jeff, it would be easy—and it's not easy."

She nodded her head as she sighed in agreement. "We've been seeing a lot of each other since you started therapy. It would be simple for us to fall into a relationship together. We've said it all before. We have a past, we share a loss, and there is a definite attraction. But I'm not over Jeff; there's still a big hole in my heart, and I'm not ready to move on."

"I don't mean to push you, Jen," he said softly, offering comfort, gently stroking her cheek. "I want you to have all the room you need. It's just that when we get together…"

She picked up where his words trailed off. "I know, I feel the same way, and it's confusing the heck out of me. Besides my own feelings, I have to consider my son first. He needs stability and permanence in his life—and that's not who you are. I can't let crazy emotions get ahead of what's right for my son."

"I would never hurt your son, Jen. I'm wild about the kid—even when he's coated in macaroni and cheese."

She couldn't prevent a grin from touching her mouth. "I know, and I think that's great. But for all of our sakes, I think we need to back off for a while. Things are moving too far too fast."

"What are you asking me to do?"

"I need time, I need space. No more drop-in visits, at least for a while." A knot tied in her throat as she took a deep breath. "We owe it to each other, and we owe it to Jake."

****

She received a clean bill of health the next day, and spent the rest of the weekend with Jake. The following week and the week after that included a very heavy patient load, and she barely had enough time to think about Paul, much less spend time with him outside the therapy room or on the jogging path. Every free instant she had, she spent with Jake. That was just fine with her.

They went to the beach, playgrounds, parks—the kinds of places they'd been with Paul—and had a terrific time. Not that anything was any clearer, but she was certain—well, almost certain—they'd both soon see what a mistake it would be to consider a serious romantic involvement.

On Friday morning, before she began working with her first patient of the day, Jennifer ambled over to the small kitchen near the nurses' station on the orthopedic wing. She hadn't slept well the night before and she needed a cup of hot, black coffee to get her motor running.

As she reached for the pot of hot liquid, two nurses entered the kitchen. They were both young and pretty; one was a redhead, the other had curly dark hair.

"Boy, that Paul Davis is one big flirt." Jennifer overheard the redhead chatting to her co-worker, and her ears immediately perked up. "He knows just what to say and goes on and on and on." She giggled as she spoke, and seemed to preen as she said his name.

"He sure can make the ladies smile," added the other nurse.

The redhead went toward the coffeemaker and quickly spied Jennifer.

"We're talking about one of your flyboys."

"Oh, really?" she asked as nonchalantly as possible.

The woman nodded, and poured a mug for herself. "Paul Davis. You are so lucky to work with him. I wish I had an excuse to—any excuse. He is one good-looking man." Jennifer forced a smile on her face. "Don't you think?"

"Ah, yes," Jennifer stumbled over the words. "He's attractive."

"Attractive?" She clapped her hands together and

shook her head slowly from side to side. It was obvious she didn't agree with Jennifer. "That's an understatement if I ever heard one. He's gorgeous." Her eyes grew wide and her voice lowered as if she were about to share a secret. "He's got half the women on the floor drooling after him, for goodness' sake."

"Oh?" Jennifer felt the muscles in her neck stiffen, and she bit down on her lower lip. Damn him.

"Virginia Mason, the lady in 402, is ready to walk down the aisle with him."

"Is that so?"

"She said that yesterday, just after Paul took her for a walk." She took a sip of coffee and grinned. "I think that was right after his therapy with you—during the lunch hour. She was simply glowing the rest of the afternoon."

Jennifer's fingers clenched around the foam cup.

The nurse sauntered out of the kitchen toward the reception desk. "In fact, I think she's still glowing. There she is."

The nurse lifted her slender hand and pointed across the room toward an elderly gray-haired woman chatting quite vivaciously with two other older patients. "Mrs. Mason's a recent widow. She and her husband were married for forty-seven years. Can you believe that? His death has been hard on her. Paul's been visiting with her, and it's made a real difference."

Humility rushed to her face, and Jennifer tried to keep the surprise from showing. "That's really nice of him."

"There are more than a dozen nurses on this wing under thirty, and I swear each and every one of us has made a play for that hot flyboy. He's sweet as can be, but he gives his attention to a senior citizen. Can you beat that?" The redhead shrugged good-naturedly. "Wait a minute and I'll introduce you to the lucky woman." Before Jennifer could stop her, the nurse took her elbow and led her over to Virginia Mason.

"Mrs. Mason, excuse me for interrupting," the nurse said, as she approached the older woman and her two friends. "This is Paul Davis' therapist."

"Jennifer Wade?" The older woman's eyes sparkled as she gave Jennifer her attention.

"Why, yes," Jennifer replied, more than a hint of surprise in her voice. How did she know?

"He's told me all about you." She turned to the other patients and the nurse, and chuckled. "He says you're a slave driver."

Jennifer didn't realize she'd been holding her breath until her lungs relaxed. "That's just because he doesn't want to work for the result. No pain, no gain."

"He's also said some other things." The older woman's eyes sparkled again and Jennifer felt her heart lurch. Mrs. Mason shifted several times on the soft leather chair. "I think I've been sitting too long. Ladies"—she turned to the nurse and the others—"if you'll excuse me."

"I'd just like a few minutes of fresh air." Her gaze landed on Jennifer, and there was a definite lilt in her voice. "I could use a strong arm to lean on while I walk, Miss Wade."

"Certainly," Jennifer said, offering her arm as the older woman stood. "And it's Jennifer."

As soon as they were out of earshot, Mrs. Mason spoke, a soft, feminine quality to her voice. "Thought I was going to spill the beans, didn't you?"

Jennifer cleared her throat. What had Paul been saying to her? "Excuse me?" she sputtered.

With soft, wrinkled fingers, she patted Jennifer's tanned skin. "It's all right, my dear. I wasn't going to give anything away. Besides, it's much more fun keeping information like this to myself."

Jennifer stared down at the woman. "Mrs. Mason?"

"I must tell you I'm quite fond of your Paul Davis. He's as good a listener as he is a talker."

Jennifer felt the urge to say that he was not her Paul Davis, but she was more curious about what the older woman was going to say to interrupt.

"My husband died about six months ago." She closed her eyes and sighed deeply. "I never loved anyone the way I loved John Mason. He was a pilot, just like your Paul Davis. Why, I remember seeing him off at the start of the Vietnam War, and I kept a stiff upper lip. That's what we did in those days. I was pregnant with my first boy, so big with him I could barely walk. And as I stood at the pier, I prayed John would come home to me and our child." Her arm hugged Jennifer's a little tighter. "I never told anyone, but I was so mad at John that day. I didn't want him to leave me."

"But it was war. He had to go."

"I knew that, of course," she said, slowing her gait a bit. "But every time that child kicked in my stomach, I hurt all over. Now, I was lucky, John came home safe and sound. And I treasured every day we had together." Her feet moved slowly beneath her, and Jennifer had to take tiny steps to keep up. "I understand you weren't so lucky."

"No, I wasn't."

"Must be a horrible thing to lose the man you love."

"It is."

"An old woman's allowed to talk out of school every now and then, I've decided. The privilege comes with age. Now I don't know what it was like to lose my husband when I was young. But I do know he would have wanted me to go on with my life and find somebody else."

Jennifer's eyes narrowed. "Did Paul tell you to talk to me?"

Mrs. Mason tossed her head back and laughed louder than Jennifer would have thought possible. "Goodness, he'd probably kill me if he knew all the forward things I was saying to you right now." A mischievous smile crossed her lips, and then her eyes turned thoughtful. "Things haven't felt right since my John's been gone. One day turns into the next. Early this week I was sitting outside. They make me sit outside sometimes, you know, around lunch time. Then I see this handsome young man who looks a lot like my husband and he's playing catch with a boy in a wheelchair. The next day, around the same time, I see them out there again. I asked one of the nurses if he was the boy's father. When they said no, that he was a patient, well, I got rather curious. You had to see that look of excitement in that boy's face. The attention meant the world to him. I called Paul over the next day, after he was done playing with the boy." She slowed a bit as the walk made her tired. Still her face shined with amusement and pleasure. "In just a few days, we've become the best of friends. He's perked up my spirits more than you can imagine. The attention of a nice, attractive man is always welcome—even when you're my age. Not that you have anything to worry about my dear. As the saying goes, he only has eyes for you."

"Mrs. Mason, I appreciate your insight, but I must tell you I've known Paul a long time, and he's always been quite a ladies' man."

"Maybe so, but he's in love with you."

Jennifer pulled back. "Did he tell you that?"

Mrs. Mason muffled her words for a minute, as if deciding whether to tell the truth or not. "Well, not in so many words, but you don't get to be my age and not know a little something about human nature." She watched as Jennifer's expression grew wary. "Believe what I'm saying. He's your second chance, Jennifer Wade. He might not know it yet and you might not believe it, but it's true."

****

He's in love with you. The older woman's words drifted through her mind and lingered there. She didn't know what to think or feel. And, with Paul coming in for therapy three times a week, she didn't have the space she needed to sort it all out.

She glanced down at her schedule and rolled her eyes. Paul was her second appointment for the day and the only thing that made it worse was that Scott Montcliff was first in line this morning.

Scott Montcliff. Great. The cheery pilot had become frustrated and disagreeable during therapy. He wanted a quick fix for his bad ankle and she could only offer him hard, time-consuming therapy. She'd scheduled him for twenty minutes of water therapy in the whirlpool. He was dressed in swim trunks when she arrived.

Jennifer turned on the whirlpool and instructed him to sit in the bath. This whirlpool was different from most she'd used in the past. Most whirlpools were small, just large enough to comfortably accommodate an arm or a leg. This one was very large, big enough to comfortably hold two or three people. The water came up to Scott's waist as he got situated in the large, pulsating steel tub. His hands rested on the edge of the tub for additional support.

"This is great. I can't believe it's going to help my leg, though," he said with a smirk. "I could almost fall asleep in here."

"You won't have time to sleep, Scott. We have too much work to do." She sat on the edge of the big metal drum, careful to avoid getting too close to the swirling water. "If you're comfortable, we can start. First, I want you to flex and extend your leg, feeling the tension with your bad ankle." She kept her eyes on his leg in the water, and ignored the way he stared at her. "Okay. That's fine. Now do some flutter kicks."

"What?" He smiled like a sly dog.

"Like this." She demonstrated the kicking motion, ignoring the amount of leg she was showing. He followed her lead and then stopped abruptly.

"You know, I don't feel much like therapy today." He leaned back and fully relaxed, sweat starting to gather at his brow. "This is too much like a Jacuzzi, and I always have company when I'm in a Jacuzzi."

She didn't want—or have time for—game playing, and she didn't like patients exercising their oversized egos with her. He was having a hard time dealing with his disability, and she was trying to handle him in a patient, professional manner. She'd dealt with bigger babies and bigger egos during her career, and Scott Montcliff wasn't going to throw her off course. She was going to help him fix his leg if it was the last thing she did, but she wouldn't coddle him in the process.

"I'm sorry you're not in the mood to work out, but this isn't a Jacuzzi, it's a therapy whirlpool. I'm your therapist, not your Jacuzzi partner. If you don't feel like therapy today, just get out of the pool. I've got a busy schedule. On the other hand, if you want to get better…"

"Sure I do, but I've got other things on my mind right now." He moved his hand and reached out for her wrist. She tensed under the firm pressure. "You need to loosen up. Let down this gorgeous blonde hair." His eyes drifted over her hair, pulled back in a tight business-like knot. "Why don't you change out of that lab coat? I know I'd like what's underneath that shapeless white jacket."

"What's under my lab coat is none of your business. Let me go immediately."

Again, she tried to yank her hand away but he wouldn't budge. "This isn't funny. Release me now."

"I wasn't intending to be funny. I had something else in mind." As he pulled her down to capture her mouth, she yanked away again, but instead of falling toward the ground, she flailed head first into the pool. The swirling water was momentarily disorienting, but Jennifer found her footing and stood up instantly. With water dripping from her like a faucet, she shook with rage. She pushed her blonde mop off her face and stared at the startled man in the whirlpool. She was so furious she could feel steam coming off her skin. "Of all the pompous, arrogant things to do. I could…"

"What the hell is going on here?" Jennifer tore her eyes away from Scott to find Paul standing in the doorway, dressed in PT workout clothes. His eyes darkened as he took in the scene. "What the hell did he do?"

For a short moment, she was speechless. It wasn't often she lost control of a work situation. "Lieutenant Montcliff forgot this wasn't a fun spa," she said, finding her voice. "Everything is under control."

"Just wanted to have a little fun, Pauly boy," Scott said, rising from his watery seat. "You know what I mean." He smirked, his lips curling up slightly. "A looker like our physical therapist is too good to pass up. Don't tell me you haven't noticed? We all need a little R&R once in a while. I decided to take what I want."

Jennifer knew Scott had just made a huge mistake. She watched as every muscle in Paul's body tightened with rage. His fingers slowly knotted into fists. He bounded across the room, his intention crystal clear.

"Keep your damn hands off of her."

"Who is going to make me? You?" Scott asked with a sneer. An instant later, he yanked Jennifer into his arms and held her.

With wild fury blazing in Paul's eyes, Jennifer reacted on impulse. "No, I am." With all her strength, Jennifer twisted and pulled out of his grasp. As she flung around to face him and give him a piece of her mind, Scott skidded backward and lost his footing. He reeled sideways into the water, making it look like a tidal wave when he hit the small pool. His right cheek caught the hard side of the basin with a solid smack.

Water rippling around him, Scott caught his breath. He shot up and angrily nursed his jaw.

Jennifer almost tumbled from the pool as Scott veered back into the water to right himself. She caught herself on the ledge and worked to fix her balance.

"Ignore him, Jen. I've got you." Paul's arms steadied her shaking shoulders. With a firm grasp, he helped her out of the tub.

Jennifer took a deep breath to calm her agitated nerves. While she wanted to walk away and not look back, she needed to grab control of the situation.

"Lieutenant Montcliff, I will be reporting your actions and your behavior to Commander Taylor. You'll go to Captain's Mast," she said, holding her head high and ignoring the water that dripped down her wet face. At Captain's Mast, he would go before his commanding and executive officers for a non-judicial review. He might lose his current rank because of this. "However, I will not suggest that you withdraw from this program. I'm here to help you with your leg, and I intend to continue doing so. But I will insist you seek professional help from a trained counselor. Otherwise, you will be wasting my time, and I won't allow that to happen again." She then turned away and marched out the room.

"Hold on a second. Are you all right?" Paul asked with concern as she walked quickly from the whirlpool room and headed for the staff lounge.

"Yes, I'm fine. A little shaky, sopping wet, but perfectly fine," she said, feeling a little chilled as damp clothes clung to her skin. Her feet felt squishy as she walked and she was annoyed a perfectly good pair of work shoes were destroyed.

"God, I hate guys with silly male pride and oversized egos," she mumbled under her breath as they reached the lounge.

"So I guess you're pleased that I didn't knock him to the floor?"

Jennifer slid him a sideways glance. "I was afraid you might. You looked angry enough."

"I *was* angry enough," Paul said. "But you took care of the situation yourself, before I could react." She held her head high, and he smiled from ear to ear. "I didn't realize you were such a tough chick."

"Tougher than you can imagine," she replied, as she reached her locker in the lounge. "I know how to take care of myself, Paul."

"That is perfectly obvious to me. I'm calling you Rocky from now on," he said as she grabbed a pair of sweat clothes from her locker and ducked behind a changing curtain. "But that doesn't change the fact that I wanted to wipe that lousy smirk off his face."

"Well, I'm glad you restrained yourself," she called from behind the curtain, throwing dripping wet clothes in the corner as she discarded them. Completely stripped down, she realized she hadn't pulled all the clothes she needed from her locker. "Uh, I need a favor." From the top of the flimsy curtain, she reached her hand over with a small key. "I seem to have forgotten to get a dry pair of underpants. Would you please get a pair for me, please? And don't laugh. Not one chuckle, or you'll be sorry. I'll give you the workout from hell in a few minutes if you're not careful."

"I'd never turn down a lady in distress." She could hear the wry humor in his voice. A quiver ran through her fingertips as he took the key from her. She heard the key in the lock and the shuffling sound of Paul going through her things. "The pink silky ones?"

"Any one will do, thank you." Her cheeks warmed with embarrassment. "Please hurry. I'm cold standing here without anything on."

"That presents an enticing image," he said as he closed the locker and walked over to the curtain. Pink silky panties dangled over from the other side. "Here you go."

"Thanks." She grabbed the little pink undergarment from him and finished dressing in record time. When she emerged from behind the curtain, she was garbed in baggy workout clothes, and her hair, now dangling loose around her face, was almost dry.

"All set," she said, stepping next to him. "Are you ready to start your therapy session?"

"Why don't we sit down for a few minutes first?" Paul suggested, gesturing toward a little beige Formica-topped table in the lounge. "I know a tough lady like you doesn't like to miss a beat, but that scene with Montcliff…it's okay to take a breather."

"No, it's not necessary," she said, inhaling deeply for an instant, leaning against the counter in the small kitchen area.

She was touched by the obvious concern in his dark green eyes. It seemed like such a very long time since a man had looked at her so protectively. For the past eighteen months, she'd adjusted to life on her own. While her parents had offered their support and love, Jennifer felt it was important that she stand on her own two feet. Life was too uncertain to rely on others, even if they had the best of intentions. For Jake's sake, she needed to set the right path and stick to it.

"Well, at least let me get you a glass of water,"

Paul offered, striding over to the sink, reaching for a foam cup.

"I think I've had enough water, thank you," she answered with a grin. The smile he returned warmed her all the way to her toes.

It would be so easy to fall into a relationship with Paul. He was kind, caring, and as gorgeous as sin. But Paul wasn't a relationship kind of guy. Not that he didn't have feelings for her. She was certain he did. At the same time, fire and excitement didn't spell the kind of relationship she needed for her future and Jake's. She knew it would be hard to keep all the facts in perspective when Paul made everything seem so darned easy and comfortable.

"I think I've rested for long enough," she replied as she righted her stance. "Ready to give that leg a good workout today?"

His grin was crooked and totally disarming. "I don't think I have a choice. My PT is worse than a drill sergeant."

She chuckled as she directed him from the entrance of the large therapy room to the equipment area. "Don't you forget it. Your commanding officer expects results from all the men in his unit, and I have no intention of letting him down."

"You've always been driven, haven't you?"

"I think it's critical to set goals and go after them," she replied, her tone matter-of-fact. "Now that I've got Jake, I think it's even more important for me to have a plan."

"God, I hate to plan even five minutes in advance."

"Yes, I know," she said, raising a wary eyebrow. "It's always been part of your charm."

He stopped mid-step, forcing her to come to a standstill. "Hey, you think I'm charming?"

She watched the teasing twinkle in his eyes, and then sidestepped around him. "Hm, you've got your moments, I suppose. Come on."

The therapy room was filled with therapists and their patients. Each piece of equipment was being used to help mend injured arms, legs, and backs. As they entered the main part of the room for Paul to begin leg work on the universal machine, she saw Billy Wilder come into the room from the main hallway.

"What are you doing here, young man?" She looked from the little boy in the wheelchair to the list of patients at the desk near the door. "I don't have you scheduled until this afternoon. You weren't trying to have an unsupervised workout, were you?" She tried to keep her tone scolding. This was against the rules and he knew it.

"Well, sort of." He hung his head low for a second, a hesitant smile starting at his lips. "Can't you spend a little time with me this morning?"

Jennifer glanced back down at her schedule. After Paul, there was lunch. "This is Lieutenant Davis' time. You'll have to ask him first."

"Sure, Billy, I don't have to report to the squadron until after lunch." Paul winked at the young teenager. "So tell me, from your point of view, is Miss Wade a good PT?" he asked as Jennifer wheeled the little boy to the raised floor mat. She automatically lowered the mat to accommodate Billy.

"Like I told you, she's the best," Billy replied, his tone laced with admiration. "I had a bunch of other therapists before Miss Wade took me. I could barely move my legs. It was awful. She made me work so hard. She made me stand when I didn't want to. It may not sound like much, but I was scared I'd never do it again. Miss Wade's going to make sure I walk again, too."

"No, Billy, *you're* going to make sure you walk again," she interrupted and helped the little boy raise himself out of the chair and onto the mat. "I'm just a coach. Let's make this a little higher." She pushed a button and the mat raised six inches. "This is better than a ride at Disneyland. Lieutenant Davis is going to make himself useful now. Lieutenant, hold this bolster under his knees while Billy starts his exercise. I'm going to check his blood pressure."

When she'd finished with the blood pressure gauge, Billy worked with Jennifer and Paul to stretch and exercise his legs. He sat up, looking winded and anxious. "I want to stand again today," he announced, shifting his legs to the edge of the raised mat.

"Let's take it easy, pal. Everything takes time, remember?" she said absently, reviewing his chart of activities. His legs were getting stronger. With some more hard work and a little luck, he'd be on his feet again soon.

"I can do it," he replied stubbornly, moving his legs to the floor. "I've done everything I'm supposed to do, and Paul's been helping me."

"He has, has he?" Jennifer arched a single brow and cast a slightly irked look at her adult patient, who suddenly looked quite sheepish. "Since when have you become a physical therapist, Lieutenant?"

Billy rushed to Paul's defense. "We haven't done anything I'm not supposed to do, I swear. He just helped me practice all the exercises I do with you."

"You shouldn't do that," she said, scolding Paul with a dirty look. "He might hurt something and you wouldn't know what to do."

"I'd come looking for you, of course," he said with a wink.

"Come on, Miss Wade, don't be mad," Billy said.

"Yes, come on, Miss Wade," Paul repeated softly, and a tingle shot up her neck. "If anything, we took it too easy." He grinned at Billy. "If anything, I just helped him get pumped up."

"So watch me now, okay?"

Jennifer glanced at the eager boy and sighed. He wanted to show off in front of Paul. "Okay, but let me give you a hand." She reached out and grabbed his hand, and placed a harness around his middle. "If it hurts, stop. Don't push yourself too hard."

Billy breathed deeply and shifted his weight to his feet. He beamed as his legs stood straight and his back stiffened. "Watch." Before she could latch on to him tighter, he shifted his right foot and then his left.

"I'm walking. Look, I'm walking! I knew I could do it!" His face flushed as he cried out. A half year of therapy had led up to this moment. He could walk.

Chapter Seven

Jennifer watched in amazement, her breath trapped in her lungs. He had waited so very long for this moment. She forced herself to swallow and took an instant to control her emotions. It wouldn't be proper for Billy to see her cry, even if it was out of joy.

"Oh, Billy, you are walking!" She held the harness around his waist a little tighter, still giving him the room he needed to feel independent of her. "Be careful," she cautioned, almost afraid to talk and break the spell.

The first time she'd met Billy, he'd been flat on his back, barely able to move much more than a toe. She'd had her doubts, real doubts, he'd ever walk again. But he'd been a fighter, not someone who'd easily throw in the towel.

"You're doing great," she said encouragingly, but still she didn't want him to push too hard. "I'm going to help you back down again. Billy, I'm so proud of you." It was moments like this that made her feel triumphant. While he'd done all the hard work, she'd been the guide that had helped him on the journey.

He was tired from the activity, so she helped him lower himself first to the mat, then back into the wheelchair. "Before long, you're going to be getting rid of this thing. I'm going to call your doctor right now. We'll want to vary your program just slightly. Why don't you go give your mom a call? She's going to be thrilled."

"Yeah," he replied, his cheeks pink and excited. "When my dad gets home, I'll be doing even more."

"That sounds great, but let's wait until tomorrow before we start planning for that marathon."

****

"So when are we going to go for that flight, Lieutenant Davis?" asked Billy. "You haven't forgotten your promise, have you?"

"No, Billy. How could I forget that?" He'd just witnessed something spectacular. He'd done some things in the air that would stun most people, but right now he was stunned. Nothing he'd ever done equaled what taking two steps meant to the thirteen-year-old in front of him. And for the first time in a long time, his insides didn't turn upside down at the thought of flying again. If the kid could do what he did, Paul could certainly take the next step and keep his promise to the boy. "Soon, I promise."

"I can't wait." He almost jumped out of his wheelchair. "It's going to be so cool."

Paul's laugh came from deep in his stomach. "Great. When Miss Wade tells me you're ready and your folks say it's okay, I'll make all the arrangements." He patted Billy's shoulder, man to man.

"Now, young man, I'd like to see you get back to your room and get some rest." Jennifer bent down and gave Billy's hand an affectionate squeeze. Then, as if she couldn't resist, she kneeled down and gave him a big bear hug. "At your regular session this afternoon, we'll talk about how we can keep improving on that incredible performance."

As the young man wheeled out of the room, his excitement showing in his speed, Jennifer lifted her young patient's chart from the mat, scribbled a few notes and put it back where it belonged. "Are you ready to start, Paul?"

****

Paul jumped on the mat and fell flat on his back, arms and legs stretched out as far as they could go. "What do you mean, 'are you ready, Paul?' I still can't get over that kid. It was amazing. I'm so glad I could be a little part of it."

A big smile stretched across her face. How could she pretend she'd witnessed anything short of fantastic? And Paul had the right to feel proud too. He'd given Billy the extra push he'd needed to take that scary first step. "Okay, okay, I confess." She dug her hands deep into her pants pockets. The smile on her face grew bigger and bigger. "That was really something, wasn't it?"

"Something? God, did you see the look in his eyes?" Paul's face beamed with admiration. "I'm truly impressed with both of you."

"I'm pleased to hear that, Lieutenant." She cocked her head to the side, excitement radiating from her face. "Your role in this event is not insignificant. If you won't get a swollen head, I'll admit I'm impressed, too. You made a big difference in his life and his recuperation. Motivation is key in this business, and you gave him something to get excited about. You've never struck me as a kid person, but I've certainly done an about-face on that." She also never pegged him as someone who'd spend his free time listening to the memories of a lonely old widow.

Paul slid off the mat and stood at attention when he noticed his commanding officer in the doorway. In a dress khaki uniform, the senior officer looked as fit as a man Paul's age. Only a touch of gray at the temples of his short dark brown hair hinted at the reality.

"Since you're so impressed with Miss Wade, I suppose it won't be too much of an imposition to accompany her to the carrier this afternoon." He smiled genially as he turned to Jennifer. She wished she was wearing something nicer than sloppy workout attire. "I know we didn't discuss a time and day earlier, but I'd like you to come down to the ship and look over a few charts of some of my other men. I've told the medic you were coming. I was able to reach your partner, Ms. Hampton, and she said her afternoon was light and she'd be able to take any of your patients here."

Commander Taylor was too important a client to turn down. If she and Lori were going to be successful, they had to be flexible and accommodating—especially to military brass like Paul's superior officer. And he'd already taken care of everything.

"That's fine, Commander," she said, knowing she'd have to go find Billy before she left for the base. While he'd worked with Lori on a number of occasions, today was special for the both of them. She didn't want this change in schedule to deflate his excitement, or make him feel dismissed. He knew about her interest in building Navy work, and she was certain the situation would be fine with him. Still, it was important to keep him informed personally. Thirteen-year-olds could be tricky creatures sometimes. "I'd be more than happy to do some pre-evaluations."

****

The *USS Valiant* looked more like a traveling football field—several football fields—than anything else. An aircraft carrier was the largest type of ship in the Navy, dwarfing all other vessels by comparison. At any point in time, five thousand men and women called the *Valiant* home. The top of the carrier, called the flight deck, was used by pilots to take off with the aid of steam-powered catapults. On landing, the catapults captured the vessel in what was known as a controlled crash.

Jennifer knew all about it. It all sounded so simple, and so thrilling, but if the catapult didn't work, the pilot died. God, there were so many ways for a young pilot to die. Just yesterday, she'd picked up a copy of the Naval Academy alumnae magazine. She'd read about Curt, her brother's old roommate at Annapolis, who'd died when the catapult failed to hold him and he'd plummeted into the water. She'd choked when she'd noticed that almost all of the deaths reported of young officers were pilots.

As she and Paul approached the big gray ship, Jennifer was reminded of a time when a trip to an aircraft carrier was an exciting, thrilling event. That was before she'd known all the dangers and experienced the pain. Gone was the thrill of watching one of the most powerful vessels in the world in action. It wasn't all glamour.

Inside the ship, it seemed like a strange hotel, encased in steel, with long narrow passageways and pipes everywhere that seemed to lead all over the place.

"Watch your head, Miss Wade. The hatches start to feel pretty narrow at times." A young petty officer third class, a doctor's aide, escorted them to the sick bay. It took more than five minutes to journey through the dozens of passageways, hatches, and steep metal stairs to reach the small on-board health center.

For the trip, she had changed into heather gray slacks and an ivory-colored blouse. While she kept a variety of shoes in her locker, she purposely chose the lowest heeled walking shoes she could find. It had been a long time since she'd been on a fighting ship, and she remembered the deck grating and metal stairs. In pumps, she might become a casualty, maneuvering on the decks and halls made for flat soles.

Along the way, she ducked many times as she passed the engine room and many small cubicles of work areas. "Here we are," the young enlisted man said as they reached their destination. "The doc is inside waiting for you." The petty officer saluted at Paul and descended back down one of the narrow tunnels.

Jennifer was surprised to find this sick bay to be the size of a large broom closet. Typically, carriers like the *Valiant* were filled with health facilities to rival small hospitals. Stepping inside the small room with a pull-down desk attached to a wall, a pint-sized examining table, and a tiny medicine cabinet, Jennifer felt like Alice in Wonderland. The doc, sitting on a fold-out chair at the desk, was scribbling notes in patient charts. He looked to be in his late thirties with short black hair, a slender build, gray eyes covered by smart-looking wire frames and a bony, somewhat angular face that looked stern until he smiled.

"Miss Wade? Lieutenant." He greeted his guests with a friendly, assuring manner. When he extended his arm, Jennifer accepted it and his warm handshake. "I'm Mark Gordon. Sorry, we don't have a larger room to meet in, but this is the best we can do, I'm afraid. We had a little pipe problem this morning and this was all they could give me on short notice."

"This is fine, Doctor." Jennifer quickly scanned the room for a place to sit, and finding none, remained standing. "Commander Taylor said you had some patients to discuss with me. Since we don't have a lot of room to spread out, why don't we just go over the charts, and I'll schedule time with the men you want me to see for therapy."

Paul excused himself and during the next twenty minutes, Jennifer rested on the examining table and flipped through a dozen medical files as the doctor gave a quick rundown on each of the patients he felt could benefit from therapy.

"When we go out to sea months at a time, our men don't get much of a chance to exercise," the ship's medical officer explained as Jennifer finished scanning the patient information. "We have the facilities, mind you, but the schedules are pretty rigorous. Most would rather sleep when they get off duty than work out. We don't blame them, really, but unexercised muscles aren't as strong as exercised ones. Some of the work is quite labor-intensive. If a sprained ankle or pulled ligament doesn't heal quickly, the man's no good to us. Even if he just suffers from chronic stiffness, he won't be performing his best. All the men in these charts have had some kind of injury in the past six months or so. While they're healed, there's a lot of work I still wouldn't want them to do. Since we're in port for the next four months, I want them started in a therapy program that will bring them up to speed one hundred percent."

"Sounds good to me." Jennifer met the man's strong gaze and ignored the feeling of claustrophobia that was starting to creep into her thoughts. She should be excited and happy. This special pilot program was expanding already, and soon she and Lori would need to hire other physical therapists to help with the patient load. "Just give me a call when you have a tentative schedule worked out. I'm sure we can accommodate all of your men."

"I was hoping you'd say that." The doctor took off his glasses and rubbed his tired eyes. "It's great to get some help. With a crew this large, it's difficult to make sure everyone gets the treatment they need. We see some of the officers and enlisted men, but I have to send a lot of them over to the hospital or up to the doctors and therapists at the base. It's hard to keep track. I've been impressed with your work. All the men you've been treating have shown considerable improvement. They're not even complaining anymore about the therapy, except for this semi-vegetarian, anti-inflammatory diet of yours. They even see and feel the difference, so most of them are trying to stick to it." Jennifer thought of the recent run-in with Scott Montcliff. Apparently the disgruntled young pilot hadn't been sharing his complaints about the therapy program with the ship's doctor.

Paul popped his head back in the sick bay. "How are we doing?"

"We're done, Lieutenant," said the doctor over his shoulder. He turned to face Paul. "I was just commenting to Miss Wade that the therapy seems to be working very well for you. And I haven't heard any recent complaints from the other men, so I assume this pilot program, excuse the pun, is a success so far."

Paul grinned as the medical officer spoke. "You know it, Doc. Miss Wade's a real expert. That's because she threatens us," he said with a grin. "When we're all stretched out and completely vulnerable, she grabs our legs and twists. We don't dare not improve. Who know what she'd do to us then."

"Well, if it works, I won't question her methods. Unorthodox practices are often the best, I've discovered over the years." He chuckled as he picked up the files and locked them away in a cabinet near his feet. He shook her hand again as Jennifer gathered up her purse and prepared to leave. "Thanks a lot, Miss Wade. I'll be sending over the files in the next day or two, and I'll be calling you about the therapy appointments."

"Nice man," Jennifer said as they were out of the doctor's office, heading back to the flight deck where they could leave. "He's really interested in you guys."

"Yes, he is." Paul seemed distracted as they walked back the way they came. He missed it. Being attached to a desk when he wasn't in therapy wasn't why he'd become a pilot. He was restless and flying again would be the only medicine that would truly work for him.

****

"Paul, Paul Davis." The voice was coming from the floor above.

Jennifer twisted her head and looked at the balcony behind them. A lean blond man in a navy blue work jumper, called a poopy suit, waved his hand like a flag fluttering in the wind. "What are you doing here?"

"Trying to get into trouble," Paul retorted, cupping his hand over his eyes to avoid squinting in the afternoon sunlight.

"I thought, maybe, you came down to see the FX-21, the new demo job. Did you know it was here?" Paul's response to the question was to grab Jennifer's hand and pull her through a short hallway and up a flight of metal stairs into the hangar bay where planes not on the flight deck were kept. She was more than a little winded when they reached their destination.

The handsome blond officer laughed out loud as Paul ran toward him and the sleek new experimental fighter plane. Paul's eyes showed genuine appreciation for the FX-21. He smiled as he approached the plane and ran his fingers along its shiny exterior.

The FX-21 was the newest, sleekest fighter plane in existence. The sexy silver bird was designed to be one of the fastest aircraft in the flying Navy. It was also equipped with state-of-the-art radar-avoiding devices—and was considered to be the most dynamic plane ever designed for an aircraft carrier. Ever since he'd heard the plane had been tested and was ready for the fleet, Paul had wanted to fly that baby. He clenched his jaw with frustration and excitement. If he didn't get in the cockpit again soon, he'd never get the chance. *Get over your fears. Don't let them eat you alive. If the kid can do it, so can you.*

"Jennifer, this is Doug White. Doug, Jennifer Wade. And this"—he turned to Jennifer, his face filled with excitement and admiration—"is the FX-21. A plane built for me."

"Hey, Davis," his friend chided easily, giving him a friendly nudge. "You're not the only one whose been waiting for this baby. Boy, it sure is one beautiful plane, isn't it?"

Paul walked from one end of the plane to the other,

seeming to examine every inch, every nut, every bolt. "Anybody flown her yet?"

"Nope, not yet." He patted the silver bird with respect. "So how's your therapy going? Your walk looks pretty strong."

The pleasure of seeing the plane waned for an instant. He glanced at Jennifer from the corner of his eye and wished she could share in his excitement, or even his anxious frustration. "Jennifer is my therapist. Came down here today to talk to the doc about some of the other guys. I'm doing so well they want to get some others onto a good thing."

"So how's he doing really?" Doug turned and winked at the blonde standing more than a foot shorter than himself and the dark-haired officer. "Listening to him, he'd tell us all he was fit to run a marathon."

"Actually, he's not doing bad at all—not for a troublemaker, that is." She kept a smile across her mouth as she looked from one man to the other. "And if he could only get as motivated about therapy as he just did about your little plane here, he'd be all set."

"Hey, Davis, listen to the lady. We all miss you and your antics." He glanced down at his watch and then at the clipboard on the chair beside him. "I've got to go. It was nice meeting you, Jennifer. Take good care of that character."

****

It was just before twilight when they left the *Valiant*. A gentle breeze brushed against her body and caused her shirt to flutter in the evening wind. Her blonde hair curled around her face trying to ease itself out of her barrette. The low setting sun still shined brightly as its rays lit up the base and the ships as they floated on the ocean.

As they continued down the dock, walking lazily among the anchored ships and into the shadows they cast, she looked onto the glimmering city lights in the distance. The city was built on and around several hills and valleys. At the top of the hilltops, the red tiled roofs of the white stucco homes shimmered in the late afternoon sun, and the dark, dreamy ocean beneath glistened as the waves rolled onto the beach. She looked over at Paul. The distant look in his eyes told her that he was also distracted.

"What are you thinking?" she asked.

"A lot of things," he replied.

"Such as?" she coaxed.

"It's almost crazy how much I want to fly that plane." He'd spent most of his life waiting to fly a plane like the FX-21. It was part of him, like his heart and his soul. "And the thought of getting into its cockpit scares the hell out of me."

So he was going to share with her and open up. Jennifer slowed her pace and lightly touched the hem of his sleeve. "It's to be expected, Paul."

"Jen, you know Jeff and I were flying an experimental fighter plane similar to this one when it went down." There was razor-sharp tension in his voice.

She took a deep breath and nodded slowly. "Yes, I know."

He shook his head from side to side. "You think I'm a lunatic, don't you?"

"Frankly, I'm not sure what to think. It scares me, though. I do know that much."

"I can't explain, but my life won't feel right until

I'm flying again. I've been out of the cockpit a long time. Being here today reminds me just how long." He quickened his pace.

"It's all right to be afraid. In fact, it's normal and sane to be afraid," she said in a light tone, trying to keep up with him. She wanted to say that it was all right for him to walk away from the whole thing, but she knew it wouldn't be okay for him.

He stopped and stared into her eyes. "I know it's hard for you to sympathize."

"Not at all," she said as she bit back a sigh. This had always been his dream. "I get it, of course I get it, but nobody would blame you if you didn't…"

"It's what I do." He cut her off. "It'll be all right." He forced a smile on his face. "Really, it will. For both of us, I swear. Come on."

A few minutes later they were back in his car, speeding along the busy highway. Jennifer sat quietly, her head swimming with a million confusing thoughts. She was being pulled in two different directions. In such a short time, Paul had become such an important person to her. And his need to fly was as great as his need to breathe.

She listened to the logical side of her brain, the part she wanted to follow. *He doesn't belong in your life. He lives in a different world than you've built for yourself and Jake—and the two of you can't live in his. It's full of danger and uncertainty. It's not for you or your son.*

Unfortunately, the other side of her brain fought for equal time. *How can you tell him to get out of your life? You want him there; you need him there.* She'd been beyond panicked when she thought he'd been injured in the hospital fire. Her temples began to pound.

"It's almost dinnertime. Want to stop somewhere for a bite?" Paul had lowered the top of his convertible, inviting the late afternoon light to cast its rays on them. He patted her hand lightly to get her attention. "I know a nice little seafood restaurant just a few blocks from here. The food is great. It's kid friendly too."

"No, I don't think so." Even to her own ears, her voice sounded distracted and faraway. "I don't feel like eating out tonight. I need to go pick up Jake from the sitter. Thanks anyway."

"Okay, then we'll eat in," he said, not giving up. "I'll drop you off at your place, then I'll pick up a few things." He looked at the gold Seiko at his wrist. "We should be at your place in ten minutes. Give me half an hour to get the food I need, then I'll cook you up a fabulous gourmet meal."

"You're a gourmet cook?" She looked at him suspiciously. "Since when?"

"Since…you'll have to see for yourself." He smiled and then his expression turned serious. "There are some things I think we should talk about."

None of this was a good idea. She knew she was tempting fate again. The more time they spent together, the more time she wanted them to spend together. It was never going to work in the long run, so why couldn't she just say no?

"All right."

****

"I am such a mess, sweetie," Jennifer said to Jake as they dashed into their apartment. The place was quiet as Becki and Tyler were visiting Becki's mom for a few weeks. "That car ride blew Mommy's hair all over the place." She was thankful Jake was such a happy baby, and her apartment complex was filled with wonderful grandmotherly ladies dying for a baby to spoil and love. Mrs. Martin, a woman in her mid-sixties, who lived on the floor below, had good-naturedly taken on babysitting duty for the day. Her grandchildren lived back east, so she loved to get her fill of little ones with Jake.

Jennifer glanced in the hallway mirror, surveying the damage. "What do you think, baby boy? Does Mommy look like a disaster?" She held out a handful of windblown hair for the child to examine, and he gave a wayward curl a toddler-sized tug.

"That bad?" she asked with a laugh. Jake giggled, too, and Jennifer hugged him tight. "Mommy missed you so much today. How about we take a quick shower together and get ready for our dinner guest. He promised a gourmet meal, but between you and me, I don't expect much. You may be the lucky one tonight with your strained green beans and apricots."

Fifteen minutes later, they'd showered and Jake was dried and dressed. Jake crawled about the floor of Jennifer's bedroom. A soft groan escaped his small mouth as he grasped onto her comforter and pulled himself up to a standing position in a surprisingly expedient manner. He grinned broadly at his feat, obviously pleased with his accomplishment. "Look at you. It seems like just yesterday you were rolling over for the first time," Jennifer exclaimed with a motherly sigh. She bent down and placed a quick kiss on the top of his downy head. "You'll be running all over the place before too long. I don't know if I'm ready for this yet, Jake."

She smiled again as she turned back to her open

closet. "What to wear for a gourmet meal?" she murmured aloud as she scanned her wardrobe. Her eyes caught a silk dress in robin's-egg blue with puffed sweetheart sleeves and a loosely belted waistband. She'd forgotten all about the dress. It seemed she had no use for pretty clothes anymore—just the occasional suit and comfortable work clothes. Well, the dress would have to wait for another occasion, she decided as she grabbed a short peach-colored cotton dress and pulled it over her head. With Jake, wash and wear was a prerequisite, gourmet meal or not.

The doorbell rang exactly one minute after she'd yanked a brush through her almost-dried hair. When she opened the door, her eyes met his in a welcoming smile. Even though she knew this dinner—like every dinner they'd had together—was a mistake, she couldn't help but look forward to his company. She glanced down at his arms and saw he carried a bouquet of coral roses and a heavy bag of groceries from an area gourmet food store. She stepped back so he could move from the foyer into the living room. Until they were situated, she placed Jake in his playpen. He was immediately content when she helped him locate a colorful plastic toy phone.

"Hi, Jake," Paul said with a friendly grin before his eyes came back to Jennifer. "I keep forgetting to tell you how much I like your place. It's very pretty, like you."

Jennifer's cheeks flushed slightly as she smiled a thank-you. The living room was nice, and distinctively feminine. Slate blue antique satin curtains framed two large front windows. The sofa was beige chintz, and two side chairs, surrounding an oval brass and glass coffee table, were covered with a blue and rose satiny fabric. At the back of the apartment was a large travertine marble dining table and finely carved pickled pine chairs. The adjacent kitchen with bleached oak cabinets had plenty of counter space. It normally went unused due to Jennifer's fondness for rabbit food or the occasional fast-food splurge.

"I think the kitchen is yours tonight." She gestured him forward. "If you don't mind, I'll watch." She followed and moved over to the side wall where she and Becki had put together their own version of a minibar. "Can I get you something to drink while you're getting everything ready?"

"I'll have a scotch and soda, if you have it," he said, making himself comfortable in the kitchen, starting to pull containers out of the brown paper bag.

"Not on your life." Jennifer reached behind the bar, and pulled out a bottle of club soda.

"What's that?"

"A new kind of scotch and soda," she said, stifling a grin that pulled at the corners of her mouth.

"It looks to me like you're forgetting something."

"Oh, you're right, I am forgetting something." She strode to the refrigerator and pulled a fresh lemon from the vegetable crisper.

"That wasn't what I had in mind," he said dryly.

"Liquor isn't good for you. It increases inflammation and dulls the senses."

"So you care about my senses?"

She wasn't sure how to respond to that, so she quickly poured two glasses of soda water and carried them into the kitchen.

"To Billy." Paul raised his glass to hers.

She returned the toast as their glasses clinked. "What's going on here? I thought you said you were a gourmet?" The containers in front of him held prepared gourmet foods—escargot, stuffed mushroom caps, poached salmon steaks, green beans with almonds, twice-baked potatoes, and more pastries than they could possibly consume in a week. "This is cheating."

"Hey, come on, this is great. I said I was going to make you a gourmet meal—that didn't exactly mean from scratch." He good-naturedly shrugged his shoulders, and kept his lips from turning upward. "Anyway, this is much better than those greasy burgers and fries you used to eat."

She wouldn't admit it out loud, but she was impressed by his ingenuity. She sat on one of the stools beneath the raised kitchen counter. "Okay. This does look pretty fantastic. And salmon is one of my all-time favorite foods. Need some help, or can you handle it alone?" She lifted Jake from the playpen so he could also enjoy the evening's festivities. When the phone rang a moment later, she picked up the receiver with a friendly greeting. "Hello."

Her wide smile quickly faded. "Yes, yes. I'll be right down. Don't worry. Yes, he'll be just fine."

She dropped the phone onto the receiver and glanced quickly from Paul to Jake and back to Paul again. "That was Mrs. Martin downstairs. She often babysits for Jake and always comes through in a pinch. Her husband's been having some painful back problems lately."

Her mind was moving a mile a minute. Through pure motherly instinct, she grabbed a glass from Jake just before his little fingers tipped it over. "The first time it happened, they went to the emergency room and he wasn't seen for hours. It was terrible, so the last time they called me. I, uh, was able to work the muscles in his back and he was fine. I'd bring Jake with me, but their house isn't entirely childproofed. Normally, she just keeps a close eye on him. Right now, she sounds too upset to do that and Jake's getting into everything lately. I, uh…"

"Go, go," Paul said, practically pushing Jennifer toward the front door. "I can watch him for you."

"But you don't know how to take care of a baby," she began. Her options were somewhat limited at the moment and she didn't want to keep Mr. Martin waiting. He and his wife had both been too kind to her and Jake to not respond promptly when needed.

Paul lifted a hand in protest. "I'm sure I can handle it," he said with confidence. "I know how to fly an F-18. Taking care of an infant can't be that complicated. He's not even a year old yet. I'll read him a book or something."

Jennifer saw the self-assuredness in his eyes and wanted to laugh, but the Martins needed her. Paul had no idea what he'd just volunteered for. Poor dear. "It's more work than you think. He's into everything, and he's faster and sneakier than he looks. That angelic face is really quite deceptive. Don't let him out of your sight for a second," she said as the door behind her closed.

****

Paul quickly realized Jake had his own agenda while his mother was out of sight. The baby wasn't interested in any of the books that sat in a neat pile on the coffee table. He also couldn't be less interested in any of the dozen toys Paul plucked from a nearby toy chest. No, he obviously had other plans as he scanned the room and decided to attack an issue of *Parent's Magazine* that rested helplessly on the end table near the sofa.

Five minutes later Jake had ripped the covers off the six publications that had been placed near the parenting periodical. As Paul reached for one in Jake's tiny insistent grasp, the baby was already working on destroying another. Three minutes after that, every pot and pan in the lower kitchen cabinets was strewn throughout the apartment. Then he reached for the pantry door and the real trouble started.

Quicker than Paul could blink, Jake was covered from head to toe with the contents of a box of cornstarch. Immediately, tears began to roll from his big blue eyes down pink, chubby cheeks. He choked and sputtered, trying to wipe the powdery mixture from his face, becoming totally frustrated that his efforts were only making matters worse. Paul grabbed for the box of white fluff and righted it on the kitchen counter. "Cornstarch? What the heck is this? Why would your mommy have something like this?

"What do you do with it anyway?" he pondered aloud, totally frustrated by the growing mess. How had the baby even reached that high, Paul wondered with an astonished sigh, totally perplexed as he put aside a pan and reached for the crying child.

"Hey, it's okay, big guy," he said, pulling Jake into his lap as he sat cross-legged on the linoleum floor. He brushed the white powder from the baby's blond curls and groaned as the powder further settle onto his head. "Uh, what a mess you've created, Jake. Who would have expected such a disaster from such a cute little boy." He continued to survey the damage. "And I had my eyes on you the whole time. Boy, if the enemy ever gets a hold of a few like you, we're really going to be in trouble. You should have the words *search* and *destroy* written across your chest."

Taking a deep breath, Paul blew cool air onto Jake, trying to dislodge the cornstarch that had taken root into each crack and crevice of his face. After an initial frown of surprise, Jake's mouth spread into a wide grin and he squealed with delight. "I don't know why you look so happy now, little man. Your mom is not going to be pleased with either one of us when she sees this."

"Now stay put for two minutes, just two minutes," he implored, placing the baby beside him and rising to his full height. Jake looked up at him, cornstarch still dotting his long lashes, with the sweet expression of a cherub. "Don't pretend you don't know what I'm talking about. I may be a little slow about these things, but I've got your number now, buddy boy. Looking innocent won't help you out next time."

Jake giggled amiably, seemingly content to follow Paul's actions. "Okay, so we have an understanding," Paul said as he reached for a dishrag near the sink. Not wanting to give Jake an opportunity to plan his next attack, Paul soaked the cloth and approached the powdery mess on the floor. He quickly realized a wet towel might not have been the best method for cleanup, because the flour-like mixture soon turned to a sticky paste before his eyes. "Ugh, this is worse than what I started with."

As his shoulders drooped, Paul considered his next step. Whatever he needed to do, he needed to do it fast. He couldn't let Jennifer come home to a disaster like this. How could he admit that an eleven-month old could get the better of him? He'd never live it down.

All of a sudden, he heard the shower of little somethings behind him. He spun around and caught the last Cheerio leaving its box as Jake cheerfully turned the container of breakfast cereal upside down. "Jake, no," he groaned aloud and futilely pulled the now-empty cardboard container from the baby's grasp. The little o-shaped oat cereal crunched under his feet as he plucked Jake from the mess. "Why did you do that, kiddo?" He frowned into Jake's relaxed face. "Your mommy is going to kill us."

Paul watched as Jake took in his annoyed expression, and seconds later, the baby burst into fresh tears.

"No, no, don't cry," Paul said, pulling Jake into his arms. He patted his back and gently ran his fingers through the baby's curly cap of hair. "It's okay, I swear. See, I'm happy." Paul plastered a smile on his face, and grinned broadly into Jake's reddened face. The gesture made Jake cry that much harder.

When Paul heard Jennifer run up the steps to her garden apartment, he felt his heart skip a beat. As he saw the knob of the front door rotate, Paul jumped up with Jake in his arms and ran to the apartment entrance. He quickly flung the door open. "Come back in five minutes. Just turn around and come back in five minutes," he said before she could open her mouth. Jake continued to sob loudly as he curled into Paul's shoulder.

Paul tried to close the door, but Jennifer stretched out her hand and used her palm to firmly hold it open. "What happened here?" Her mouth dropped open in surprise and her eyes narrowed in stunned disbelief. "Paul?" Jake turned from Paul and stretched out his chubby hands for his mother. He sniffled loudly as she reached out for him.

Settled in Jennifer's embrace, he quieted immediately.

****

"I...I...I thought I had it under control," Paul began slowly, running a hand through his hair. "I read him this book about these guys named Elmo and Grover. He wanted to get down from my lap and then everything just..."

"I can see that," she said, eyebrows lifted, scanning the room and the disastrous mess that awaited her. "But I've only been gone for fifteen minutes, Paul."

"He's just so fast and tricky."

"I warned you." She smoothed back Jake's hair, taking in the cornstarch.

"But I didn't believe you."

"Taking care of kids is hard work," she said, enjoying the way Paul was truly flustered and baffled by the events of the last quarter hour.

"You're telling me."

"If you'd like to call it a day, I'll understand." She walked into the apartment, continuing to take in the torn magazines strewn about, and whatever it was that had taken over her kitchen. She knew he'd jump at the opportunity to flee. "We can do this some other time."

"No way. We men take responsibility for our messes, right, Jake?" Jake chuckled as Paul tickled him under his chin.

"You really don't have to. I shouldn't have left you with Jake anyway. Taking care of a baby isn't always a lot of fun." She stopped suddenly as she came upon the spread of white powder and paste in the kitchen. Her brows drew together. "What were you doing with the cornstarch?"

"Ask him," he said, pointing a teasing finger at Jake. "I don't even know what it's for—cooking or laundry."

"Cooking," she supplied with a grin. "You are such a bachelor, Paul. So you'll take a raincheck?"

"Hey, I'm not going to desert you and Jake. Jen, I'm like gum on the bottom of an old shoe. It takes a lot to get rid of me, when I want to be somewhere." He lightly ran his fingers down her cheek, and her skin flushed underneath his touch. "I don't know much about devilishly clever babies, but I'm learning."

"Okay, then," she said. "If you're certain you don't want to take this opportunity and flee the scene of the crime."

"I'm staying, Jen." He smiled back, his feet firmly planted.

Seeing his intent, she pointed to a small pantry door. "If you'd like to help, my wet/dry vac is over there. You'll be amazed how fast it takes care of the whole messy affair. I'll give Jake a quick bath and then we can pick up where we left off…if you want."

****

She thought he was going to turn tail and run with a little hiccup like this. He leaned over and planted a quick kiss on her cheek. "I want."

Minutes later, he smiled as he heard the joyful sounds of water splashing, Jennifer's sweet laugh and the baby's happy giggles. It felt homey and intimate as he ventured down the hall and poked his head through the bathroom doorway. "Hi," he said, not chancing into the tiled room.

Jennifer was elbow-deep in soap suds as she wiped bath water from her face.

"Hi yourself." She smiled. "Jake has discovered the joy of splashing and thinks it's great fun to get me soaking wet. I get drenched every time we do this."

"Need some help?" Paul offered, slowly stepping into the bathroom. "Turns out I'm a whiz with your wet/dry vac." He paused and gestured to the baby in the tub. "Now that I've learned his tricks, I'm sure I can be trusted with the squirt."

"We'd really scare you off if I took you up on that one," she replied with a wide smile as she rubbed golden-colored shampoo in Jake's curly, wet head. "Don't worry. Baby bathing is beyond the call of duty. Besides, we're almost done."

A few minutes later, Jennifer lifted Jake out of the tub, evidence of his early adventure thoroughly rinsed away. "Nobody would believe what a mess you were earlier," she said with a laugh as she towel-dried Jake and lifted him in her arms and carried him into his bedroom.

Trains in bright primary colors decorated Jake's bedroom. Paul grinned as Jennifer explained that Becki's son Tyler was wild for trains and couldn't wait for Jake to get old enough to share his passion for choo-choos.

As Paul scanned the child's cheery room, his eyes froze as they landed on a photograph prominently displayed on the sturdy bureau adjacent to Jake's crib. Jeff and Jennifer. Jeff and Jennifer looking so happy and in love. Jennifer beamed brighter than any sunshine in a dressy pink suit and a smile as wide as a mile. Jeff, in his service dress whites, looked every inch the dashing young officer, full of promise and glory. They looked happy, so happy.

Jennifer noticed Paul eying the photograph. She took a deep breath as she grabbed a diaper and began to dress Jake. "I know he'll never know Jeff, but I want him to see how happy we were together." She secured Jake's diaper and pulled his PJ bottoms over his wiggly legs. "I don't think he understands yet when I point to the picture and say 'Daddy,' but one day he will. I need to keep Jeff's memory alive for him."

"Of course, no one can take his place, but…" Before Paul could finish his thought, they watched as Jake grabbed for an open container of baby powder, ready to wreck havoc in this room as he'd done in the kitchen and family room.

Like a commando, Paul shot between them and recaptured the dusting powder before any damage could be done. "An old dog can learn new tricks. Not bad for a novice," Paul said with a satisfied smile.

"Not bad at all," Jennifer agreed.

After all the food containers were emptied and their contents placed in the oven or microwave for warming, Paul finished the last of his drink and helped Jennifer place plates, silverware, and napkins at the dinner table. He also offered to help feed Jake, but Jennifer assured him it would be better for her to complete the deed and put the baby down for the evening. Twenty minutes later, Jake was settling in for the night and Jennifer and Paul were alone again.

"I learned a number of new things today," he said as they began to complete dinner preparations.

"Like what?"

"That babies can be tricky, but they can be outsmarted." He folded a napkin and put it under a knife. "That cornstarch is for cooking something, but I haven't figured out what yet, and bathing babies, while certainly a wet affair, looks like a lot of fun."

Jennifer rolled her eyes as the sides of her mouth slanted upward. "Paul, you were frantically waving a white flag a half-hour ago, and you and Jake were alone for only fifteen minutes. I think you might be being a bit premature about considering yourself a baby expert."

He ignored the wry expression on her face, and continued unfazed. "I also learned you have a soft spot a mile wide for your patients—especially the teenage variety."

Her eyes warmed for a moment. "Guilty as charged. I won't deny that."

"And, of course, I already knew about your interest in tearfully sad late-night movies, moonlight strolls on deserted beaches, and waterfalls. We can't forget waterfalls." He smiled as he noticed heat rising in her fair cheeks. God, she was cute when he threw her off course. "Sorry, I couldn't resist that moment of nostalgia."

****

Her cheeks continued to warm as she went to the cabinet for wine glasses. Why had he mentioned waterfalls? "I believe that proves you know entirely too much about me."

"Oh, I don't know about that. I'm sure you know more about me from all those records from the Navy than I know about you."

She tossed her hair behind her shoulder and smirked. "Hm…Let's see. Of course, your medical chart reveals some mighty fascinating information: height, weight, blood type. None of the good stuff is written on any official piece of paper. The most important facts I already knew, of course."

"Such as?"

"Paul, you were best friends for years with the man I was going to marry. You can safely assume that what he knew, I know."

"Oh, God." He grimaced.

She enjoyed watching him look a bit uncomfortable. It was good for him to squirm once in a while. "Yes, some of those stories are quite…what is the word? Colorful? Shocking?"

"I'm sure he exaggerated," Paul suggested.

Jennifer shook her head as her eyebrows rose. "I'm sure he didn't."

Paul took an exaggerated breath and looked helplessly around the room. "There's no need to dredge up the past, is there?"

"But there were sweet stories, too. He told me how the two of you plotted for him to meet me on that trip to South Padre Island." She laughed at the memory. "My father was stunned and impressed by the lengths you went through to get him invited to our beach house for dinner that first night." She paused and met his glimmering green eyes. "He later confessed you were the instigator."

"Guilty, I'm afraid," he said, with a light chuckle. "What else do you know?"

"Not much, at least nothing I'm willing to share at the moment. I'd rather have you worry about what I know or don't know for a little while." She smiled at the idea of letting him wonder.

"No tiny crumbs?"

Poking her tongue in her cheek, she thought for an instant. There were a lot of things she couldn't say—things that were just too personal for the both of them. Sometimes it was just better to play it safe. "Well, I know you've become the latest heartthrob on the senior wing at the hospital. I recently become acquainted with Virginia Mason."

"Oh?" His eyes crinkled as he smiled. "She is one interesting lady, a real one-of-a-kind charmer."

"Well, you could both join a mutual admiration society. She's very taken with you, too."

"What did she say?"

"Now, *that* I can't tell you." She chuckled as Paul rose to retrieve their warmed meal.

"I hope you like everything—even if it wasn't made by my hands. The lady at the gourmet store said it was a nice variety of foods."

"A dinner in a fancy restaurant wouldn't have been nicer," Jennifer said as lovely plates of well-prepared food were placed on the table. Although the meal wasn't homemade—a thought that secretly pleased her since she'd sampled Paul's cooking before—he'd gone to some trouble to arrange a nice evening for them. And he'd surprised her by not jumping ship when Jake decided to start World War Ill in her kitchen and living room. Many guys would have run from a toddler mess like that.

An instant later, Paul dimmed the lights and lit two tall graceful candles. Then, he put on a DVD and the soft, gentle vibrations of a harp embraced the room in music. The bouquet of roses looked most impressive as the centerpiece in a Lenox vase.

It was obviously a setting made for romance. Romance that Jennifer swore she didn't want, but couldn't convince her heart of that fact. Waiting for Paul to open the bottle of white Riesling—she'd decided after some gentle prodding that one glass wouldn't hurt—she looked forward to sampling some of the delicacies he'd bought for their meal.

She briefly remembered a tropical meal of barbecued fish, papaya, and poi. Yes, she sighed, she even had fond memories of poi. Instead of flowers in a vase and warm candlelight, they'd had a marvelous feast on a worn beach blanket, with island wildflowers growing all around them. Nothing had ever tasted that good.

Jennifer picked up the delicate bloom that fell to the table. She inhaled the floral scent and gently chided herself for thinking like a silly romantic. Why did she have to dwell on something that could never be? While their past brought them together, it would always come between them as well. Tonight, she was tempting fate, but she couldn't help herself.

He was getting better, nearing the one hundred percent his commanding officer wanted. Just yesterday afternoon, during a short jog together on the dirt running path, she'd realized how fit he was becoming. Her mind drifted back to their conversation on the dirt course…

Only if she were blind could she have ignored the fact that Paul was an incredibly masculine male. His hair was dark and waved loosely over his forehead. His legs were lean and fit—firm and sinewy as he jogged at a quickened pace. With broad shoulders and strong ropy arms, he was hard to ignore. Her heart skipped a beat.

Jennifer stopped suddenly. "Ow, I've got a pebble in my shoe." Awkwardly, she limped to a nearby tree to balance against while she shook the small stone from her running shoes.

They were both breathing hard as she slipped the sneaker back on and retied the laces.

"I think I've had enough anyway, Ms. Drill Sergeant." He rested his hands on his hips, while his eyes flickered as he teased her.

Jennifer spotted a group of benches a hundred yards from where they stood. "There." As they jogged over to the benches, she noticed the sweet smell of freshly cut grass and wanted to toss off her shoes and run barefoot. Nothing, she considered easily, was better than the light tickle of soft grass on bare feet.

"Mind if we join you, Mrs. Carson?" Paul spoke to one of the elderly women sitting across from them on the line of benches.

"Of course not, young man," she said, clearly happy for the disruption. "No matter how old I get, I still enjoy the company of a handsome young officer."

Jennifer smiled broadly, remembering Paul had become friends with just about everyone at the medical facility over the age of five. No, he'd been a hit with the preschoolers too, helping them make paper airplanes.

"Is this your girlfriend?" the woman asked slyly, putting aside her knitting and crossing her hands in front of her.

Jennifer coughed. It was an honest mistake, with her being out of her white lab coat and in jogging clothes. "No," Paul said, shooting Jennifer an irresistible grin. "This is my warden."

"I see," Mrs. Carson replied, nodding with a complete understanding.

"Actually," Jennifer interrupted, smoothing back her windswept hair with the back of her palm, "I'm a physical therapist, and he is one of my most ornery, troublesome patients. Won't listen to a thing I tell him—so I've got to keep an eye on him personally."

The old woman tossed back her head and chuckled. While her face was heavily lined and her hair was snowy white, her eyes were a bright, sparkling blue. They told of living eighty years with much happiness and few regrets. "I understand completely, my dear. I had one troublemaker like that in my life. He was a pilot, too." She winked openly at Paul. "He was an ace during the Vietnam War. Shot down more than a few enemy planes. But you couldn't tell that man anything."

"What happened to him?" Jennifer couldn't help ask, intrigued by the story.

"I married him, of course."

…Jennifer blinked as images of Mrs. Carson's kind face faded away. She shook her head slightly, trying to put yesterday in the back of her mind.

"Here's your wine." Paul handed her the cool crystal glass. When their fingers touched for a moment, little sparks of electricity tickled Jennifer's arm. He had that effect on her; he always had that effect on her. She shifted uneasily in her seat. He said he wanted to talk tonight. It would not be a light and easy conversation.

"Good wine?"

"Very good."

A stray blonde curl floated over her eye. Paul

reached to straighten it, lingering a moment to ease it back into place. The gesture was intimate, like a kiss or a caress. His light touch made her stomach jump, so she focused on the feast before her. "I think I'll pass on the escargot, if you don't mind and stick to the mushrooms." Jennifer scooped up three of the six mushrooms and left the escargot untouched.

"Why don't you take them all?" He moved the remaining mushroom caps to her plate. "I've always wanted to have escargot, but I've never tried them." The little snail shells stared back at him. He raised dark expressive eyebrows and narrowed them. "I think I know why. Wanna share?" He pointed to one of Jennifer's mushrooms with a helpless look.

"Sure. Mom always taught us sharing was nice." She had to admit that snails, even those dripping in delectable garlic butter, didn't quite suit her fancy. With the help of her salad fork and a spoon, Jennifer carefully lifted three mushrooms off her plate and onto Paul's. He moved the escargot off to the side and presented her with a grateful smile.

"Next time I'll have to follow your lead."

Jennifer chuckled until she thought of his words. Next time, the two little words echoed in her brain. If her head had anything to say about it, there wouldn't be a next time—at least not a next time with candlelight and roses. She kept showing very poor judgment where Paul was concerned. Jake certainly needed more than Paul could give and so did she. While Paul's intentions were heartfelt, there were far too many obstacles to overcome.

The only problem was her heart. It was looking at the situation and the man seated across from her in an entirely different angle. And it wouldn't stop pounding. She decided to talk instead of mulling over the situation to death in her mind.

"You know who really loved escargot?" She stabbed a piece of mushroom heaping with crabmeat and placed the morsel in her mouth.

"Jeff. He would devour the little creatures."

"And want more." She laughed and her throat tightened at the same time. Her eyes clouded for an instant. "It's hard to move on, Paul."

"I know it is." His eyes brimmed with tenderness and compassion. "I wish I could take away the pain, Jen."

"Sometimes it feels like I'll never be whole again. Like the world just caved in and I'll never feel like me again." She shuddered as she felt the emotion.

The heavy weight of Jeff's death had been with her a long time. "Then, I feel guilty when he's not on my mind. When you and I…" She left the words unsaid. "I felt so disloyal. He's the father of my son. I can't forget him."

"You don't have to forget him. I never will."

"I wish it were that simple. I owe Jake more laughter in his life." She looked deep into Paul's eyes and was torn from conflicting feelings. He'd brought more fun and laughter into their lives, and she'd pushed him away. It felt like the only sane thing she could do. "It's hard to know all the answers."

"Especially when you're so hard on yourself." He cocked a knowing brow.

"I'm not," she disagreed. "I just understand my responsibilities." Her mind drifted to the letter she'd received from Jeff's mother only days before. It just reaffirmed all the reasons she should never let herself become too involved with Paul.

She hadn't meant for their dinner conversation to take on such a serious tone. She'd wanted to keep their chatter light and friendly. Then she remembered a joke gift she'd picked up for him at the grocery store. She knew that it would lighten the conversation. "I got you something the other day."

"A gift?" He leaned back in his seat, looking at first startled, and then pleased.

"Well, kind of."

"Kind of a gift?"

She pushed her chair from the table and went to a cabinet in the kitchen. "I noticed something about you a couple weeks ago," she explained, setting the stage. "It's really silly…"

"Okay, what is it?"

She was silent for a moment, until she spied Paul's fork looming close to her plate. "Are you planning to steal my mushroom?"

He grinned widely and stabbed at her plate. "We have ways of making you talk. If you don't tell me now, I'll be forced to take your last remaining mushroom and hold it hostage."

She quickly moved to the table and pushed his arm away. "Okay, okay, you win," she said with a laugh as she tossed a packet of Breathe Right snore relief strips near his dinner plate. "You have a bit of a snoring problem."

"I snore?" He cocked his head to one side and choked back a laugh. "I don't snore. Do I?"

"I noticed in the hospital. Actually it's kind of endearing, in a snoring sort of way." Jennifer chuckled under her breath. She'd gone into his room the morning after the fire. He'd been tossing and turning every few moments, like a man who didn't want to stay in the same place too long. She'd made the observation and grinned as she'd tiptoed out of his room, leaving a covered plate of bacon and toast for his breakfast.

"So snoring can be endearing?" His grin reached his eyes.

"Sometimes."

"That's nice to know."

"Now can I have my mushroom back?"

Chapter Eight

The evening turned out to be more fun and relaxing than Jennifer had expected.

Chatting over a delicious meal, she remembered how much they had in common. He mentioned an upcoming concert at the Folger Theater. It sounded fun, she said. And how about hiking in the desert at Boreggo Springs? In the early summer, the slightly eastward desert bloomed bright like a botanical garden.

But summer was months away. The eastern desert would have to bloom without the two of them together. Paul would be a memory by then; he'd be back on the carrier, back in a military plane, and out of her and Jake's life.

As they lingered over sinfully rich chocolate mousse and cappuccino, Jennifer was surprised how comfortable she was with Paul. Even with all their history—and they had a lot of history, good and bad— she still found him an easy person to talk to. He knew her, understood her. If only things could be different.

"Want to put on some music and dance?" He indicated to the DVD in the other room. "It's nice outside. I could open the patio doors for a breeze."

"I don't know if that's a good idea."

"Worried about the last time we danced?" He raised an inquisitive eyebrow.

"Maybe." She nibbled on her lower lip as she

glanced from him to the open space in the living room just made for slow dancing.

"I'll be the perfect gentleman, promise." He raised his right hand and placed his left one on his heart. "You have nothing to worry about."

Without waiting for her response, Paul rose from his seat and strode over to her DVD player. He started flipping through her collection and stopped when he found one of her old 1940s tunes. "This is great. You love this type of music, too, don't you?" he asked, as he put in the disc and "Moonlight Serenade" filled the room.

"Come on." He beckoned her to join him. "Dance with me."

****

He'd wanted to have some quiet time with her. It seemed like they were either spending their time together kicking his butt during therapy or figuring out how to outsmart a one-year-old. Then, there was always the occasional hospital fire to contend with.

While he loved spending time with the one-year-old—who would have thought playgrounds and bath time could be so much fun?—he also wanted some time alone with her. She'd spent a lot of time focusing on why they couldn't—or shouldn't—be together. He got it. He understood her worries and fears. But he could make her and Jake happy. The quiet rumblings that had started in Hawaii had exploded during the short weeks they'd been worked together in San Diego. She was still cautious and apprehensive. He wanted her to forget he was a pilot—just a man—but her seeing him in his uniform every day didn't help matters. She had so much hurt inside—and he wanted to take it all away.

When Jennifer opened the sliding glass door to the balcony, her body swayed in the breeze. His eyes followed her gentle motion, and his heart thumped. He was falling in love with her thoroughly and completely—and he couldn't tell her, couldn't show her. She'd bolt. But he was finding it almost impossible to wait any longer.

"I'll bring some more wine out to you," he called as she stood against the railing, taking in the perfect San Diego evening. Later, he'd be able to tell her everything, but now wasn't the time. Now was the time for gentle wooing and easy flirting—not passionate lovemaking or powerful declarations and commitments. He prayed his control could last that long.

Her apartment balcony provided a perfect view of the ocean. The cool night wind ripped through the air, making Jennifer's blond tresses dance with the evening breeze.

"You know, I just love the ocean." Jennifer spread her arms wide and swung them around her. Paul caught one of her hands, and her whole body spun, following the breeze. She looked free, so free. As she twirled about for the second time, Paul grabbed her shoulders and pulled her to his chest. A kiss couldn't hurt, could it? His heart beat next to hers as he brushed his lips over her mouth. Who was he kidding? A kiss could never be enough.

Then he kissed her again. This kiss was different from the last—urgent, wanting, needy. His mouth eased hers open, and his tongue searched hers, seeking more, needing more.

With a desire just as great as his, her lips parted willingly, and her mouth met his with as much joy as there was longing. Slowly, her arms went around his shoulders, holding him close.

As his kiss became more demanding, Jennifer's body responded. It was as if she was filled with the same unbearable need to possess him, the way he wanted to possess her. Her body was flat against Paul's, her breasts buried in his chest, their legs tangled together. She molded perfectly to him. The wind seemed to flow around them, as the barrier of their bodies kept the night breeze from passing through.

He broke the embrace for an instant. He loved holding her face; it was like holding all the beauty of the world in his hands. At the moment, it was impossible to pretend she wasn't everything to him. She sent his emotions spinning out of control.

"I want you, Jennifer. I need you." His lips trembled as he spoke the truth. "I've never wanted anyone the way I want you. We've been dancing around our feelings for weeks now, trying to pretend them away. They're not going to go away, Jennifer, they're not."

****

Jennifer stared up at him, her eyes ablaze. Her heart pounded so fiercely, she was unable to move. It was as if time had frozen the instant their mouths met, and nothing else would ever matter again. She couldn't explain how a kiss could have so much power and authority, but it did. No man had ever aroused such a hunger, such a desire in her.

She'd kissed him back softly. She wanted him, but in a small corner of her brain, a doubt continued to nag. She had made a promise to herself, a promise she hadn't made lightly. Resolve melted when Paul kissed her, and no one else, nothing else seemed to matter. She moved away and rested her head on his chest.

Why was this happening to her? Steadying her breath, she struggled to sort out the thoughts snarled in her head. The sad truth was she didn't know what to do. At this very instant, she wanted Paul, she wanted to make love with him more than anything she had ever wanted. But what about tomorrow?

She squeezed her eyes closed, hoping it would help her concentrate. It didn't. Of course, Paul kissing and nuzzling her throat and neck didn't help either. She didn't want her body to override her mind. She had to keep control of the situation. For such a logical person, she was acting awfully emotional.

Abruptly, she broke from his grasp. It was impossible to meet his eyes.

"Paul, no." She spoke barely above a whisper, hoping he wouldn't be hurt and angry. Finally, when she looked up and caught his gaze, she saw a mixture of desire and understanding.

"You've changed my world, Jen. I felt empty before you came back into my life." He shook his head with disbelief. "It's hard to explain how I feel. My heart. My head. You're doing something crazy to me, and I can't walk away from it or you. I know I promised to give you time. I want you to sort out your feelings—and I know I need to do the same—but you're driving me crazy. I need to know what I should do."

His touch was driving her crazy. She was flip-flopping inside, and all she wanted was for him to hold her tight. But the fear, the anxiety, kept pressing. "I don't know, Paul. I feel so confused. I want to give us a chance, but I'm afraid what could happen if I do. Your life, your dreams. They're not good for me, and they're not good for Jake."

His arms tightened around her. She knew he had no intention of giving up. "I can't pretend away my feelings for you or Jake. How could I? You know how I feel. I want you next to me, in my arms, around me, inside me. And I adore your son; I have since the moment I saw your smile and Jeff's eyes. But I want it to be right for you. Yes, I'm a Navy pilot, and it's not as safe as being an accountant or a bookkeeper or whatever other guy sits behind a desk, but there are no guarantees and promises for anyone, anywhere."

"I know that, but it's not that simple."

"Give us a chance." He took her hands and held them. "I want you to get to know me—not me, the Navy pilot or Jeff's best friend, but me, the man who wants to be with you."

He was putting his cards on the table. Give us a chance, he asked. Get to know me, the man. But weren't the two intertwined? Wasn't being a pilot part of him? Could she go into this with her eyes open, all the time knowing that one day he might fly away and never come back? Wasn't he asking too much? And what if Jake started to care about him, too? It would only be natural for Jake to look up to the man in his mother's life. It wasn't just her heart, her life at risk, but his, too.

"I need more time to think this through, Paul. When Jeff died, I fell apart. It's taken a long time to put the pieces of my life back together. I don't think I can look at things clearly between us when we're working together…"

"You're making excuses, Jennifer," he said, trying to reason with her. His touch made her sizzle, made her hunger for his arms, for his touch. Slowly, he pulled her back into his cocoon. His mouth was on her throat and neck, increasing the emotion that was growing between them. "Days, weeks, months. It's not going to change what's happening between us."

"Please, no. I can't," she said, denying everything her heart and body wanted. There were too many questions that did not have answers. She couldn't walk blindly into something that might tear them all apart later. "I just can't."

If she let him make love to her now, there would be no turning back. That was a commitment she couldn't make. If she let her passion overtake her, she would be lost forever. She wouldn't go through the pain again.

"No, Paul." Her voice was strained as she spoke. She couldn't stop herself from running her fingers down his cheek. His jaw was tight, and she wanted to soothe it, to brush her hand over his nubby face. She wanted him, oh God, she wanted him. "I think I've been unfair to you. I haven't meant to lead you on."

Paul raked a frustrated hand through his hair. He put his hand under her silver hair and found the nape of her neck. "You're lying to yourself, Jen, and you're lying to me. We're on the brink of something incredible." He shifted his fingers and lifted her chin as he spoke. His tone was gentle and reassuring. The wind whipped through her, and Jennifer felt transparent standing there. "Are you cold?" Paul had noticed her shiver and placed a comforting arm around her shoulders.

It would only take a moment, no more than that.

One more word, one more look, and she wouldn't be able to be reasonable again. She looked sideways to glimpse his profile and turned away. She'd come too far to get hurt again. She had to end it now. "I got a letter from Carol Lyons a few days ago," she said abruptly.

He breathed deeply and briefly closed his eyes. "Jen, I know how upsetting…" He paused for an instant as if to find his words. "I carried a lot of guilt around for a long time. But I've gone over it a million times in my head. He wanted to be with me that day. I couldn't have stopped what happened."

Jennifer walked to the living room and pulled a tattered envelope from a drawer in her coffee table. She slipped out the letter. "Read this."

Paul took the pages and immediately recognized the handwriting. Jeff had often shared his correspondence from home when they were out at sea.

Dear Jennifer,

I know I've taken too long to write this letter. It's taken me a long time to get up the courage. I know you tried your best to comfort me after Jeff was killed. Back then I was inconsolable. I've spent the last six months in counseling, and finally I'm beginning to feel like my old self again. While it's been a very hard year and I'm still taking it one day at a time, I can see more clearly. To think that I haven't seen my only grandson yet is inexcusable. I plan to remedy that situation in the very near future. Please kiss that sweet little boy for me. I realize now that it wasn't Paul Davis who killed my son. I understand that accidents happen. I owe that young man an apology. Still, I can't help feel that young men like my Jeff and Paul are reckless. It's crazy what they do for a living. I don't think I'll ever understand what drives them to take the kinds of risks they take. If only they knew what it does to the people who love them, the people they leave behind. I hope life is treating you well and you have found the peace that I am searching for.

Love,

Carol Lyons

Paul folded the thin note paper carefully. "I don't know what to say."

"I saw the way you looked at that plane today. Even though I know the thought of flying makes you uneasy right now, you looked at it as if it were something priceless, something to be cherished. You live on the edge. You push too hard, take too many chances. I know it. I can see it. I've been through it before, and I can't do it again." Life was more than heated passion, and she had to do what was right. "I feel what you feel. Jake and I..."

"I'm crazy about your son, Jen," he broke in.

A small smile crept across her lips. "I know," she said softly. "And that just makes this so much harder. Jake is going to adore you, and there's going to come a time when you won't be there."

"I'll be there," he said with confidence.

"Paul, you can't make that kind of promise," she said with a thorough shake of her head. "First of all, there's no way you're going to remain stationed at Miramar and my physical therapy practice is here. We both know the Navy doesn't work that way." He didn't respond, so she went on. "And what if one of those stupid controlled crash contraptions doesn't work? What if you die, Paul? What if you die?"

"Nothing is going to happen to me. I'm a good

pilot, Jen."

"So was Jeff," she cried out, then stopped mid-breath as she watched a strange darkness move across Paul's eyes. "What? What's that funny look about?"

He paused, and then cleared his throat. "Nothing, Jen. Of course Jeff was a terrific flyer."

"And so were a lot of other good men who are now dead," she continued on, her mind and heart racked with hot emotion. They could work through the other problems—Jeff, her practice, their past—but they couldn't work through this. She couldn't jeopardize her son's future on her feelings for this man.

"I think you're fooling yourself if you think we can just walk away from what we've started, Jen."

"Maybe, but I need to think what's best for me and my son." His expression softened, and she could see the amber flecks in his green eyes glimmering in the evening light. Jennifer twisted the thin gold chain around her neck, and her brow tightened. She squeezed her eyes shut; it wasn't a matter of her needing more time, not really. She'd known the answer from the start. They didn't stand a chance, not in the long run.

Her heart pounded furiously in her chest. Paul was a good man. It was too bad he wasn't a good man for her. "I think we should call it a night. It's late." Their lives and dreams were too different. He wanted to spend his life in the clouds, and she wanted to be on solid ground.

For a second, his grasp on her shoulders tightened, but then he released her, almost pushing her away. He turned away, and stared out into the ocean.

"If that's how you want it, Jennifer."

Although she tried to keep her face forward,

Jennifer couldn't resist glancing at Paul from the corner of her eye. He, too, was staring straight ahead, his chin high, a hardness in his jaw. "Good night." He grabbed his jacket, and an instant later was out the door.

****

"Lori, I don't want to go to this thing. Couldn't you tell Commander Taylor I was sick with malaria or something?" They had just pulled inside the parking area adjacent to the Navy commander's home, and there was no turning back.

But there was no reason in the world she couldn't pout about it for a moment or two longer. It had been three days since her last evening with Paul, and she was still annoyed at the world.

"Come on, Jen. It'll be fun." From behind the wheel of the car, Lori offered her partner a reassuring smile. She turned the key to the ignition, and the motor died.

"Even if Daddy couldn't make it, we'll have a good time, right girls?" She shot a quick look over her shoulder at her two daughters, Christina and Gina, strapped securely in the backseat. Gina giggled happily as she clutched her favorite doll, Heidi, who traveled with her everywhere. Lori then grinned at Jake, who was toying with a wispy curl on top of Gina's dark head. "And Jake's ready to party, too."

Jennifer gritted her teeth but didn't want to spoil the girls' outing. "I can't wait."

Lori clutched Jennifer's hand and gave it a friendly squeeze. "Look, we only have to stay a couple hours. Then you have the rest of the weekend to yourself, right? Aren't you taking Jake to your aunt's house later today?"

"Yes, I suppose." Even though she loved spending time with Jake, she enjoyed having the occasional day all to herself. Her Aunt Susan lived about fifteen miles away, in a pleasant beach retirement community; Jennifer's aunt, still active and youthful at sixty-six, was one of Jake's favorite people and he seemed to love her doting attention.

"Hey, don't sound so glum. She'll be spoiling her favorite great-nephew rotten, while you get some needed breathing space for a full twenty-four hours— no work, no pilots, and no baby messes to clean up."

"All right, I'll try to look cheerier."

As they got the kids out of the car, Jennifer wondered how she'd gotten lassoed into coming to this little gathering. Of course, it would have been terribly impolite to refuse when Commander Taylor invited them to an informal get-together at his home to meet his wife and children. He was pleased with the work she was doing with his squadron, and wanted to talk about a bigger, expanded therapy program. It wasn't until after they'd accepted that he'd added, "I've also invited some of the men from your group. It'll be a nice party." How it had moved from a small little get-together to a party was beyond her.

"I'm so glad you and your families could make it." Commander Taylor greeted Jennifer and Lori with firm handshakes when he answered the door. "We're in the backyard," he said, leading them through his house. "Let me get you drinks. Miss Wade?"

"Just a ginger ale, please. Nothing for Jake." Her eyes scanned the roomy backyard looking for familiar faces. There was Jack Herman, Mark White, but not any dark haired, green-eyed surprises. For a moment, she calmed. Maybe he wasn't coming today.

"Ms. Hampton?"

"A beer. Whatever you have. The girls like anything sweet."

Grabbing the drinks, Commander Taylor escorted them to one of several well-shaded picnic-style tables. He was warm and friendly as they spoke about the therapy program he wanted for the men in his command. "I think it's important to be physically fit. It's not only good for the body, but the mind, too.

"People don't know how to keep in shape. They start running or begin a strength-training regimen, but don't follow through." He picked up his beer mug and took a gulp. While he appeared to enjoy a good beer, it was obvious Commander Taylor didn't overdue it. Lean and trim, he had no semblance of a beer belly.

"The program you've got a lot of my men on is very smart—they can keep with it for the rest of their lives. Why, in just a little over a month, they've been showing a real difference. Like Lieutenant Davis here." Jennifer twisted her head to find Paul greeting his commanding officer. "Paul, I know you already know Miss Wade, but this is her partner, Lori Hampton."

The two men shook hands; no salutes were necessary as they were out of uniform. Jennifer wished she were anywhere but there. She needed more time to adjust to the way she needed to think about Paul. Every time she turned around, he was there, so deep under her skin. Her plan to distance herself from him wasn't working at all. She picked up her tall glass of ginger ale and swirled the ice with her straw.

"It's nice to see you, Jennifer." He lightly rested his hands on the back of her chair, then moved to meet her eyes. His brows arched, and his mouth eased into a smile.

She counted to ten silently as Lori asked Paul about his thoughts on the therapy program. He would be gone in a minute, since the table was only so big.

While she did nothing to call attention to herself, Jake obviously felt no compunction about keeping still. As soon as he saw Paul, he lit up, little fingers reaching upward for Paul to pick him up.

The rest of the afternoon was bound to be a disaster when Commander Taylor turned to Paul and excused himself. "Lieutenant, since you're obviously on such good terms with our young visitor here, why don't you sit down. I've got some business to attend to. You can keep our guests company while I'm gone. We'll talk later. It's good to have you onboard, Miss Wade, Ms. Hampton."

It was like a bad dream, and it was going to get worse. Paul was going to join them for the duration.

"It's nice to finally meet you, Lori." Paul plopped down in the seat beside Jennifer and casually lifted the impatient Jake onto his lap. Jake grinned victoriously, and Jennifer couldn't prevent a smile of resignation from crossing her lips. How mean a mommy would she be if she tried to keep Jake from spending a little time with his best buddy? "Jennifer has spoken frequently about you and Steve and the girls." He smiled widely at Christina and Gina. "It sounds like your business partnership is doing very well."

Lori's mouth lifted as she reached over to give Jennifer's wrist a chummy squeeze. "It's actually a lot of fun." She leaned back and rested in the high back lawn chair. "Jennifer and I have known each other a long time. Years ago, I used to date her older brother. My family was military, just like Jen's. Our fathers were in the same squadron." Her gaze shifted to Paul. "Flyboys like you, you know."

Lori reached for her beer and swirled it. "It seems like such a long time ago, but I can still remember when Jennifer decided to become a physical therapist. I was in PT school at the time, and she wanted to know everything. Bob, her brother," she said, glancing at Jennifer, her mind full of memories, "had me teach her how to do therapeutic back rubs. Then he convinced her that she needed lots of practice and he'd sacrifice his back to her education." Lori laughed as the Taylors' teenage daughter, Chloe, graciously refilled drinks and placed bowls of popcorn and pretzels on the table. "Poor Jennifer. I've tried to make it up to her, but I'm not sure she forgives me yet."

Paul lifted his glass and sipped, hiding a grin. "So studious at such a young age."

"Was she?" Lori offered, more than willing to fill in the details to Jennifer's chagrin. "If it weren't for Jake, she'd be willing to put in twelve or fourteen-hour days. Me, I need the sleep."

Jennifer dipped her hand into Jake's diaper bag and retrieved large sunshades from a side pocket. She placed the glasses on her eyes and hoped it would hide the blush she knew was quickly coloring her face. While her fingers haphazardly toyed with the fringe on the checkered tablecloth, she gave Lori a scolding glance. "Thank you very much. I just love people to know what a nerd I was."

Paul winked. "Don't worry, your secret is safe with us, Jen. I didn't realize whom I was dealing with before." He jostled Jake slightly on his knee, and the little boy immediately giggled and rocked up and down, begging for more. "Jake, what other things don't we know about your mommy?"

While she was afraid Paul would spend the rest of the afternoon being her shadow, he surprised her when he scooped up Jake, intent to introduce her baby to some of the other toddlers who had recently joined the party. "Jen, Jack and Mark have some little ones about Jake's age, do you mind if I introduce him around?"

She glanced over her shoulder and saw a small group of toddlers playing on some well-used plastic play equipment. She frowned a little as she quickly assessed that Jake would easily be the youngest child in the group. "I don't know, Paul."

She gnawed on her lower lip as she took a second look, unsure if she was being overprotective or sensible in her uncertainty. "They look a little big for Jake."

"He'll be safe. I won't let him out of my arms." Heat ran through warm veins as he winked at her again. He snuggled Jake in his strong embrace. "I'll take good care of our boy, Jen."

Our boy. She swallowed hard as she nodded her head and familiar warmth continued to spread through her body.

"Can we go, too, Mommy?" Gina asked her mother, grabbing Heidi as she began to ease out of her seat.

"Sure, have fun, but don't drive Paul crazy," she answered pleasantly as both girls scurried after Paul and Jake.

"God, he is so good with Jake," Lori murmured, as soon as Paul was out of earshot.

"I know," she faltered, her eyes peeled as Paul gently eased Jake onto a small baby slide.

"You're not going to let go of him, are you?"

"I have no choice, Lori."

"There's always a choice." She cocked her head to the side. "You just have to decide if you're ready to take it."

"You make it sound easy." She toyed with the fringe at the edge of checked tablecloth.

"It is, if you're ready to move on—for Jake's sake, as well as your own."

"Paul doesn't want what Jake and I need. As soon as he passes his PT test, he'll be on to his next assignment."

"Well, all I know is that your footloose and fancy-free bachelor is up to his elbows in taking care of your baby and loving every minute of it."

"I don't know."

"You can't fool me, partner. I see the way you look at him and the way he looks at you." She nudged her. "This guy is good for the two of you."

Jennifer shrugged, unable to come up with a good verbal response. Paul was terrific with Jake; there was certainly no denying that—but then she couldn't deny the problems either. Before she could think on it further, she heard the delightful sounds of her son having a terrific time playing in a large plastic cube. A smile pulled at the corners of her mouth as she turned and watched Jake play a little game of peekaboo with Paul. Her eyes moisten as Paul moved his palms on and off his eyes. God, how could a guy like Paul, who had no use for children in his life, be so good with her little one?

Paul spent the next hour with Jake and the other kids who apparently knew a sucker when they saw one. Jennifer joined in for a good portion of the time, not able to resist playing with Jake when he was having such fun.

By the time Command Taylor announced the burgers and hotdogs were ready, Paul had helped each of the kids—a good dozen times—slide down slides and swing on swings. He looked noticeable tired when he finally plopped down next to Jennifer and Lori for the barbecued lunch.

"What? Not giving up yet, are you, Paul?" Lori chuckled as she watched Paul swipe the hem of his T-shirt across his moist forehead. "I think most of the parents here owe you some babysitting money."

"Nah, we were just having a good time with all the kids, weren't we, Jake?" He relaxed with Jake comfortably in his lap.

With her son sitting contentedly with his adult pal, Jennifer quickly rose and got plates of food for herself, Paul, and Jake. "I'll take over now," she said when she returned. "You've already gone above and beyond the call of duty."

Jake protested slightly as he was transferred from Paul to Jennifer. "Hey, young man, I'm the one who carried you for nine months. No fair changing allegiances midstream."

"Jennifer, I have the touch." His voice was low and smooth and completely unsettling.

Her stomach rumbled, and it had nothing to do with hunger. She looked down at Jake's plate and began tearing up small pieces of a hot dog.

"For a single guy, you're very good with kids,

Paul," Lori commented, cutting up a hamburger for her preschooler. "Isn't he, Jen?"

Jennifer nodded, but continued to focus on the tiny piece of meat in front of her. "Uh huh."

"I mean, my husband Steve took a long time to get that comfortable being with the kids. He always thought they'd break or something."

"I guess I'm just a kid at heart, Lori," he replied with a grin, as he reached over to tickle the underside of Jake's knee.

They continued to chat amiably during the rest of the meal, and Jennifer laughed when the main topic of conversation was the amount of food Jake could put away.

"He really can pack it in, can't he?" Paul commented as Jake polished off one and a half hotdogs, and a good helping of potato salad.

"He's a growing boy," she defended as she reached for a paper napkin to wipe Jake's messy face. "I wouldn't talk if I were you, though. That *snack* you had at the hospital that day was enough to satisfy several growing boys."

"A healthy appetite." He jovially patted his firm stomach.

"I don't think you have much to worry about," Lori chimed in with a grin.

"Especially with Jennifer's warden-like exercise program," he tossed back and looked pleased when Jennifer's face cracked into a wide smile.

"I have my methods," she retorted as a newly-cleaned Jake worked his way out of her lap and into the pile of large Legos Christina and Gina had brought to their nearby picnic blanket. Commander Taylor had enough toys and games to satisfy the entire group of youngsters; like a good military man, it seemed he was always prepared...even when he was out of uniform.

"Look, Jake wants to help with our castle," said Christina, who couldn't wait until she was old enough to babysit for Jennifer's son.

"Maybe he has a little engineer in him, like Jeff." Paul leaned over to wrestle Jake's curly top.

In college, Jeff had majored in electrical engineering. Even though he'd enjoyed the difficult discipline, he'd been happy to put it aside and learn aerodynamics. "I also have good math and science skills, thank you very much," Jennifer added in a pretend huff.

"I remember." His smile reached his eyes and held her gaze captive.

It was getting harder and harder to ignore him. That way he looked at her, like he could see right through to her heart. She shifted uncomfortably, rearranging her legs beneath her. This was going to be a long afternoon.

Her head jerked suddenly, when she heard Christina cry out in alarm, her arms flailing in front of her. "Mommy, Jenny, something is wrong with Jake. He can't breathe."

Jennifer's eyes shot to her son, and she practically tumbled off the picnic bench seat to reach him. His mouth was clenched tight as his eyes ballooned. His skin quickly turned from sheet-white to a pale drawn blue. He couldn't utter a sound, but he was crying, rocking back and forth on the palms of his small hands. "Oh, God, Jake."

Panic trapped in her throat as she screamed in fear.

Her legs twisted underneath her as she scooted toward her baby.

Paul was faster. In a blink of an eye, he grabbed the heaving child and hoisted him onto his lap. Turning the baby around in his capable hands, Paul fixed Jake's jerking body over his outstretched forearm and thumped five times between his tiny shoulder blades. Nothing. Paul repositioned his hands and took a firmer hold and repeated the process. His hands clenched as he worked to dislodge whatever was trapped in the infant's airway.

Although it seemed like hours had passed, a tiny round object flew from Jake's small mouth an instant later and landed yards away. A fierce terrified howl followed as Jake seized his first clear breath, tears running down his frightened face in enormous droplets. "Ma ma ma ma," Jake repeated again and again, his teary eyes searching for his mother's comforting embrace.

"I'm here, sweetie, I'm here," Jennifer cooed as Paul eased Jake from his arms into her welcoming touch. She rocked him gently in her embrace, stroking the back of his now-damp head.

While she worked to calm the distraught baby in her arms, she tried to still the frantic pounding of her own heart. One minute he was just playing with some big colorful plastic blocks, and the next he was unable to even gasp for breath. She could have lost him, too. Jennifer tried to focus on Jake and ignore the feelings of dread that enveloped her. Her lower jaw quivered as she whispered sweet nothings to her cherished armful.

"Jen, you're shaking." Paul's reassuring arms wrapped around her shoulders. His hands skimmed up and down her trembling arms. "Do you want me to take him for a little while?"

"No, no, I'm fine." She held Jake tighter, more protectively, then eased her grip when she saw the emotion in his dark green eyes. "Thank you."

"I guess I can be good to have around sometimes." He shifted his hands from her to Jake's quivering body. "You're going to be okay, buddy, I promise," he whispered into the small boy's ear.

"It was a doll's eye." Mark Gordon, the doctor Jennifer met at the aircraft carrier, snatched up the little round plastic object from the well-manicured lawn and held it out in his open palm.

"Oh, God, it's Heidi's eye," Lori cried as she reached for her daughter's favorite doll that lay prone on their picnic blanket. A few loose strings dangled where an eye had been. "I'm so sorry."

"It's not your fault...or Heidi's. It just happened." Jennifer breathed in deeply, still trying to relax the tremors quaking through her muscles.

"Jennifer, why don't you let me see him," Mark Gordon wedged his way next to Jennifer. "Let's sit down inside the house. You can keep him on your lap."

She nodded as her hands continued to stroke Jake's baby fine hair. As they started toward the house, Paul was right beside them. "You don't have to," she began, but his eyes stopped her.

"I know," he said simply, and stayed by her side.

****

Dr. Gordon gave Jake a thumb's-up after a thorough on-the-spot evaluation. He didn't think it was necessary for Jake to go to the hospital, but recommended they postpone his overnight with

Jennifer's aunt as a precaution.

Several hours later, Jake was laughing and giggling again. It was as if the horrible scare had never happened. But it *had* happened, she thought anxiously as she prepared Jake for bed that night. As a medical professional, she knew how easily it would have been to lose him today. Life was so precious and fragile.

She finally relaxed after Jake was snug in his crib. Her heart calmed as she watched him take slow, rhythmic breaths in his sleep. She wanted to hug him again, but he needed the rest especially after the day's activity. Jennifer wrapped her arms around her shoulders, hugging her robe close to her body. She was glad the day was finally coming to a close.

Lost in her thoughts, Jennifer barely heard the chime of the doorbell. She wasn't surprised to open the door moments later and find Paul on the other side.

"I was worried about Jake," he said without preamble. "I needed to be with you."

"I'm glad you're here." While she'd spent the past six hours totally focused on Jake, she hadn't been able to prevent her mind from drifting to Paul—his swift action, kindness, and concern. And she'd wanted him beside her while the doctor had examined Jake. She couldn't quite figure it all out in her head, but Paul had become an integral part of their lives.

For the first time in a long time, she wasn't alone and isolated. She had friends and family, of course, but too often it was just her and Jake against the world. With Paul, she could relax; with him, she felt content. She'd fought the feeling—as if being happy and at ease with someone meant she was being disloyal to Jeff and his memory. God, what was she going to do? "You saved Jake's life tonight." She opened the door wider so he could enter. "I owe you so much."

"Jen, you don't owe me anything," he replied, shaking his head, "at least not for anything that happened today."

"No, really, I'm grateful…"

"Damn, I don't want your gratitude." His voice was hoarse as he faced her. His hands rose and clutched her shoulders. "I have training; I would have aided anybody who needed it. What I want from you, need from you, is honesty." He released his hold and started pacing short steps in her entryway. His face knotted with building frustration. "I went home after you left. All I could do was stare into nothingness. I knew that I should be with you, but you've said you don't want me. I know it's a lie, and I couldn't stay away."

She took a deep breath, then exhaled. "Okay, it is a lie."

The tight muscles in his face and body relaxed. He lifted his hands to cup her face, then twined his fingers through her hair. "I've never pushed so hard with anyone before, but I've never cared for anyone the way I care about you." He released a long, raspy sigh. "I know you're always going to love Jeff and that's all right. He was my best friend, and I'll always love him, too." His eyes were bright and full of compassion. "I'm going to get my chance to fly again soon. I'm really scared, but I'm not going to run away. I'm gonna do it because I won't let it cripple me."

"I know you'll do it, Paul."

"I need you, Jen. I need you to be with me. And you need me, too." He wrapped his finger around the back of her neck and gently kneaded the sensitive skin there. "You're right that I can't promise you forever. But sweetheart, nobody can." He wiped a tear from her cheek and brushed tangled bangs from her eyes.

Her heart had stopped, she was sure of it. She tried to breathe, but it was close to impossible. "I made a promise to myself, Paul, no more pilots," she uttered in a tone barely above a whisper. "Never."

"That's just an excuse to keep hiding. I know you're afraid to feel what you feel. It's understandable with the kind of pain you've had." His eyes searched hers with intensity. "But Jennifer, you can't live in fear all the time. You don't always choose the people you care about. It just happens sometimes. That's what makes it so great. You've got to take a chance."

Jennifer shook her head slowly from side to side. She tried to pull from him, but he held her tight. "You make it sound so easy."

"Easy? No. We both have demons to conquer. But it's so hard to do alone. We have so much to overcome, but we can do it together. I'm not asking for forever—I know you're not ready for that—just a chance, a real chance, to see if we can work. I'm not going to make this easy for you. I care too much about us."

Her brows knit together, and her face tightened. Her voice quaked as she spoke. "Why are you doing this to me? Why can't you let it be?"

"I can't. I love you."

The words were so simple. The delivery so easy. Her life had just changed, and she would never be the same. Her shoulders slumped with his confession. He loved her.

A streak of bright lightning shot through the black sky. "Paul, I can't pretend I don't care, but I don't know if I can do this again." Her voice shook, and her eyes watered as she spoke. She couldn't return his words. "I can't make any promises."

"Come here." His tone was gentle but firm. He wasn't the kind of man that reached for the brass ring and missed. "Jennifer, I just can't let you walk away from me. I love you too much. You're too important, we're too important."

"No promises, Paul," she said firmly, unable to resist the need to be near him.

As his grip tightened on her shoulders, willing her close to him, the night grew bright and the sky outside opened up. "Okay, no promises, Jen."

Lightning sliced through the room through a crack in the curtain, illuminating the dark, quiet night. He closed a finger around a disobedient curl and brushed the nape of her neck. "I dream about being with you."

She leaned back, enjoying the rough feel of his hands. "I want to be with you, too."

Slowly, his mouth closed on hers. Her lips opened willingly, longingly, as his tongue caressed the softness of her mouth. His hands tangled in her hair, until they moved over her back, tracing every curve as if committing them to memory. As her mind filled with thoughts of pleasure, she willed him to possess her body. His palms felt rough and manly as they ventured over her shoulders and tingled the soft skin there.

She remembered the first time they'd been together like this. They'd been soaking wet with minds and hearts racing. That moment had been a mix of wild lust and desire. This time the passion was mixed with love and compassion. It made the sensations he was stirring in her more arousing and overwhelming.

Gently, he reached into her robe and cupped her breasts. She gasped and slowly closed her eyes when his fingers brushed over her nipples. The tips of her breasts ached as she welcomed those magic fingers.

Jennifer sighed when Paul eased the terry robe off her shoulders. As the fabric slipped from her arms, the cool air tickled her skin. His breathing was hard and sporadic, and she smiled. She was doing this to him, making him wanting and hungry. Needing to fulfill that desire, Jennifer held him close, as if they were meant to be one.

As if their clothing were a hindrance, Paul untied the loose belt around her waist, and she reveled in her near-nakedness. He took her breath away as his tongue tickled the tips of her breasts; they grew hard and taut in his mouth.

Jennifer needed to feel his skin against hers. It was like needing water, needing air. Forcing his hands up, she lifted the cumbersome T-shirt over his head. He chuckled softly as she ran her hands over the tan hair on his chest, and skimmed an eager tongue over his nipple.

When she reached to unbuckle his pants, he lifted her quickly and carried her into the bedroom. She sighed as he placed her on the bed and joined her there. The sheets were crisp and seductively cool. Rolling on a downy quilt, she reached for his belt again to finish what she had started, what they had started. This was it. She greedily kissed his neck, refusing to think of tomorrow, of flying. Tonight, only tonight mattered, this instant, this frozen moment in time.

She tried to speak, to say his name, to say she loved him back, but only a groan escaped her lips. His hands—such special wonderful hands—rolled over her slender hips and caressed her thighs. She wanted him inside her, God, she needed him. He was making love so slowly, she feared she would burst with anticipation. He stripped his jeans from his legs, and his hard athletic thighs wrapped around her. She closed her eyes and the merry-go-round whizzed faster and faster.

Paul moaned as he nuzzled her neck and nibbled on the lobe of her ear.

"You make me so happy, Jen."

She wanted to enjoy every moment, to savor and relish the wondrous feelings he was bringing out in her. She needed to touch, taste, and examine every hard line and angle of his body.

He wanted her, he needed her. His gentle, yet thorough touch made her feel wonderful and alive. As his fingers traveled up her thighs and between her legs, he brought her to the brink and beyond, way beyond. She leaned back on the pillow writhing with desire, and arched her back as the journey of pleasure continued.

Still, she hadn't forgotten him and his need. Her hands went to him and stroked him sensuously, listening to his breathing, watching what made him hunger for her. In a rush, he grabbed for his jeans and pulled a foiled packet from his wallet. He unwrapped the condom and had it ready to go in seconds.

A bright streak of lightning entered the room with a thunderous clap as he gently moved over her. She was waiting for him as he moved into her slowly, treasuring the sensation of his body filling hers. They moved together with sweet, delirious friction. His hands brushed her cheek as his fingers dragged through her hair. As the bright light continued, his mouth was at her breast, her neck; their lovemaking became everything.

She cried out with pleasure as she reached the peak, and he followed.

He loved her, God, he loved her.

Chapter Nine

It was the sweet hum of a robin that woke her the following day. Light cascaded through a slight crack in the closed bedroom drapes, sending a gentle glow in the dim room. Morning.

As she yawned, she noted the distinct sound of water running. Automatically, her hands stretched to the other side of the bed, searching for Paul. Through smiling, sleepy eyes, she turned her attention to the closed bathroom door.

She yawned again, happy to be where she was, content to stay there all day. He hadn't woken her when he'd risen for a shower. The bed was lonely and big without him. Memories of the previous evening whispered in her mind. Had it all been a wonderful dream? Although the moments were no promise for tomorrow, she'd been willing to grasp the brass ring, too. She pressed the thought of tomorrow, of later, from her mind. They had now and today. That had to be enough. Tomorrow, he could be…

Her head popped up as the bathroom doorknob turned. Dressed in fresh clothes he kept in his car, Paul entered the room smiling. "Sleep well?"

She returned the smile, her body still pulsing with memories of the night before. "Wonderfully well."

She giggled as Paul slowly walked toward her, opened the drapes to let the morning light rush in, and proceeded to leap on the bed. She pretended to pull away, but allowed herself to be captured in his arms. A more wonderful location had never been created.

"What do you want to do today?" he asked, after touching his lips to hers. He pulled his hands through her sleep-mussed hair and massaged the nape of her neck. She reciprocated with a leisurely kiss in the hollow of his throat.

The answer came to Jennifer quickly. She twisted out of his reach to face him. "Let's go flying."

"What?"

"You heard me," she replied, gathering her nerve. "Let's go out to Montgomery Field, rent a plane, and go flying."

"Right, and next you'll say you want to go to the moon." He soothed her hair and rested his hand on her shoulder.

She shook her head, feeling more certain by the minute. "I'm serious, Paul. I know you're anxious about it, and so am I. I was just thinking that maybe if we did this together, it would help. We can drop Jake off with my aunt; he was doing just great when I put him to bed last night, so I'm sure he will be fine with her."

He quickly bent down and kissed the tip of her nose. "You're really something." He swallowed hard and breathed deeply. "But I'm not sure if I'm ready."

"Are you going to feel any readier with Commander Taylor and the rest of your squadron watching?" She caught his eyes as he considered the idea. "With me, it would be easy. Besides, you made a promise to Billy. I can just imagine his face when you see him next week and tell him you went up."

He gnawed on the thought. "I did make that promise, didn't I?"

"Yes, you certainly did."

He kissed her softly on the lips. "I can't believe you'd do this for me."

Jennifer could hardly believe she'd made the offer, but it was something he'd have to face sooner or later. He'd be miserable otherwise, and she couldn't ignore that fact. She wanted him to be happy. "Well, I wouldn't do it for anybody else." As he rolled his palms up and down her sides, from her shoulders to her hands, a flicker of excitement, a memory of recent passion, sped through her. "I've only got one condition." She lined his jaw with baby-fine kisses.

He lifted a brow and drew her closer, his voice deeper and husky. "It's a sacrifice," he said lightly, starting to undo the top button of her nightshirt. "But I surrender."

She ran her tongue over a tender piece of flesh at his throat. "I'm glad you see it my way," she growled.

The hunger hadn't decreased; she wanted him, needed him. The first kiss didn't quench, only inflamed. Jennifer barely noticed her shirt come apart and slip onto the bed. His hands tightened around her hips as she shifted to be closer to him. She relished the electric bursts of desire that rushed through her body. She yanked the cotton shirt from his broad chest, delighting in the clean, soapy scent of his body. His jeans came next, and her appetite for him increased. His stomach was hard and lean as she yanked the denim off his body. No hindrances. Soon they were flesh to flesh and the craving, the thirst for more, shot up like an explosive.

His hands sought every inch of her, and she urged him on with soft butterfly kisses from his face to his neck on down. His heart beat rapidly; she could hear it as she continued her journey. He needed all she could give.

His tongue slid from her neck to her breasts, and she arched as little tremors coursed through her system. Each nerve was in tune.

But it got better and better. His hands gently spread her legs. If it weren't an involuntary function, her breathing would have ceased long ago. She reached for him, and he sighed again. The thirst was contagious.

Their bodies met again, and her heart left the ground. She was drugged and energized as their bodies moved together. Then they were soaring in the clouds, falling, drifting. When they touched ground, his body shuddered over hers, and she cried out. This couldn't be the end.

****

Montgomery Field was the smaller, non-hub airport in San Diego. Most of the city's private pilots maintained their aircraft there. In the early morning, maintenance crews were servicing small and large planes on the quiet and peaceful airstrip. The sky was true blue, vast and welcoming.

During the short drive to the airport, Paul chatted anxiously about flying. He'd learned to fly as a teenager. His father's youngest brother was a pilot— and took his favorite nephew flying at every opportunity. From the very start, Paul had been hooked.

Her eyes followed a sea gull gliding through the sky and wondered if it knew how hard man strived to compete with it in the heavens. It terrified her, utterly and completely. Just an hour ago, her hands had shivered as she'd slipped on faded corduroys and a warm billowy cowl-neck sweater. She wanted to trust him, but out of his secure arms, she had her doubts. What had she been thinking? He'd even expressed doubts, and she'd pushed him on. Her head needed to be examined. She couldn't let him down, though. He was counting on her, now.

"Which one is ours?" she asked, getting out of the car. It was cool outside, yet she was starting to sweat. Her eyes cautiously surveyed the group of small propeller planes.

"That one," he said, pointing at a small blue two-seater propeller plane. It was unlike the large, somewhat reassuring Boeing 747 she was used to traveling in. It reminded her of the type of plane, open and airy, that Wilbur and Orville Wright probably flew. She was going to humiliate herself and get sick right then and there. There was no way in the world she was getting off the ground in that plane.

****

Seconds after they were off the ground, a fear greater than she had ever imagined ran up Jennifer's spine and clutched at her throat. She'd been kidding herself. There was no way she was going to make it. They were going to crash, she just knew it.

It had been years since she had gone up in anything but a large commercial carrier. As a little girl, she'd flown in her father's small twelve-seater passenger plane. It had seemed bumpy then, but compared to this plane, the other rides had been almost soothing.

Her initial reaction was to jump and abandon ship. But looking down at the ground, she abandoned that idea quickly. The wind whipped at her face, and the goggles Paul had presented her with felt tight and hard. Her seat belt didn't feel secure. If he did anything but fly a completely even course, she'd probably tip right out of the plane.

Quite startlingly after a few moments, her back began to relax. The wind, the feeling of weightlessness, of being on top of the world, was strangely pleasing.

She looked down at the earth and felt at peace. It was not terrifying or death-defying. She smiled, thinking of her father. Flying had kept him alive. He had never felt more vital than when his feet left the ground. Jeff had felt the same way. And Paul—they were all from the same mold. It was a part of her, too. Her heart warmed as she thought of the times she would sit and listen mesmerized by tales of her father at thirty thousand feet. It had been exhilarating; this was exhilarating.

Jennifer adjusted her goggles and lifted her chin to feel the shock of cool wind envelop her body. She glanced down again at the world below her. From the sky, she could feel and smell the sea breeze when they passed over the Salton Sea in Borrego Springs. The desert was dry and beige, with hints of dark green vegetation here and there. From her bird's-eye view, everything melted together. Instead of pieces, she saw the whole picture. "A doll's house," she murmured, watching the miniature cars, the tiny houses, and the difficult-to-see people. They flew into a cloud, and it was as if nothing else existed.

For the first time since they took flight, the small plane finally stopped climbing at twelve thousand feet. As it straightened and became parallel to the ground below, Jennifer breathed deeply, inhaling the fresh brisk air, and looked straight ahead at the clear blue morning sky.

She had almost forgotten about Paul sitting behind her at the main controls. With the wind whipping at the loose curls that had escaped her ponytail, she strained her neck to face him, but found it impossible.

As she turned back, her gaze caught a large thundercloud. The white billows meant there might be showers before the day was over. There had been a time when she could have recognized every cloud she saw in an instant. It had been a favorite game. The memory made her smile.

****

He was flying, and it felt great. His stomach had grown uneasy when he'd taken his seat inside the small cockpit. He'd done the safety check with extra care and patience. The radio, engine, and the rest of the instruments were in perfect working order. His palms had sweated like a geyser when he'd started the engine and began taxiing down the runaway. For a quick moment, he'd wanted to turn around and forget what it was like to soar. But he couldn't turn back. Jennifer was risking so much to join him.

She didn't want to be here. It didn't take a brain surgeon to figure that out. She was doing it for him, despite all of her fears and reservations. He couldn't let her down. He needed her to understand why he flew, and why he took the risks and the chances. God, he loved her so much. Once they were airborne, he'd choked back a deep breath and piloted the plane. His hands had trembled when he took the controls and guided the small propeller craft into the air. For a minute, he'd operated on autopilot. He knew the instrument panel like the back of his hand. Then his pulse began to relax, and he breathed a long-sought sigh of relief. He could do it.

****

Jennifer was startled when she felt a strong, firm hand grip her shoulder from behind. It was strangely reassuring and familiar. Her spine straightened, and she glanced backward, still seeing more of her left wing than her pilot. Since she was unable to meet his gaze, she slowly raised her right arm and reached over her shoulder, fighting the strong determined wind. Seconds later his hand reached hers and squeezed it. Warm and tingly currents of electricity flowed between them. They'd made it.

The flight lasted no more than twenty minutes, but for Jennifer, who had reopened and stared fiercely at a painful door in her past, it was like an eternity. As they touched down, Jennifer tore the obstructing goggles from her eyes. The fear, the anxiety, was gone.

"How was it?" Paul called anxiously from the ground. He'd hopped from his seat onto the tarmac when the plane had stopped taxiing. The answer beamed from her face. She was flushed from the wind and the excitement. She'd closed the door to a painful chapter in her life. "You don't look any the worse for wear."

She jumped into his outstretched arms, too excited to ease herself from the plane. "It was wonderful. I feel wonderful." Playfully, he spun her around, not permitting her feet to touch the ground yet. She hugged him tightly, and slightly regretted when her feet landed on solid turf again. "I'd forgotten how exhilarating it can be." Her arms circled his neck, and she felt utterly content and victorious. "How about you?"

"It's a great first step, Jen." He continued to hug her. "I couldn't have done it without you."

She softly touched his cheek with her fingers. "Yes, you could have."

"Are you still afraid for me?" he asked, reading the hot emotion in her eyes.

"Of course," she answered with a sigh. "But like you said, it's a great first step."

"Oh, Jennifer." He squeezed her lightly as he whispered her name. His voice was barely audible above the noise of an incoming jet. "You are the woman of my dreams."

They spent the rest of the afternoon sailing and relaxing in the comfort of each other's company. The sky was a deep midnight blue and the sun had long since vanished, when Jennifer and Paul tied up the sailboat and returned the water gear to the boathouse.

Jennifer stood at the top of the pier and gazed out past the horizon. Her body swayed rhythmically in the gentle night wind, her heart crowded with a million emotions. To get the pot at the end of the rainbow, she had to take chances.

When it was time to go, they automatically linked fingers and walked hand in hand down the pier to his car. Jennifer stopped suddenly on one of the boardwalk planks that separated the shoreline from the dock. She spun toward Paul.

"Let's walk on the beach," she suggested, kicking off her sandals, and jumping down from the wooden walkway to the sand.

Joining her, Paul sat down on the pier. His legs

draped over the edge as he took off his shoes and socks. "No more jumping for me."

The sand was soft and fine. Their feet sank into the powdery down as they padded down the shoreline. A strong ocean breeze blew between them, and Jennifer's body braced from the chill. With a big smile on her face, she playfully swung her shoes from side to side in the hand Paul did not possess.

"Let's stop here for a minute."

Paul drew her under the boardwalk, away from other moonlight strollers. Under the pier, away from the lights of the dock, he pulled her into his arms and held her close. His body, though chilled on the outside, radiated inner warmth. Then, his mouth was on hers, at first gentle and prodding, but then with power and urgency. As they kissed, Jennifer's knees buckled and she sank into the soothing sand. Paul's mouth followed, never leaving hers.

Jennifer was dizzy with passion, her mind and body floating on the clouds. His mouth devoured hers, hungry to taste. Her body ached for his strong, generous hands.

Slowly, his hands, then his mouth, began to explore her body inch by inch. With each kiss moving lower and lower, Jennifer felt every nerve in her body ignite. Paul moved Jennifer backward, so her hair splayed against the pale sand. With her cooperation, he raised her pale top, and her bra was gone in an instant. Her breath grew shallow and the tips of her breasts tightened as he toyed with them with his hands and his mouth.

In a flurry of building passion, Jennifer reached between her breasts and found the small buttons of

Paul's shirt. In her quick and efficient fashion, she stripped him of his garment in seconds.

Balancing himself easily on his elbows, Paul raised his mouth to find her lips once again. As he kissed her longingly, his hands caressing her face, her neck, her breasts, and her stomach. Jennifer relished the delicious warmth of her bare skin against his chest.

"Oh, Jen," he moaned. "I want you. I can't stop wanting you."

"Don't try," she answered and met his mouth again. In a moment, they were both completely undressed, and she gasped awaiting the intense pleasure yet to come.

Paul held her tightly and moved skillfully, placing himself between her slender thighs. A moment later, they were moving as one—one heart, one spirit, one soul.

Chapter Ten

She never would have pegged him as a man who liked the theater—especially Shakespeare. But he had surprised her one morning with matinee tickets to the Folger Theater's production of *As You Like It*. Then again, she hadn't dreamed he'd enjoy spending a Sunday afternoon feeding the elephants and the bears at the San Diego Zoo. He'd thrown a peanut at Chester the bear and coaxed the furry animal into sitting up and begging and rubbing his stomach. He was a man of many surprises. Most of the time Jake joined them, and it warmed her heart as she loved how patient Paul could be with her son.

The May afternoon was warm and breezy as they descended the stone steps of the theater, walking hand in hand. His hand was becoming as familiar as her own as she squeezed it. It had been three wonderful weeks since their day at Montgomery Field, yet it seemed a lifetime ago. Had they only been lovers since then? She knew his body the way a musician knew his instrument—intimately, completely. His fingers around her waist simply belonged there.

They strolled through nearby Balboa Park, relaxing as if the day were a thousand years long. The sun above was strong and unyielding, causing eucalyptus trees to throw curious shadows on the walkway.

The park was filled with the chatter of children and

she wished Jake was with them now. Of course, her little boy was years away from appreciating any work by William Shakespeare. A Frisbee soared in their direction, and Jennifer caught it in mid-air. She tossed it back to the teenagers playing in the open, grassy field.

Jennifer was glad she'd worn her powder blue sundress. Her shoulders welcomed the feel of the sun, helping to deepen her tan. Life couldn't get any better.

As they reached the car in a lot on the outskirts of the park, Paul walked to the back of his Camaro and opened the trunk. To her surprise, a large wooden cooler occupied much of the rear. He reached down to pick it up and carried it in both arms.

"This seemed an appropriate way to finish an afternoon of Shakespeare. Just pretend the River Thames is over there, and the streets are cobblestone. Want to get the blanket?" She reached for it at the foot of the trunk and held it in her arms.

Pleasure flooded through her. Jennifer loved surprises, nice surprises. With the edge of his elbow, Paul playfully nudged her along. "I put plenty of ice in here this morning, but let's not press our luck."

She toyed with a belt loop on his khaki slacks. "Sounds good to me." They set up the picnic on a rich thatch of grass partially shaded by the full leaves of a mature oak. Dramatically, Paul pulled out the contents of the cooler one item at a time. First produced was a bottle of Laurent Perrier champagne, and two tulip-shaped champagne goblets. Then came a small tin of caviar, a matching one of pâté and a container of cocktail rounds.

"I feel completely spoiled," she said, wanting to clap. "What a wonderful way to spend a Sunday afternoon—with champagne and caviar." He picked up the champagne bottle, and popped the cork. The bubbly drink splashed energetically into the waiting glasses. He handed one to her and filled the other for himself.

He raised his glass, and she followed suit. "To a beautiful blonde with blue eyes." Jennifer sighed as their glasses clinked.

"To us and champagne," she returned, touching his glass again after the first wonderful sip.

While she took another taste, and grew accustomed to the delicious bubbles that tickled her nose, Paul produced item after item from the seemingly bottomless container. First came individual cups of gazpacho, red and spicy and full of tiny vegetables, and then matching lobster tails, perfectly cooked with bright red shells and moist white meat. A mixture of sliced strawberries, apples, and melon was in a large covered glass bowl. And a tin of salted cashews, her favorite, was cushioned in the corner of the basket.

Finally, Paul scooped out the bottom of the cooler and produced a small lacy tablecloth, two Colport china plates and a setting for two of polished silverware.

Jennifer picked up one of the plates and ran her finger over the blue and gold lines that rimmed the outer edge. "Where did these come from?" While they didn't eat at his apartment often, they normally dined with plastic utensils and paper plates when they were there. He was a man who ate out often.

"They've been stored away," he said grinning, running his fingers through hair the breeze had already jumbled. "They were my grandmother's. She had no granddaughters, so I inherited them. I haven't really had any use for them. I thought they might be nice for today."

Touched, she scooted over to be closer to him. "Well, there's no better time for china and silver than with lobster."

"Actually, it was the company, not the food, that I thought was pretty special." He leaned over and gently nibbled on her lower lip. The same thrill, the same excitement she felt the first time he'd kissed her happened all over again. "But then, you taste a lot better than the lobster."

This time, Jennifer circled his neck with her fingers. She kissed his mouth, his throat, his neck. Each time they kissed, each time they touched, she knew him better, more intimately. There was always something else, something exciting that hadn't been uncovered yet. His hands wrapped around her waist and held her. As they started to creep up, he suddenly released her, placing her firmly on her backside.

His voice was deep and throaty when he spoke. "I almost forgot where we were." A hundred yards away, they turned and saw an elderly man walking with his granddaughter. "Why don't we hurry up and finish this lobster and go to my place?"

"What, and not savor every bite?" Jennifer raised her brows then allowed her eyes to crinkle with laughter. She picked up a fork and dug into the lobster.

Thirty minutes later, they were enjoying the last bit of champagne and the final piece of melon. The sun had started to lower in the sky, and the air was slightly crisp. Things were falling into place so precisely, so wonderfully. Jennifer rested in the crook of Paul's arm while they leaned against the trunk of the tree. This was the kind of day that should last forever.

"Paul, Paul Davis." Jennifer blinked up into the faces of two strangers. A couple, probably picnicking like them. She wiped the lazy dreams from her eyes and turned to Paul. He recognized the man instantly.

Paul stretched out his hand and greeted the man who had spoken. "It's good to see you, Ken. Enjoying the day?"

For some inexplicable reason, Jennifer sensed the man was not a completely welcome sight. Paul's jaw set, and his eyes were fixed and intent.

She shifted from her relaxed position, smoothing out the wrinkled blanket beneath them, eyes focused on the newcomers. "This is Jennifer Wade."

The man shook her extended arm and introduced his wife, Denise. They immediately joined Jennifer and Paul on the blanket. "That's quite a spread you fixed, Jennifer."

"Actually, it was all Paul's doing." She grinned and ran her fingers along his forearm. His muscles tightened and she tensed. "I'm probably the worst cook in the world—so we both have to be inventive when it comes to food."

"Boy, that certainly is a change." Ken tilted his head to the side and chuckled. He had a deep Texas accent and a slow, confident smile. "I thought his idea of a great date was pizza and beer." His eyes crinkled, obviously enjoying the memory.

Jennifer glanced over and offered the couple what remained of the fruit. "Actually, Paul and I have never had pizza and beer together. I guess he's upgraded to champagne. A change I'm very happy about."

"We were at flight school together, real hell raisers back then." Ken reminisced aloud, pulling a cigarette from his front pocket and lighting it. "I'm glad to know we're going to get the chance to work together again, Paul."

"Are you a pilot at Miramar, too?" Jennifer asked curiously, barely aware of the tense look in Paul's eyes.

"You bet."

"So, you're joining Paul's squadron? That's nice." That would give them a chance to rekindle their friendship.

He laughed. "No way, I'm out of the F-18 business for a while."

Jennifer's eyes narrowed in confusion. "Ken, what do you fly, then?"

"Why, honey, I'm a Blue Angel. Didn't you know?" He picked up a nut and popped it in his mouth. "Was that what this is all about? Going to tell her the good news?" He stopped at the stunned expression on Jennifer's face. "Oops. I guess I ruined the surprise."

He grabbed his wife's hand and helped her to her feet. "Well, I know you two want to celebrate, so we'll leave you alone. Congratulations, buddy."

Paul swallowed hard and tapped his index finger on the blanket as Ken and Denise disappeared down a narrow path leading out of the park. Then, he grabbed her fingers, ready with a quick explanation. "Don't jump to any conclusions," he urged. "I haven't joined the Blue Angels—yet."

"What's going on?" She tried to stay calm, to keep her composure, but it wasn't working. "If you're not joining the Blue Angels, then what was that all about?" She gestured toward the walking path where Ken and Denise had departed. "Your pal seems to think you're a new member of his flying fraternity."

"I was selected. I haven't made a decision yet."

Jennifer's eyes narrowed, and she shook her head with disbelief. How could he keep something like this from her? He grabbed for her hand again, but she shifted from his grasp. "I didn't even know you were interested in the Blue Angels. When did you start all of this?"

"Before Hawaii," he said, trying to backpedal. "It was a pipe dream. I never imagined I'd ever really have a shot, especially after the accident."

"How lucky for you," she muttered, not attempting to hide her sarcasm.

"Jen, just listen."

"What? What are you going to do?" she asked, not bothering to hide her anger and frustration. She already knew what he'd say. No one turned down the Blue Angels. They were a troupe of flying acrobats that entertained troops and civilians worldwide. They were flying daredevils, performing the kinds of death defying stunts that brought ohhs and ahhs from the open-mouthed crowds below. It was every Navy pilot's dream. It was every Navy pilot's wife's nightmare. She wished she could be happy for him, but she couldn't. "You're going to join them, aren't you?"

"It's what I've always wanted, what I've always wanted to be. It's one of the biggest challenges for a pilot. The best tour of a lifetime. I thought we could talk about it—weigh the pros and the cons."

She shook her head and dragged a shaking hand through her hair. "Paul, if you expect me to say go ahead with my blessing, I can't."

"I thought you'd come to terms with my flying."

"How can you say that now?" she accused, as a

hard knot gathered in the center of her forehead. "This is a whole different story entirely. Apples and oranges. How long have you known about this?"

"A few days."

The words stung. She hated secrets, and he was asking more than she was capable of giving. "Paul…"

"Look, I don't have to make up my mind for a few days. I wanted to know what you thought first."

"Well, now you know," she threw out fast, her heart pumping. "What are you going to do?"

He hesitated. "I don't know yet."

She pulled at a clump of grass near her hands. Her stomach was tied up in knots, and she didn't know how to say what she needed to say. He'd given her a push, a shove, and she didn't like it. She could handle his flying—sort of. She'd finally started to heal. But the process was slow, and she needed more time. Joining the Blue Angels wasn't the answer.

The words came slowly, painfully. Her voice wavered as she spoke. "Yes, I felt better about you flying after going up at Montgomery Field. But remember I grew up in the Navy. I know how dangerous it is for the Blues. I don't think I can do it. I've seen too much. I know too much. There's been too much heartache. I love you, and Jake loves you."

She finally said what she'd been too afraid to say, afraid of the commitment and the promise in the three little words. She tried to swallow the knot that had lodged in her throat.

Paul took her hand and urged her to rest her head on his shoulder. He stroked her hair and the back of her neck. It would be a difficult decision for Paul, but for their sake, she prayed he'd turn down the Blue Angels.

****

Jennifer hadn't planned on putting on a big to-do for Jake's first birthday, but everyone else in her life had other ideas on the matter. Becki grumbled that it would be downright criminal not to host a huge affair in honor of Jake's big day. The fact that the event would mean nothing to the baby didn't faze her any.

Lori jumped in on the act and offered the use of her home and her large, fenced-in backyard. When Paul got the fever and offered to arrange for a clown, she knew she was a goner.

"This really is too much," Jennifer exclaimed an hour before the party as she surveyed the preparations underway in Lori's amazingly hectic backyard. "I can't believe I let myself be talked into this."

Lori's husband, Steve, was setting up two gas grills, neon-bright balloons were tied to every possible chair and table, and a clown practiced face-painting on Lori's six-year-old Christina. Gina, Lori's three-year-old, giggled with delight, waiting patiently for her turn. "I'm glad your girls are enjoying Paul's clown, because I'm sure Jake would rather eat that pretty face paint than wear it."

Lori laughed as she placed two firm arms on Jennifer's shoulders and ushered her to a shady Adirondack chair under an old leafy oak. "We'll take lots of pictures and show him what a blast it was. Why don't you kick back for a few minutes? I'm sure Jake will be up from his morning nap in a little while and all the guests will be arriving soon."

Jennifer raised a weary brow. "Sounds like a lot of fun to me."

"Hey, I forgot to tell you. Paul said he'd be a little

late," she added before turning to her husband, who was working to contain a small fire. "Steve, don't burn down the house yet, honey. At least wait until all the burgers and hotdogs are cooked," she called over her shoulder.

"What is it about men and barbecue?" Lori released a breath and focused her eyes on Jennifer again. "Paul said he had a meeting at the base this morning and that he had some surprise."

"Surprise?" Her brows lowered and narrowed.

"Don't look at me. I don't think he trusts me to keep my mouth shut."

"Not if he knows you."

"Hey, I can almost keep a secret."

Jennifer glanced down at her watch and ran her fingers anxiously down the arms of the sturdy wood chair. Jake would be getting up from his morning nap any moment, and she just hoped all the festivities wouldn't overwhelm him. Her head jerked up as she heard car doors slam on the street in front of the house and knew their first guests were arriving. She slapped a big smile on her face and rose to greet the arrivals.

Her fears were immediately put to rest when Jake made his grand entrance fifteen minutes later. The opposite of his mom, who was a little uncomfortable and off-balance at large gatherings, Jake was in his element as he smiled charmingly and greeted all the people who had come to help him celebrate his big day. He was thrilled when he moved from his mother's arms, and was given the grand opportunity of showing off his newly developed walking skills on the freshly mowed grass in the Hampton's backyard. Jennifer smiled widely as she watched a handful of children kneel around Jake, offering him encouragement and advice.

Jennifer kept her eyes glued on Jake, very aware that a one-year-old could be playing innocently one minute and making mayhem the next. In the background, Lori fussed at Steve as he put hotdogs and hamburgers on the sizzling grill. She grinned when Steve gently nudged Lori away from the fire and his manly grilling responsibilities.

"Men, they think they know everything," Lori said as she grudgingly left her husband's side and strolled over to Jennifer.

"Christina, Gina, let the other kids have some of the balloon animals," she called out to her girls. She rolled her eyes and crossed her tanned arms. "Poor Steve spent about an hour discussing the merits of sharing with them this morning. With the party being here, it can be easy to forget that they don't have center stage today."

"Oh, don't give it a thought. Jake would never notice."

"Well, we're working with them on good manners. Of course when I talk they just zone out. Now, if Daddy speaks, well that's a totally different story. For them, the sun rises and sets on that man." Catching herself, Lori bit her tongue and swore under her breath. "Stupid, that's what I am. Stupid. God, Jen. I'm sorry. Sometimes I suffer from foot in mouth disease."

Jennifer affectionately clutched her friend's forearm and smiled. She'd known Lori and Steve for years, and it was no surprise to her that the girls adored their father. "It's all right. It's no one's fault that Jeff is dead. I certainly don't begrudge your girls or anybody else for having a great relationship with their father. I...oh my God." Jennifer knew her mouth was hanging open, but when she saw the birthday surprise that Paul was bringing in, she couldn't help herself from looking absolutely stunned.

He'd come directly from an early morning meeting at the base, so he was still dressed in his service dress whites. In one hand he held a rope and at the other end of the rope was a beautiful chestnut brown pony. A man, who she presumed was the pony's owner, followed closely behind.

"Paul Davis, what do you think you're doing?"

His expression turned a little sheepish before he presented his best killer smile. "I saw this rent-a-pony ad in an area parenting magazine, and I couldn't resist. Isn't he great?" Paul added as he stroked the pony's mane and the young horse neighed, enjoying the attention.

Jennifer's brows narrowed as she stepped back a pace. "Since when do you browse through parenting guides?"

"Since I fell for you and your kid." He reached over to gently cuff the back of her neck as he nudged her forward to touch her lips with his own.

"Paul...it's very sweet," she began, moving away, not wanting to dull his enthusiasm, but needing him to understand reality. "But no one brings a pony to a one-year-old's birthday party. No one."

"I do," he replied simply. "Now, let's see if the birthday boy wants the first ride." Before zeroing in on Jake, who was still demonstrating his balancing skills to Lori's girls and other older children, he turned to Lori. "Don't worry, the pony has a little pouch in the back.

He won't be leaving any calling cards in your backyard."

"Hey, there's my best buddy." Paul zoomed over and scooped Jake up to carry him over to the pony.

Jake stared into Paul's warm face and yanked on his regulation white hat. "Daddy, Daddy," he said, clear as a bell, then pulled out of Paul's arms to grasp the little horse.

Jennifer froze.

"It's okay," Paul whispered in her ear. "It's just the uniform. The picture of Jeff you have by his bed. We all look alike to kids his age."

"I know," she replied, as Paul held Jake's hand to stroke the chestnut-colored animal. She sighed deeply as she tried to shake the sadness that flowed through her. Jake would never know his father, and nothing could ever change that. She took another breath to regain her composure. Kids were so perceptive, and she didn't want Jake to see she wasn't as happy as he was.

Paul situated Jake in the pony's saddle so he could begin a short circuit around the Hampton's backyard. Jake patted the horse's mane with Paul's guidance and smiled lovingly into his face. Her son absolutely adored Paul Davis. It was only natural for Jake to become attached to the people in his mother's life.

But Jake's affection for Paul was tempting fate, and she was numbed by the reality. Jake had to be her first priority; his happiness, his needs had to come before anything or anyone else. The only problem was that Paul loved Jake as much as Jake loved Paul. She'd found a man who could truly love her son as his own. If only it could last forever, it would all be so easy. Unfortunately, life was rarely that simple.

****

During the next week, Jennifer pretended as if their discussion about the Blue Angels had never happened. It wasn't like her to avoid a problem like this, but she didn't know what else to do.

At first, she'd been angry. *How far does he think he can push me?* But he wasn't doing this to hurt her. In fact, if it weren't for her, he'd already be making plans for El Centro, the Blue Angel training base east of San Diego.

She was trying to concentrate on the Sunday paper's crossword puzzle when the doorbell chimed. Paul was performing surgery on his microwave, so Jennifer got off the sofa and ran to answer it. "I'll get it," she called, when she heard Paul curse as he dropped a heavy tool.

"Are you expecting anybody?" she called over her shoulder as she reached the doorknob, still grinning over his lack of mechanical ability with household products. Without waiting for his reply, she flung the door wide open. Startled, she blinked into familiar dark eyes, eyes just like Jeff's. "Carol," she said, practically tripping over her own feet as she worked to get her bearings. Jeff's mother was just about the last person she expected to see on the other side of Paul's door. "Wh…what a surprise."

For a short moment, Carol Lyons appeared as equally startled as Jennifer, but quickly regained her composure. "I could say the same thing," she said with brows raised, standing stick-straight at the door's entrance. "I didn't realize you and Paul…" She paused for an instant as if looking for the right words. "…had kept in touch."

Jennifer clenched her teeth and slapped a smile on her face. "Well, actually, it's not like that. You see…" She breathed a sigh of relief as Paul loudly dropped his tools on the floor in the other room. It would be difficult to explain her relationship with Paul, since she didn't exactly understand it either.

"Where's my grandson? He is here, isn't he?"

"He's sleeping right now. He'll be getting up soon and you can see him then."

"Jen, sweetheart, who is it?" Paul called out before he reached her.

Jennifer grimaced at the endearment.

"If it's a salesperson, tell them we're not interested."

Like Jennifer, he was dumbstruck when he reached the door and discovered his surprise visitor was Jeff's mother. "Mrs. Lyons." He nodded a greeting, and her lips turned slightly in return.

"Paul, I must apologize for dropping in on you like this." She swallowed hard and tightly clutched a small black purse between her fingers. "I know it's very rude, but after what happened, I was afraid you wouldn't see me if I called."

"That's silly," Paul answered, relaxing a bit. "Please come in." He gestured for her to enter his home.

Carol hesitated. "I really don't want to interrupt."

"You're not, really," Jennifer piped in.

"Well, all right," Carol agreed after a moment's delay.

Paul ushered the older woman into the living room. "Can I get you something to drink?" he asked as she took a seat on the sofa and Jennifer sat down beside her.

Carol nodded. "Water would be nice."

When Paul stepped into the kitchen, Carol turned to Jennifer. "Have you and Paul been involved for very long?" she asked matter-of-factly.

"Uh." Her mouth opened and at first nothing came out. "Paul's one of my patients," she said, after finding her voice. It was best to avoid directly answering the pointed question.

"It's none of my business, of course. It's just I'm surprised."

****

Paul returned with Carol's water, and immediately sensed the heightened tension in the room. "Everything okay here?"

Jennifer nodded numbly as Carol picked up her glass and took a long sip. She slowly placed the cup on the coffee table and appeared to gather her thoughts. She leaned back in the sofa and crossed her legs. "I need a favor from you, Paul."

"What's that?"

"You know Jeff's younger brother, Keith, my baby." She spoke with great warmth in her voice. "He's a senior at the Academy this year."

Paul slowly shook his head from side to side. "Time certainly does fly." Just yesterday Keith was trailing after his big brother, wanting to be just like Jeff. It had been Keith to whom he'd finally returned the gold bands intended for Jeff and Jennifer's wedding. He was a good kid. A kid with a lot of brains and a bright future.

"To get right to the point of my visit, Keith wants to fly jets like his brother." Her faced was stoic as she met his eyes. "I want you to talk him out of it."

"What?" Paul frowned as he leaned toward her.

The older woman cleared her throat and her words and intent were unmistakable. "I want you to tell Keith he shouldn't fly like his brother, that it's a selfish and dangerous thing to do." Her eyes were like sharp lasers.

Paul lowered his head and then lifted it to face her. "I don't think I understand."

"Of course you understand," she spat out, tapping her tense fingers on her purse. "You just don't like what I'm saying."

Paul leaned back in his chair and released a long, jagged breath. "What I meant was that I don't understand what you hope I can accomplish. Keith knows how I feel about flying and how much Jeff loved it, too. I don't think I'm the one to offer up advice or a testimonial on a flying career or not." He saw her lips thin into a small straight line. God, he wanted to help, but..."Have you told him how you feel and how worried you are? Maybe if you sit down with him and explain, he'd..."

"No!" Carol bit back a grimace. It was obvious she was having a hard time maintaining what composure she could muster. "You're the one. You were there. You know what a horrible death Jeff endured."

Paul flinched at her accusation and the gasp that escaped Jennifer's lips. He turned to face her, to comfort her, but he couldn't find the words.

As Carol witnessed the exchange, she altered her plan of attack. "And you, you're the biggest fool of all, aren't you, Jennifer? You must be a real glutton for punishment." She grabbed Jennifer's forearm and held it tight with strong, thin fingers. "How can you do it? You must hate the fact he flies. I know you felt pain when Jeff died, I know it. Could you bear to go through it again? And what about your son? Could you do that to him? Think about it, could you?"

Jennifer's face flushed. "Carol...I..."

"You don't have to say anything to me. I already know," Carol tossed out, a hint of triumph in her voice. "Make him talk to my baby. Tell him what it was like. Hearing the news, the hours afterward. Tell him about the pain."

Paul stood up and pulled Jennifer out of Carol's reach. "Mrs. Lyons, please calm down, you're upsetting Jennifer."

The older woman's eyes darkened as she held her chin high. "I'm upsetting her?" Her tone was drenched with sarcasm. "What do you think you do to her? But you don't think about that do you, Paul? You don't think about the people who get left behind." Her eyes continued to turn cold and hard. "Well, I'm one of them and I'm telling you, it's hell."

What she was saying came from a bitter, but honest heart. Like a mother lion, she wanted to protect her cubs any way she could. "If you'd like me to talk to Keith, I'll give him the pluses and minuses of flying— my honest opinions. I can't tell another man how to lead his life, though."

"No, no, that won't do." Carol shook her head back and forth in short, terse motions. She glanced down at the watch on her wrist. "He'll be here any minute, and I need to know you'll tell him what I need you to tell him."

"He'll be here?" Paul asked, his head rocking back in astonishment.

"Keith?" Jennifer echoed, surprised as much as

Paul.

Carol nodded her head. "I told him you wanted to see him."

"Oh, God." Jennifer gulped and the doorbell rang a moment later.

Keith Lyons was a younger, even more handsome version of his brother. They possessed the same dark good looks and killer smiles. When he burst through the door an instant later, he filled the room with energy and excitement. That was his way. He hugged and kissed Jennifer and his mother and offered Paul a big bear hug.

It didn't take him long to sense unease in the room. "Something is wrong with this picture. What's up?"

"Paul has something to say to you," Carol offered quickly, when Jennifer and Paul were silent. When Paul didn't speak up, Carol continued on. "Paul thinks you shouldn't even consider flying, not after what happened to your brother. He thinks it would be a selfish thing to do to the people who love you."

Keith stepped back a pace. Confusion was written all over the young man's face. "What?" His eyes moved from his mother's to Paul's. "What's this all about?"

Paul sighed heavily. "Keith, why don't you sit down?"

Carol pursed her lips together. "He doesn't need to sit down. Just tell him what you need to tell him."

Paul placed his arm on Keith's shoulder. "Sit." When the young dark-haired man complied, Paul sat down beside him. "Your mother has asked me to talk to you about flying—about how frightened she is for you."

"No," Carol barked. "That's not what I wanted you to say."

"Mom." Keith rose and took his mother's hands. "What's going on here?" His tenderness made her crumble.

She buried her face in her fingers, trembling and shaking as if she feared for her life. "I just can't go through it again. I can't," she sobbed. Her makeup was streaked as she looked up. "A mother is supposed to outlive her children. That's the way it's supposed to be. I can't lose two sons, I can't, I can't."

Keith bit back a curse. "I'm so sorry, Mom. I didn't mean to hurt you by thinking about going jets." He put his arms around his mother. "I should have told you yesterday, after I talked to my commanding officer." He offered a slight grin as he presented news that would take away her anguish. "I've decided to go subs."

"What?" Carol swallowed as she faced her second son.

Her voice still trembled as she accepted a tissue from Jennifer and blotted her watery eyes and nose.

"I wish you'd told me how much my flying would upset you. I knew you weren't crazy about the idea. I just didn't realize."

"What made you change your mind? Jeff's accident?" Paul asked. Keith had wanted to fly since the day his older brother had announced his intentions to soar with the eagles.

"Partly him, and partly my mother." He rubbed his mother's shoulder, since she needed the support. "A lot of things, really." He shrugged. "I guess when it comes down to it, I don't have the edge. I know what can happen up there, all the things that can go wrong. It's not worth it to me."

From the look in the younger man's eyes, Paul

knew the decision had been a tough one. "So you've decided to be a bubblehead." He gave Keith's shoulder a friendly yank. "I think I can live with that." His eyes softened for an instant. "I know Jeff would have been proud of your choice."

"Yeah, well." He winked at Paul and Jennifer. "Now don't you two get mushy on me." Then he gave his mother a warm, reassuring hug.

Carol, more composed, met Paul's eyes squarely. "Paul, I'm sorry." She swallowed hard. "I know it was horrible of me to come here. I was at the end of my rope. I'm still seeing a counselor, trying to put all the pieces back together again." She lowered her chin. "Sometimes I lose it."

"It's all right, Mrs. L." He took her hand and squeezed it.

"And, Jennifer, after all you've done for me." She turned to the young woman who would have been her daughter-in-law. "I'll understand if you never forgive me."

"Don't give it another thought." Jennifer leaned forward and embraced Carol with a warm hug.

"But do yourself a favor." She clearly found it impossible to withhold final words of advice. "Save yourself from heartache and get him out of the air."

"Mom," Keith cautioned.

"All right, I'm sorry. I can't help but care." At the same moment, she took Paul and Jennifer's hands in her own. "Be careful, be safe. I love you both."

A moment later, a short howl pierced the air as Jake proclaimed that he was up.

"Now, it's about time you met your grandson," Jennifer announced with a short smile and led the older woman into the bedroom.

****

When Paul hadn't spoken about the Blue Angels in a week, Jennifer hoped that meant he'd made a decision. The decision she could live with. It was an honor even to be asked to join the flying acrobatic troupe, and she prayed that had been enough.

The hospital had more than a little excitement during the week. Billy Wilder walked again, more than a few steps this time. During a session, he'd crossed half the room under his own power. The kid had guts. He said he'd walk again, and he was doing it. That wheelchair was going to start collecting dust before too long.

Paul had been as excited as she'd been when he'd heard the news. "Let's celebrate. You and I will go out first, and then we'll take Billy out later."

Later that evening in front of the mirror, Jennifer primped. She giggled as she put on the finishing touches of makeup. She'd set her hair in loose easy curls and was wearing a new midnight-blue cocktail dress. The pearls around her neck were the lustrous product of years of waiting under the ocean. The most wonderful man in the world was in love with her. Color rose to her cheeks when her mind drifted to him. No one had ever made her feel so special, so desirable.

When she answered the doorbell a moment later, she was greeted by a smile that was becoming as familiar as the back of her hand.

"Wow, you don't give a guy a chance, do you?" He walked forward and stopped inches from her. Jennifer narrowed the gap even further, enjoying the clean, appealing smell of soap on his skin.

"You're a dead man." Her voice was deep and throaty.

He clutched her around the waist in a way that Jennifer wished could be frozen in time. "I don't think I could be any happier than I am with you right now." He gently bent his head and nuzzled her neck, causing tiny electrical jolts to pass from the top of her head to the ends of her toes. When his mouth finally met hers, she responded to his kiss with as much enthusiasm as she was given.

"With a greeting like that, we might never make it out of here tonight," she said teasingly.

"Did you get a sitter for Jake?"

"Actually, Becki went to visit her folks for the night and took Tyler and Jake with her. So, we've got all night."

His mouth straightened and his eyes, dark and somber, locked on hers. "I hope you feel the same way in a few minutes. Let's sit down." He gestured toward the living room sofa, and the room chilled immediately.

"What is it, Paul?" She hadn't wanted to ask. If she didn't ask, she wouldn't have to hear his response.

"I got a call from Commander Hill this afternoon. He said I needed to give him a final answer right then." His hands tried to warm Jennifer's fingers, which rested limply in her lap.

Deep down, she'd known avoiding the problem wouldn't make it go away. Paul hadn't mentioned the Blue Angels again because she didn't want to talk about it. Her voice cracked. "What did you tell him?" She felt defeated, defeated by an airplane and a dream.

He took her shoulders and forced her to meet his eyes. They told of an agonizing decision. "I told him yes, Jen."

The bubble burst. Her shoulders slumped under the weight of his hands. "I see." There was nothing she could say. The choice had been his, and he'd made it.

"Sweetheart, I've wanted to be a Blue Angel since I was a kid. It's what I've always hoped for. Even in flight school, I knew that's where I wanted to be. It's my shot to be one of the best. I just couldn't turn my back on it. I want you to understand."

Her head lowered and she slowly shook it back and forth. "I do understand. I really do. But that doesn't mean I can live with it. I don't think I can."

"You're upset," he said softly lowering his hands to her arms in comfort. "Hey, you saw for yourself what a great pilot I am. Nothing bad is going to happen to me. Give yourself some time to get used to the idea."

She stifled a cry that started in her chest. "Paul, I can't. I can't and I won't. Maybe I'm being unfair and selfish, but I can't wait around to watch you kill yourself. And my son needs a stable father figure in his life. I want Jake to have the kind of relationship with a father that Steve Hampton has with his kids. He deserves to have someone put him first."

"Jen, I love Jake. I want to be his dad in every way."

Her eyes filled with tears, and she fought to bury the inner turmoil that consumed her. Damn it, she wanted him to fulfill his dream. She wanted him to have the brass ring. "Don't you see, I've been through it before, and I'm not going to do it again," she continued speaking as her voice wavered and shook. She had seen too much. There had been so much heartache. "You mean so much to me, Paul, but I just can't live my life watching you from the sidelines, hoping and praying that you'll make it home safe and sound each night."

For a few moments he was quiet. Finally, after what seemed like several eternities, he spoke. Misery was in his darkened eyes. "I wish I could tell you that I could give up flying and never look at another plane again." He paused, forcing her to meet his gaze when all she wanted was to turn away. "But I can't. It's a part of me."

"I don't know what you expect from me." Her throat was so tight, it was hard to respond. "I can't say I'm okay with this because I'm not."

"Remember when you didn't want to get involved with me because I was a pilot. When we went flying, I think that helped. You understood how I felt, and became a part of it." She knew what was coming and couldn't stop it. "I'm a good pilot, Jen," he reassured her, gripping her hands into his and flashing a dazzling, irresistible smile.

"So was Jeff, and so was my brother's roommate. We both know that being a good pilot doesn't guarantee you anything."

"You're right," he admitted. "But it's my dream, sweetheart."

She could almost see the knot tightening in his gut. She couldn't, wouldn't ease it. "I know it is."

"They're flying over Miramar two weeks from now. I want you to be there."

"Are you crazy?" she shot back, her palms moistening and hands shaking. "I will not watch that flying show knowing you're going to be up there next."

"Jen…"

"Can't you tell them you don't want it, Paul?" she

asked with quiet resignation. She already knew his answer.

"Don't want it? That would be crazy!" His body stiffened. "Jennifer, this is what I've been working for. I would have told you earlier, but it was a pipe dream then. This is the most exclusive flying club in the world. I can't tell you what it means to me."

She wanted to beg him not to go, and if she thought it might help, she would have. But this was his life. Did she have the right to prevent his dream from coming true?

"I'II have to think about it," she said slowly, shocked by her own words. "I don't know what else to say right now."

"Just say you care about me." He wrapped his arms around her neck and bent to kiss her mouth.

She raised her head, her eyes unwavering into his. "You know I do, but that has nothing to do with this."

Dinner at the Atlantis went quickly and hours later they sat quietly drinking wine on Paul's sofa. With her heels kicked off and feet tucked under her, Jennifer leaned on the man she loved and wished with all her heart that their earlier conversation hadn't existed—that the Blue Angels didn't exist. She wanted him desperately. The need to be a part of him was overwhelming.

She ran trembling finger over his arm. These were arms that had caressed her, arms that had held her tightly. It seemed like an eternity since they'd last made love, when it really had only been the night before. She needed him now like a drug. She was addicted to him and didn't know if she could let go.

Jennifer reached over and kissed his neck. Paul

responded by leaning toward her, giving her complete access. She took his offer without hesitation.

When their lips met, it was with hunger and urgency. She frantically kissed his mouth as he quickly undid the small pearl buttons at the spine of her dress. With adept fingers, he moved the blue silk from her shoulders, and the cool material slid from her body onto the sofa. Her bra came next. She arched her back, unable to restrain her desire as his mouth and tongue flickered from her neck to her throat and lower.

While Jennifer pulled at the buttons of his shirt and twisted the garment off his body, she moaned with want. She had a thirst that needed to be quenched, a longing that needed to be filled. She wanted to forget the hurt, the pain she knew was inevitable. She wanted their lovemaking to block it out. The world didn't exist any longer. She wished she didn't love him quite so much.

When his lips brushed the tips of her nipples, her eyes closed and her breathing grew sporadic. Her mind was being taken over by the pleasure—and she wished for more. Each kiss, each touch, each caress was driving her further into the deep well of desire. She pressed into him and ran her fingers down to his belt and undid the buckle. Kneading his body with a touch that knew every muscle and inch of flesh, she reached behind his back and lowered her hands to his buttocks.

"Down, I want them down." The words sprang from her mouth. Responding to her command, Paul finished what she had started and stripped the slacks from his waist.

She craved his touch, hard, then soft, then hard again. It made her feel alive. He cupped her breasts, and then moved his mouth to her neck and her lips. He tasted of wine, fresh and exciting. Her mind was spinning so fast she felt dizzy but was unable to stop.

They were crashing into waves, each one bigger and more consuming than the last, but all she could feel were the delicious sensations he was arousing in her.

She was floating as Paul lowered her onto the carpet. He unleashed the dress that was gathered around her waist. The nubby rug felt scratchy, wonderfully so, under her sensitized skin.

He lowered his fingers to her stomach and beyond, and she reciprocated. She moaned softly as her body continued to burn, and he coaxed the fire hotter. She also took him to the edge and held him there. Their bodies joined easily, readily, with the familiarity of two puzzle parts that fit together. She cried when her body peaked with desire, mixing love and longing with the sadness of knowing it might never happen again.

****

Jennifer rose from bed early the next morning. She'd awakened before daybreak after a short sleep and couldn't keep her eyes closed. Sometime in the middle of the night, while she'd lain awake in bed, she'd realized it had to be over. She loved him far too much to spend her days and nights watching and waiting and worrying.

Maybe she was being greedy, but that didn't change how she felt. Eventually, she'd make them both miserable. And that would kill her more than anything else.

The smell of fresh coffee filled the bedroom as Jennifer carried a tray with a coffee pot and two mugs from the kitchen. Paul woke groggy, a lazy smile crossing his lips as he spotted her at the doorway. From the dreamy look in his eyes, she knew he was disappointed she'd dressed already.

"Been up a long time?" he asked, patting the bed, gesturing her to sit beside him.

Holding the tray firmly, she walked to the nightstand and laid the tray on it. Before he could reach for her, she poured the mugs full of the hot morning drink. She handed one to Paul, glad the hot mugs brought warmth to her chilled fingers. After taking a quick sip, Paul returned the mug to the nightstand, and maneuvered Jennifer's cup from her hand.

He pulled her to him. "Good morning," he whispered in her ear, sending little tiny pulses through her body. It was the kind of greeting she would have loved getting used to. His smile was irresistible. She tried not to concentrate on the waves of his mahogany brown hair, the sharp, sexy angles that made up his handsome face, or his magnetic dark green eyes. She wanted to feel detached, but jumping off a cliff would have been simpler. "Not that I don't appreciate the coffee, but I had hoped for another kind of reception this morning." He toyed with the top button at the nape of her neck and gently nibbled her earlobe. He pulled back when she didn't respond.

"What's the matter?" He put a reassuring hand over her shoulder and moved to finger her tousled golden curls.

"You know, Paul." Her voice was like ice.

"I thought we were all straight about the exhibition two weeks from Saturday."

"I wish that were true." She rose from his side and sat up. "I love you more than I've ever loved anyone."

She distractedly picked up the hot mug of coffee and sipped. She looked down into her hands. "After Jeff died, I thought my life would be over, that there would never be anybody else. You came in and turned everything upside down. I've been on this incredible roller coaster with you that I never wanted to get off. I realized last night that if I don't get off now, I'll never be able to." Tears glazed her lashes as she turned to meet his confused eyes. "I couldn't stand to just watch from the sidelines. I'd never know a moment's peace. I'd make us both so unhappy."

Paul abruptly pulled the mug from her hands. He grabbed her wrists and held tight. "Why are you talking crazy like this? I love you, you love me. It's simple."

"I can't, Paul."

"Jennifer, this is my shot. Stand by me, please, sweetheart. I need to take it."

"I know. I'm not asking you to give up the Blue Angels. I'm just telling you I can't be there."

He cupped her face in his hands. Tears wet his fingers. "Jennifer, I need you."

"I'm not enough." Her voice was even while the lump in her throat grew bigger.

"All right, I'll turn them down. If you want, I'll never fly again."

"Then you'd be miserable. I can't ask that of you. I know that now." The words crumpled deep in her throat.

"I want us to have a life together. I want to marry you, and I want to be Jake's dad." Her blue eyes shot up and faced the green ones she'd grown to love and adore. "I do, you know." His words were soft and honest and painful.

"No, not now." Her eyes clouded and she shuddered, moving backward out of his tight grip. "It just can't work for us. We're too different. We want very different things in life. I love my son, and I need to create a stable home environment for him. I know you love him, too, but you have dreams that we just can't fulfill."

She wanted more than anything else to be held in his arms. She wanted to marry him—wanted him to love her forever. In the long run the best thing she could do was to give Paul his freedom. "I want you to be happy."

His voice was strained as he moved from the bed to gather jeans and a T-shirt thrown over the arm of a chair. "You make me happy. Don't do this to us."

"It's best this way. I promise you it is." Barely able to see through tear-clouded eyes, she picked up her pocketbook and hurried from the room, ignoring the half-dressed man just feet away from her. A moment later the front door slammed shut, and the dream was dead.

Chapter Eleven

She thought it would get easier with each passing day, but it didn't. It was harder. Being deprived of his presence was like being deprived of food, of water, of air. Life was almost intolerable except for the fact that she knew she was doing the right thing.

The day after their breakup, she and Jake had boarded a plane for Washington, D.C. She needed the quiet haven of home, of her parents.

Thankfully, her program with Commander Taylor had come to a close; it would be weeks before the next crew started. If there was ever a good time to take a break, this was it. She hoped a full schedule of taking care of Jake would give her little opportunity to think and dwell on what could never be. But he still invaded her thoughts. The caress of his hand and the twinkle in his eyes were permanent fixtures in her memory.

When the early sun awakened her ten days into her visit, the thought of getting up and facing another day seemed too much to contemplate. Apparently sensing her daughter's blue mood, Jennifer's mother volunteered to take Jake on a "Grandma-and-me" day. Jennifer felt guilty, but was relieved to have a short mental health vacation.

By noon she was lying on the couch with a bowlful of guacamole and a bagful of nacho chips and was watching reruns of *Mr. Ed* and *I Love Lucy*. A half-eaten box of caramel corn lay crumpled at the foot of the sofa. Jennifer was still wearing a nightgown when Teresa, her younger sister, who worked as a nurse at the hospital, traipsed in the door at the end of her odd hours shift. Jennifer barely glanced up when the door shut and her dark-haired sibling entered the living room.

Tossing a mane of brown hair over her shoulders, Teresa stood staring at her older sister lounging glumly on the sofa. "When I heard you were taking a mental health day, I got worried. What's wrong?"

Jennifer picked up a chip, stared at it angrily, and tossed it back into the bag. "I think I've overdosed on avocado dip and tostado chips."

Teresa sat down on the chair adjacent to the sofa. She looked at Jennifer cynically. "Hmm. Caramel corn, too. That looks tasty. Is that all you've been eating today?"

Jennifer nodded her head, picked up the remote control box to the television, and turned off the tube. "I thought a day off would clear my head, but instead I think I've fried my brain and turned my stomach inside out." She leaned against a fringed pillow at the head of the sofa and rested her elbow there. Her comforter was sprawled partly on her feet, the carpet, and the end table at the other side of the sofa. She hadn't paid much attention when she'd draped it over her this morning. This was the first time in as far back as she could remember that she hadn't showered and washed her hair in the morning.

"Why don't you just call him?" Teresa reached for a taco chip and some dip before kicking up her feet on the ottoman.

"Who?" Jennifer straightened out the comforter

and brought it to her chin.

Teresa cocked her head to the side and glared at her sister, frustration written all over her face. "Who? Give me a break. Paul, that's who. For gosh sakes, he wants to see you. He's not sending those gorgeous coral roses to me, you know."

Memories of the way her heart had pounded when they'd last made love were still crystal clear. It had been ten, ten excruciatingly long days. He'd decided to step back and give her time to think—to make a move, he'd said in a letter. She'd hated to admit even to herself that she'd been hurt when he hadn't called when he'd left for Blue Angels training in El Centro. She'd made it clear that it was over—so why was she upset that he hadn't called?

"Everything is so complicated." She slapped the pillow in her lap. "I love him, and it just won't work."

"Why not? He loves you, too."

"But he's going to be a Blue Angel. My Lord, I can't imagine a crazier thing to do."

"I can." Teresa rose from her chair and headed toward the kitchen for a glass of iced tea before taking a nap. "Running away from a guy you love and who loves you and your son. That's crazy. I'd give my right arm for what you two have."

Jennifer sulked, putting her head in her lap, but continued to listen to Teresa in the kitchen.

"I know what you're afraid of. But you can't be so analytical. Not everything has to make sense and fall into order."

Jennifer raised her head when she heard Teresa close the refrigerator door and stand in the living room doorway. "Life infrequently happens the way you expect it to. It's messy sometimes. But it is your life." She started toward the bedroom and turned suddenly. "I ran into Keith Lyons at the hospital, today."

"Oh?" Her head perked up.

"Apparently, he's stationed at the Pentagon on some temporary assignment before he starts nuclear power school in Orlando. He says it's horrible. Since he's an ensign, it's considered a privilege to fetch coffee for the big wigs and do their photocopying. I mentioned you were in town, and he said he was going to stop by for a visit after work."

Teresa disappeared into the hallway, and Jennifer turned back on the television. A tearful redhead was accepting the proposal of a man she loved on a soap. Jennifer turned it off immediately and covered her head with the comforter. She didn't care if the whole world thought she was a coward. She was. She didn't like the idea of walking on eggshells. She coughed in the heavy air, finding it difficult to breath under the bedcovers.

With frustrated hands, she grabbed the top of the comforter, lifting it off her face to hold around her throat. If it was all so simple, then why did she miss him so darned much?

****

"Jennifer, it's great to see you. You look wonderful." When she'd opened the door at six o'clock, Keith Lyons burst in, grabbed Jennifer, and whirled her around. His arms wrapped around her felt good, strong and nostalgic. His face, alive and exuberant, reminded her of happier times. The night she and Jeff got engaged, he'd been a wild man, tossing her around as if she were as light as a feather.

They'd all drunk champagne until the dawn—even

the under-aged kid, who'd regretted his excess in the morning. "I didn't know you were back on the east coast." He rested her back on her feet and looked her over from head to toe. Then he grabbed his nephew, who'd toddled over, and gave him a big bear hug. "He is getting so big."

"Yes, he is. Come on in. Mom and Dad aren't here. They're at some fancy dinner with friends. But I know they'll be sorry they missed you." She linked her arm through his as they strolled into the living room. "Can I get you something to drink, a soda, a beer?" she said, as they sat down on her parent's royal blue sofa.

"No, no, nothing." He rested one arm on the back of the couch, and picked up Jake with the other. His white uniform looked as fresh as if he'd just put it on. His dark hair was cut short to regulation, and his charcoal eyes glimmered with life. He cuddled Jake in his arms and grinned widely as the baby shrieked with playful laughter. "So, what's going on with you and Paul Davis?"

"You always were one to get right to the point, weren't you, Keith?"

"It makes sense to me most of the time. Being direct saves a lot of time and commotion."

"I don't know what to say." Jennifer's eyes crept anxiously from the man next to her to the magazines on the coffee table. Though already neat, she reached down to straighten them. When she turned back to him, his gaze was full of concern. "We had something, but it's over now." The words lacked conviction.

"So Terri said." Keith reached over and rested his arm across her shoulder. "Hey, it's me you're talking to. What's going on with you? Terri said it has to do with him joining the Blue Angels. That you have a real problem with it."

She leaned against the young man who would have been her brother-in-law and shut her eyes as she shook her head from side to side. "Of course it's a problem. How can I fall in love with another pilot—and a Blue Angel at that? It's crazy to be in love with Paul. I'm certainly a glutton for punishment."

"Jen, there's something I think you should know." He uneasily cleared his throat. "Paul would kill me if he knew I was going to tell you this, but I think it's important now. You deserve to know this."

She lifted her head warily. "What is it, Keith?"

He began to speak slowly. "I know you're apprehensive to commit to another pilot, because you think flying is so dangerous."

"Well, isn't it?" she cried out. "I mean Jeff was so clear-thinking and safety-conscious. If he could have an accident flying, anybody can. And, Paul, my God, talking about a guy flying by the seat of his pants."

"Jen, Jeff wasn't quite as careful as you think he was."

"Of course he was, Keith. What are you saying?"

He swallowed noticeably. "A couple of weeks before the big flight with Paul, Jeff started having headaches. Apparently, he didn't want the Navy to know, so he went to an outside doctor. Turned out he was having migraines. He started taking some medication, pills you can't take when you're flying. Kept it a big secret."

"He wouldn't do that. I don't believe it."

"The Navy ran some standard blood tests on Jeff after the accident. At first they found nothing. Then, they did a more comprehensive blood panel. They found a high level of the stuff in his system. I dug through the box of his personal possessions the Navy had collected for us. I found this bottle, and called the doctor. It didn't take a genius to figure out what had happened."

Her mind was reeling. Why would he do something like that? Not her Jeff, her calm, cool, collected Jeff. "Why would he take that kind of risk when there was so much at stake? Our life together, he risked our life together," she murmured softly, finding Keith's news almost impossible to believe.

"I'm sure he thought the pills wouldn't hamper him, and he wanted that chance with an experimental fighter jet so much."

Words spilled from her quaking lips. "Enough to risk our future?"

"Babe, he loved you so much." His troubled eyes were on hers. "Don't ever doubt that. He made a really bad judgment call."

Jennifer sank back in the sofa, unable to prevent the hot emotions from pummeling her from every direction. Her fingers pressed tightly on her temples. She took several long breaths and tried to grasp a thread of sanity before facing Keith again. "Why didn't I know about this before? How could you have kept this a secret from me?"

He placed his hands firmly on her shoulders. An apology shone in his eyes, eyes so like Jeff's. "You were so devastated at first. We didn't want to make it worse. And then months later, when you told us about the baby, well, it just seemed like the right thing to do. I didn't know what purpose it would serve then."

"So why now, Keith?"

The words choked out. "Because I want to help you get on with your life—for your own sake as well as Jake's. I was afraid your relationship with Paul fell apart because of Jeff and the accident. I thought you should know the truth. I'm not saying that Paul is completely safe in the air, but I know he won't take foolish chances, especially after what happened to Jeff."

"Did Paul know about the migraines and the medicine?" she asked suddenly.

He shook his head. "After we received a copy of the Navy medical report and found the pills in his belongings, I called Paul. He was stunned, Jen, couldn't believe his best friend had kept such a big secret from him. We both decided it was better if you didn't know. He wanted you to keep that sterling image of Jeff in your heart." His lips raised a little. "Even now, when he knows the truth might help you move on so you can be together, he keeps it to himself. That's how much this guy loves you."

Keith soothed the back of her hair. "I don't blame you for being apprehensive," he added gently. "It would be a lie to say that Jeff's death didn't influence my choice to pass on jets. But it wasn't the deciding factor. I'm very different from Jeff and Paul. If I was like them, nothing could have convinced me not to fly. Subs are the right choice for me."

Her face tightened. "I don't know. He's going to be a Blue Angel, for God's sake. I don't know if I can accept all that comes with it."

"You love him a lot, don't you?"

The words rung in her ears. "Yes. I do, but I don't

know if that's enough."

"I guess every pilot who goes up knows he may never come down. I suppose they're all a little crazy, but that doesn't stop them. It's part of them."

He leaned hard against the back of the couch and breathed deeply. "I know Jeff would have wanted you to go on, to meet somebody special, somebody a little crazy like Paul."

"I love him, but…"

"You're afraid. I know. After Jeff's crash, who can blame you? But if he had it to do all over again, he'd still want his wings. They go up because they have to. It's what they are. He wouldn't have wanted you to run away."

"I know you're right. I really miss him, Keith." She wiped a tear that landed on her cheek.

"Don't run from your fears. Go for it. If you love this guy, don't let him get away. That would be a big mistake. Would you worry any less about him if you weren't together? Do you love him any less than you did before?" He clutched her hand and squeezed it tight. "I can tell the answer to those questions is no."

"Thanks for the advice. You are way too smart for your age." She grabbed a tissue from the coffee table and blew her nose. She hadn't realized how much she'd still been hiding, how much she'd still been running. She'd always been the master of her fate, not the other way around. When Paul Davis swooped into her life, he'd tried to make her take life by the horns, to grab for the brass ring again.

"He's going to be at Blue Angel training for the next eight weeks or so. Maybe by then you'll have it all figured out."

"Maybe I will." She reached up and hugged him tightly around the shoulders. "You're a great friend, Keith."

****

"Hey, Miss Serious, are you going to stare at that lunch or eat it?"

Sitting in the staff lounge at the Naval Medical Hospital, Jennifer was startled by a familiar female voice. Lori grabbed a paper cup from the water cooler and pulled out a chair from the table to join her. Jennifer rubbed her fingers over her knuckles. She glanced up slowly. Her head had been swimming all day.

Her first weeks back in San Diego had been filled with hours of patient consultations and therapy sessions. Then Commander Taylor's new crew started. Eight weeks had gone by quickly, but it hadn't been easy. She'd missed Paul so much. Now, in less than an hour, he was going to fly in his first Blue Angel show at the Miramar Naval Air Station. Her heart thudded with the reality.

Lori waved a hand in front of Jennifer's face. "Earth to Jennifer. Are you there?"

Jennifer nodded slowly, her mind focused elsewhere. "Yeah, I'm here."

"You look like you just lost your best friend. Anyone you'd like me to beat up?"

She shook her head and smiled wryly. "No."

"I saw Paul a little while ago. His left knee was bothering him, so he came in for me to see him."

"Is he all right?" Her back straightened and she was quickly alert. She couldn't hide the concern in her voice.

"He's fine," Lori assured her.

"I knew he'd be working that leg too hard," she said with a grumble. "I told him he would still need to continue his exercises even after his therapy ended. The man doesn't listen."

"I told him, Jen."

"Good." She nodded her head uneasily.

Lori paused before she started talking again. "He gave me tickets to take Billy to his exhibition this afternoon. The kid's thrilled to be going." Her fingers lined her jaw. "Paul really helped that boy. It's amazing what a strong dose of faith and encouragement can do for someone. He gave me an extra one in case you decided to go."

Her breath caught in her throat. "He did?" She hadn't been ready to call him, to talk to him. She didn't know what to say to him yet.

"Yeah."

"Is he counting on me being there?" Jennifer drummed her fingers unconsciously on the Formica tabletop. She and Paul hadn't spoken since that day in his apartment.

"He's not. Just hoping, I think." Lori finished the last drop of water, balled up the cup and tossed it into a trash can across the room. Her voice lowered, and she leaned back in her chair. "He really loves you, Jen."

"I know, Lori," she replied, moving her eyes away from her friend.

Lori stood up and started toward the door. She paused mid-step, spinning around to face her partner. Her actions caught Jennifer's attention. "I've been meaning to give you something since you got back, but everything has just been so hectic. I've kept them in my locker for months. I'll get them right now," she said, as she turned to her nearby locker.

A moment later, she pulled out a small envelope and shook out a handful of color snapshots. Handing them to Jennifer, she said, "These were from Jake's first birthday bash. I got them printed while you were away and figured I'd wait until you got back to give them to you. They were too cute just to stick in the mail and not see your reaction."

A warm smile touched the corners of her lips as Jennifer slowly flipped through the photos of her little star. Jake was such a happy and content little boy. She grinned at an image of Christina and Gina cheering Jake on as he put one unsure foot in front of the other. Another captured Jake's utter delight as he enjoyed his first piece of chocolate birthday cake. The icing was everywhere—in his hair, up his nose, and all over his clothes. She closed her eyes and smiled as she remembered the horrid mess and the clean-up effort afterward.

When she flipped to a photo of Jake on the pony with Paul walking protectively beside him, her heart missed a beat. The love in Paul's eyes and the delight in Jake's spoke volumes. God, they were so happy together—like they were meant to be together. Another half-dozen photos showed a bond between her son and the man she loved. Paul was a man who had accepted her son as his own. She was either blind or just foolish to think she could simply pretend away this connection. They belonged together—all three of them—for better or for worse.

Lori stood next to Jennifer as she sifted through the small stack of photos.

When Jennifer remained quiet, the older therapist shrugged her shoulders and sighed aloud. "If you decide to go, Billy and I would love the company." When the door to the staff lounge shut, warm tears flowed down her cheeks.

Ten minutes later she wiped her eyes. Of course she had to go. She couldn't miss Paul's premier performance. Maybe it was crazy, but she had to be there—not just for Paul, but for herself and for Jake.

She glanced down at the watch on her wrist. It was one o'clock, and the show started at two. She started to undo the pins holding her hair in place as she rose from her seat and headed to the staff dressing area. By the time she reached her locker, her curls hung around her shoulders. The white lab coat was tossed on the changing bench a moment later as she reached for black jeans and a short knit sweater. White Adidas running shoes slipped on her feet. A brush pulled through her hair and a moment later she was off.

The hospital parking lot was full of people coming and going. She craned her head looking up and down the aisles. Not a familiar face anywhere. Then she spotted her friend and rushed over. "Lori, Billy." Out of breath, she called to the tall woman and the little boy in a wheelchair. "I'm coming with you two."

Lori's lips curled, and her smile widened. "I didn't think you were going to make it."

"I wouldn't miss it for the world." For the first time, she absolutely meant it.

When they arrived at Miramar twenty minutes before show time, Jennifer was not surprised by the crowd that had already begun to gather. Cars that couldn't get onto the base were already parked along the highway before the main gate entrance, and onlookers sat near their cars in lounge chairs with binoculars dangling from their necks. The excitement and anticipation was building, and it was contagious. Her hands sweated as she opened the car door.

Inside the gates, in an open field where the Blue Angels would be strutting their stuff, a large group of military personnel and their dependents had gathered for the show. This was the group Paul was really performing for—the men and women that needed a boost of morale and something to feel proud about. The Blue Angels made every sailor, from skipper to swabby, feel proud to be in the service.

Jennifer glanced around at the crowd, noting the people who had made the day into a special event. Large picnic blankets were strewn about, and the distinct smell of charcoal and barbecue filtered through the air. A softball whizzed by her, and Jennifer followed it in the blue, cloudless sky.

This was the perfect day for a performance. They could fly both a high and a low show, mixing climbs and starbursts, with countless rolling and twisting maneuvers.

With tickets, they were entitled to good bleacher seats. Jennifer spied a small vacant section on the bottom row of the straight wooden planks. "Let's go over there." She pointed out the empty seats, and Lori wheeled Billy over to the bleachers.

"This is great, really great." Billy settled back in his chair and looked toward the open field where the Blue Angels would make their appearance. "I wish I could do that. As soon as I'm walking—really walking—I'm going to do everything I can about learning to be a pilot. And when I'm old enough, I'm going to fly just like Paul."

The boy spoke with such admiration, such awe, Jennifer smiled and swallowed hard. He'd given the boy a goal, something wonderful to shoot for. Paul was flying for boys just like Billy. "Maybe you will."

"Look," he cried out, pointing to the streaks of light overhead.

The program had started.

The Blues sped across the sky at impossibly high speeds, and left trails of smoke in their wake. They moved like sleek birds in diamond formation, like bursts of energy and excitement. It looked so natural, so much as if they belonged up there, Jennifer almost forgot her fear, and fell into the same trance as the rest of the excited crowd. They defied gravity and nature—with the kind of ease most people walked and talked.

While the six planes roared above the crowd in a greeting, the seventh member of the Blue Angels flight team introduced the pilots. With her eyes fixed thousands of feet off the ground, Jennifer barely heard the announcer say that plane number three was piloted by Lieutenant Commander Paul Davis. Her heart lurched for a moment. It was real. He was up there. She clutched the handle of Billy's wheelchair and kept her eyes focused. Somersaults, high dives, barrel rolls were all perfectly orchestrated as if it weren't work at all.

Jennifer had seen them perform before, years ago, in Pennsacola and Annapolis. It was like watching circus performers, only much more thrilling. Up there, there was no net to catch an acrobat if he fell. She watched the intricate moves with stunned fascination. It was so beautiful. It made her want to be a part of it, too.

They flew in unison, in diamond formation, no more than mere feet from one plane's wing to another's, and later, broke away from the line and spun and rolled in parallel formation.

She was distracted by a tap on the shoulder and glanced behind her. "I was sitting over there. I tried to get your attention a few minutes ago, but you were too absorbed in the show." With no sign of recognition, the young dark-haired woman introduced herself. "I'm Denise White. Ken White's wife. We met at Balboa Park several months ago." Her eyes were apologetic. "We're the ones who spilled the beans about all this. Listen, I know it can be a little overwhelming at first. But they love it."

It was nice to know she wasn't alone. Jennifer patted the woman's arm. "Thanks for joining me."

On a final turn, she watched the Blues do the impossible—more rolls and spins than seemed conceivable, and her breath was taken away. She held her hair back to keep it out of her eyes, and leaned over to talk to Denise. "Do you ever get scared?"

Denise's eyes widened and she nodded. "You bet, all the time," she said with a warm laugh. "It's not like my husband sits at a desk all day long. That's not who he is. That's him." Her head shifted toward the clouds and the small group of jets streaking by like lightning. Foamy puffs of smoke were released from the jets; white, red, blue. They began to perform a delta vertical break. The planes broke from formation, each traveling in a different direction. Then, like graceful birds in flight, they looped around and returned to a center point, climbing high, straight up into the cloudless sky.

The audience applauded loudly, showing their

approval. Jennifer glanced down at the excited young man in the wheelchair beside her. She brushed fingers through his unruly brown waves. He didn't notice, and she smiled. He was going to walk and run again, and her heart filled with admiration. He wasn't going to let a car accident take over his life. He'd refused to become handicapped, and she'd given in so easy. She'd allowed herself to become so emotionally disabled by Jeff's accident. It was a daunting task, but she was going to walk again, too.

Her head swam with emotions—love, fear, excitement, anguish—and the answer kept coming back the same. She and Jake loved him, and he loved them back. *Could it be that simple?*

Paul had made her feel alive again. He'd given her something back that she was certain had been gone forever. If she had known Jeff was going to die, would she have loved him any less, wanted to shorten the time they'd had together? No, she would have wanted to savor that time. If that was the case, then why was she willing to give up on Paul? It might not be easy, but she loved him with every bone in her body.

For Paul, being a Blue Angel was the chance in a lifetime. Each year hundreds of pilots applied for the very few coveted spots with the flying troupe. And he'd made it. She wanted to be happy for him, proud of him. It was an honor.

Her eyes scanned the admiring crowd. Wasn't that what love was all about? It wasn't just riding off into the sunset. It was hard work and compromise. He'd offered to give it all up for her. He wanted to marry her. Her eyes clouded at the memory of his proposal. She wiped the wetness away with trembling fingers. She'd been blinded by her fears of the past. She'd been too afraid to look beyond. Flying was his dream. She should be sharing it with him. Damn it, she loved him. Love was a gamble, and she was going to put her money on them.

As the thirty-minute show began to wind down, the planes joined together again to fly across the base and over the spectators outside the gate. They flew low where it almost seemed possible to see each individual pilot. Screams of excitement and delight rose from the audience, and then a deafening round of applause invaded the air.

The Blues landed in formation, the same way they flew. Touching down within moments of one another, they taxied on the dirt runway, stopping precisely on their assigned spaces, following the gestures and signals of the ground crew. Simultaneously, the cockpits of the sleek blue birds opened. Through the fence and the dusty fields, Jennifer watched as six men in yellow flight suits emerged from the planes. Her eyes focused on Paul as he lifted off his helmet and shook his head. She breathed a deep sigh of relief. The worst was over now. She had faced her fears—and their love was the winner.

After the cheers died down, the crowd began to dissipate.

Denise hopped off the bleacher and started toward the hangar where the men had entered a moment before. She turned when she noticed Jennifer wasn't following. "You coming?"

"Just tell him I'm here." The dark-haired woman winked, and Jennifer shifted toward Lori and Billy.

"That was the most exciting thing I ever saw. I

think Paul's a great pilot." Billy's eyes raced with the thrill of the moment. It was the kind of thing that pushed him on further, to reach that next milestone. She was proud; yes, she realized, she was proud that Paul could do something so special for the little boy.

She patted his leg and leaned toward him. "He owes you a flight, doesn't he? I think it may be time for you to collect."

"Really?" His eyes were bigger than saucers. He almost bounded from his seat.

"Of course," she replied, pushing him firmly back in his seat, "I'm sure the Blue Angels are keeping Lieutenant Davis busy, but I think we can arrange something soon if your parents give it the go-ahead."

"Hey, the lot's starting to clear out, so we better go. Want a ride?" Lori began moving Billy's wheelchair from its fixed position and headed into the nearby grass. She waited a moment for Jennifer's reply.

"No, I'll think I'll hang out here a while."

She'd almost dozed off by the time she heard heavy footsteps coming in her direction. The sun was in her eyes when she opened them, and she could barely make out the figure of a man—her man.

"Hi." Jennifer raised her hands to her brows to shield her eyes from the sun. Her voice quaked slightly, and she wished she sounded as certain of herself as she wanted to be.

"Hi yourself." His voice was warm, like a sun-drenched afternoon.

"Pretty fancy flying up there." Shivers ran up and down her spine for the promises of tomorrow. She watched his eyes as they scanned her face.

"Were you scared?" he asked, his gaze not leaving

hers.

"Of course." The words were true, but she could handle it now. She'd wasted too much time being afraid.

"Me, too." She was silent, so he braved on. "I didn't think you'd show up. I'm not sure I wanted you to."

This was the man she loved. Everything was so clear now, as if the haze had lifted and the sun was shining. There were no more conflicts. She intended to make up for lost time. "What and miss your first performance? I wouldn't think of it."

"Jennifer." The soft syllables of her name sprang from his lips. "I was so afraid I'd lost you."

"You love me, don't you?" He cupped her face with his hands.

"More than anything in the world." The words rang happily in her ears. It was music, it was everything.

"That's what I need, Paul. That's all I need. I've been living with a ghost for too long. I can't say that I love what you do, but I understand it. It's you—and I love you.

"I don't want to hold you back," she continued. "I want you to have everything." She held his hand and ran her fingers over his palm. "I've let my fears lead my life for too long. I had to let go and trust you."

She looked up toward the sky, the sky that an hour ago had been filled with thrilling, spectacular birds. "I watched Billy's eyes while you were up there. You lifted that little boy right out of his wheelchair. You're a hero to a lot of people today." Her fingers touched his cheek and lined his jaw. "I want to be a part of that with you."

When he bent to kiss her, she welcomed the touch of his mouth on hers. This was what she wanted. His love was what she needed.

"Since you're in such an agreeable mood, maybe you'll accept this as part of our new understanding," he said somewhat awkwardly, and reached in his inside jacket pocket for a small box. He slowly opened it in front of her, and displayed a beautiful solitaire diamond ring. "I wanted to give it to you that last night. My timing was a bit off."

Jennifer gasped. The stone flickered like a thousand sunbursts all at once. It was the most beautiful thing she had ever seen.

"I'd get down on my knees, but they're not too steady right now. Jennifer," he said, holding up her chin with his fingers to meet his gaze. "Marry me? Make me the happiest man in the world."

"You know I will," she responded joyfully and met his mouth in a long tender kiss.

Epilogue

Two years later

Jennifer strolled barefoot into the backyard, enjoying the smell of charcoal on the grill. The evening was brisk, and the freshly mowed grass tickled the bottoms of her feet. The sky was filled with the pink and blue colors of sunset and the mountains created a valley for the setting sun.

"I think the steaks are almost ready," she called into the house after poking at the meat with a long fork. She shook her head and looked cockeyed at the grill. I never promised him a cook in the deal, she mused, placing the fork on its hanger. Bruised and tired bones she could deal with, deciding if steak was raw on the inside was another.

"You think so?" Paul emerged from the house and checked the food on the grill. "Thank goodness you're a good therapist."

"Our poor baby." He lovingly patted the swell of her stomach. "Thank goodness I make sure the two of you eat food that's not overcooked or undercooked."

She smiled as his arms went around her. The last year had held many surprises, she recalled happily, leaning back in his grasp. Their marriage had started with the fairy-tale wedding she'd always dreamed of. All frilly white lace and the groom of her dreams. And

Billy Wilder had been Paul's youngest, but most enthusiastic usher. Back then, his walk was still a little unsteady. Now, he spent all his free time chasing—and catching—pretty teenage girls.

It was all still a wonderful dream. When she'd discovered she was pregnant six months ago, she couldn't have been happier. Jake would make a terrific older brother. Everything was the way it was supposed to be.

"Are you going to miss the Blue Angels?" she asked, turning around to face him. His tour had ended the previous week and their friends had gathered yesterday in a farewell dinner.

"Sure. I'm looking forward to joining my new squadron. And then there's the baby, you and Jake. That's plenty of excitement for one man."

Her arms circled his neck, and she brought his mouth to inches from hers. "So it's excitement you want, Lieutenant Commander?" She stood on her toes and lightly nibbled his lip. "I think that can be arranged."

A word from the author...

I grew up in the Washington, DC, area and dabbled with writing fiction for as long as I can remember. To improve, I took a creative writing class my senior year of high school. The teacher was tough and heavily critiqued everyone's work. When a classmate asked if he liked anyone's story, he replied, "Yes, I liked Nadine's." That little comment began my journey to pursue a writing career.

In college, I majored in communications and for more than two decades I've worked as a corporate communications writer/editor.

I love interviewing people and turning their stories and information into something other people will want to read.

I met the love of my life while in college. He's been a naval officer, an engineer, and an attorney—all hero material to me. We have two sons and a very spoiled cockapoo.

Visit Nadine Monaco at www.nadine-monaco.com

Thank you for purchasing
this publication of The Wild Rose Press, Inc.

If you enjoyed the story, we would appreciate your
letting others know by leaving a review.

For other wonderful stories,
please visit our on-line bookstore at
www.thewildrosepress.com.

For questions or more information
contact us at
info@thewildrosepress.com.

The Wild Rose Press, Inc.
www.thewildrosepress.com

Stay current with The Wild Rose Press, Inc.

Like us on Facebook

https://www.facebook.com/TheWildRosePress

And Follow us on Twitter
https://twitter.com/WildRosePress